TOTAL

by

LIA ANDERSSEN

CHIMERA

Total Abandon published by
Chimera Publishing Ltd
PO Box 152
Waterlooville
Hants
PO8 9FS

Printed and bound in Great Britain by
Cox & Wyman Ltd, Reading.

The characters and situations in this book are entirely imaginary and bear no relation to any real person or actual happening.

TOTAL ABANDON

Lia Anderssen

This novel is fiction – in real life practice safe sex

She tried to struggle, but once again the strength of the two was too much for her and she had no chance. They worked quickly, clearly used to using the equipment. Danni's hands were pulled above her head and cold metal manacles closed about her wrists. Once these were in place the pair did the same with her legs, ignoring her desperate protests, closing the steel bands about her ankles and holding her fast. She was immobilised now, but still they hadn't finished. Taking hold of the chains, they hauled on them, pulling them tight and stretching Danni's lovely young body into the shape of an X.

Danni tugged at her bonds, but in vain. She was quite unable to move, her slender limbs pulled tight and already beginning to ache. On the wall directly opposite the frame was a mirror. With a groan of despair she closed her eyes against the sight of her own stretched and vulnerable body.

Chapter One

'How's your meal?'

Danni glanced across the table at the man sitting opposite her, and smiled uncertainly.

'It's fine,' she said.

'More wine?'

She nodded. 'Thank you.'

She watched him as he poured the red liquid into her glass. He was quite handsome really, she mused. If only he wasn't ten years her senior she might have been very attracted to him. As it was, he was proving a charming dinner companion. Despite the fact that she had known him for only a few hours, his easy manner and witty conversation were making for an unexpectedly enjoyable evening.

In fact, he was the first company she'd had for some time. She was well into the fourth week of her trip, hitchhiking across the United States, and it was proving a somewhat lonely adventure since she had walked out on Chas two weeks earlier.

She and Chas had met at the travel agent. Both had been buying tickets to the East Coast, and both planned to hitch rides across the continent. They had fallen into conversation at once, and had soon agreed to pool their resources. At first it had seemed a good idea, travelling together and sharing expenses. But they soon found out that they did not get on at all well, and after a series of arguments Danni packed her bags and moved on. Since then she had been travelling alone, choosing her own itinerary and staying where she could afford.

Peter Bourne had picked her up that afternoon. She had just left a roadside diner and barely held out her thumb before he had drawn to a stop and offered her a ride. It was he who had suggested they stay the night in the city, and he who had found the hotel – the Hotel Astra. It wasn't the most salubrious part of town, but it was clean and the rooms were comfy. The food in the restaurant wasn't bad either, she mused as she tucked into her meal.

Peter seemed quite taken with her, and was apparently unbothered by the ruffled state she was in after her long travels. Danni glanced across at a mirror that hung on the wall opposite where she was sitting, studying her reflection critically. Living out of a rucksack wasn't that easy, and her clothes weren't exactly stylish. Her blouse was plain and white. Despite its simplicity, though, it showed off her pert young breasts beautifully. She had undone the top three buttons, leaving an expanse of cleavage on view, and the way his eyes frequently dropped to her chest showed her that he approved. Her skirt, too, had been well-chosen. It was a short one that revealed long, slender legs with finely-shaped ankles.

At nineteen, Danni Bright had a beautiful body, and she enjoyed letting men see it, though she wasn't sure why. It wasn't as if she had an active sex life. In fact she was extremely inexperienced sexually, having lost her virginity in a friend's bedroom to a fumbling youth who had come too early, leaving her confused and unsatisfied. Since then she had decided that sex wasn't for her, and contented herself with occasionally masturbating in the privacy of her bedroom when her urges became too great. She knew, though, that men found her extremely attractive with her slim, shapely body, her long blonde hair and her elfin looks. Now, as Peter gazed into her green eyes, she sensed his attraction toward her.

'Penny for your thoughts,' he said.

She smiled. 'Nothing much.'

They finished their meal and took cups of coffee into the lounge, where they continued to chat. Peter ordered brandies, and Danni found her head beginning to swim somewhat as she sipped at hers. When he rose and suggested they go up, she was a little unsteady on her feet and she giggled as he took her arm and guided her.

Once alone in her room, Danni slowly disrobed. Then she stood before the full-length mirror that hung by the door and examined herself. There was no doubt that she was extremely beautiful, her firm breasts jutting forward, requiring no support, the nipples large and succulent. Her waist was slim, and her tummy was toned and flat. Her wispy pubic bush was blonde, forming a neat triangle beneath which the furrow of her sex was clearly visible. She ran her finger down between her legs, tracing the soft flesh of her slit, shivering slightly as she touched her clitoris. The alcohol had had its effect on her and she suddenly found herself feeling oddly aroused. Perhaps she would masturbate when she got to bed.

A knock on the door made her start, and she felt suddenly guilty, standing there with no clothes on. She grabbed the T-shirt that lay on the bed and began to pull it on.

'Who is it?'

'It's me, Peter. I brought a little nightcap.'

'Hold on.'

She dragged on the T-shirt, pulling it down as far as she was able. It clung tightly to the curves of her body, accentuating the shape of her breasts, the outline of her nipples showing through. It fitted well about her lower body too, hugging her curvaceous hips and the pert swell of her buttocks. She dragged the hem down as far as she was able, but it was still very short, just long enough to preserve her modesty. She stopped in front of the mirror, uncertain whether it hid her charms sufficiently. Then the knock came again.

'Danni?'

'Okay, I'm coming.'

She opened the door. Peter was wearing a dressing-gown and carrying a bottle of malt whisky. He smiled.

7

'Thought you might want one for the road.'

'But I'm not going anywhere.'

'It's just an expression. Can I come in?'

She eyed him for a moment. 'All right.'

She stood aside and allowed him in. He walked past her and went into the bathroom, emerging with two glasses. He set them on the table and poured a generous portion of whisky into each. Then he crossed to where she stood and handed one to her. In her bare feet she stood only five foot three inches, her petite form somewhat dwarfed by the large American, but she rather liked the way he towered over her, like some large protector. He clinked his glass against hers.

'Good luck.'

'Cheers.'

The whisky was a good one, and it warmed Danni's throat as it slipped down. She eyed him.

'Are you trying to get me drunk?' she said.

'Could be.'

'So you can have your evil way with me?'

'It's not so evil.'

He reached out a hand and moved it down her cheek, stroking her face, His touch felt good, and she let him run his hands through her hair, gazing up into his eyes.

'You're very beautiful, Danni,' he said.

She didn't reply, but when he took hold of her chin between finger and thumb and raised her face to his she made no move to stop him.

His lips felt soft against her own. When he opened his mouth and probed his tongue into hers she allowed it in, a sudden tingling sensation running through her at the intimacy of the kiss. She wrapped her arms about his neck, still holding her glass, her eyes closing as she lost herself in the embrace. He held her about the waist, his hand stroking her through the thin fabric. Then it began to slide upwards toward her breast.

She broke the kiss.

8

'Don't,' she whispered.

'Why not. Don't you want it?'

'I... I'm not sure.'

He gazed into her eyes. 'What is it?'

'It's just that I've never really done it.'

'You mean you're a virgin?'

'No. I've had a man inside me. Once.'

'But?'

'But it wasn't exactly what I thought it would be like.'

'Who was it?'

'Just a boy.'

'Then you've got a lot to learn.'

He took her glass from her and placed it on the table along with his. Danni watched him, her heart beating hard. On the one hand, she feared what was about to happen. She knew the drink had weakened her resistance, and that she might regret it in the morning. But, on the other hand, there was a sense of excitement rising within her that was beginning to take control, so that when he took her in his arms and kissed her again she reciprocated willingly, pressing her body against his.

The kiss went on and on, each moment increasing the arousal within the young beauty as she responded to the embrace of this strong man. When at last they broke apart, she was almost panting, her breasts rising and falling rapidly as she fought to keep control of herself.

He reached down and took hold of the hem of the T-shirt, beginning to pull it upwards.

'No,' she said, placing her hand on his, but he brushed her aside. He pulled the garment up, peeling it from her like a second skin, revealing the pink softness of bare flesh beneath. Danni resisted for a moment longer, then she sighed and raised her arms in a true gesture of surrender, allowing him to pull it over her head. She stood in front of him, her arms hanging by her sides, as his eyes travelled over her naked frame.

'God, you're lovely,' he breathed.

He reached out a hand and closed it over her breast. Danni glanced down, amazed at how quickly her nipple puckered to hardness under his touch, unable quite to understand the way her body was responding so deliciously to him.

He pushed her gently backwards so that she sat down on the bed. She looked at him questioningly.

'Just leave it to me,' he said. 'Lie back.'

She prostrated herself, her lovely breasts standing up proudly from her chest as she gazed down between them at him. He climbed onto the bed, kneeling beside her. Then he leaned forward and took her nipple between his lips. Danni gasped aloud as he began gently to suck at it, while his hand toyed with her other breast, his fingers caressing the stiff teat.

Danni could scarcely believe how good it felt, totally different from the fumblings she had experienced at the back of the cinema with the boys of her youth. This was a real man, a man who understood her desires and how to satisfy them.

For the next ten minutes Peter paid homage to Danni's breasts, taking first one, then the other into his mouth, nibbling gently at her nipples, then sucking them hard, sending thrills of excitement through her naked body so that she writhed about beneath him. She was getting more turned on by the second now, and she could feel the wetness welling up inside her as her body responded to his lovemaking.

All at once he knelt up, his hand still toying with her soft mammaries as he gazed down at the svelte young figure laying before him. Danni glanced up questioningly at him, and he gave a slight smile. Then he began to move his hand down, over her ribcage, across her belly and on toward her pubis. Danni said nothing, but already she could feel the muscles of her sex contracting in anticipation of his touch, and she bit her lip to suppress a cry as his fingers probed down into her furrow, seeking her clitoris.

When he found her button, Danni's body lurched, her legs falling open as she responded to his touch, pressing her hips forward, giving herself up to the exquisite pleasure of his ministrations. She could barely believe what was happening to her, splayed naked in the strange room while she abandoned herself to a relative stranger's caresses. All she knew was that, when he slipped a finger into her, it felt delicious, and she moaned with pleasure at the intimacy of his touch.

He started to frig her gently, his finger slipping slowly back and forth as he watched her face. Danni felt the muscles deep inside her contract about his probing digit as the wetness in her flowed anew. As he worked her, he moved down the bed, dropping to his knees between her thighs so that she knew he was staring straight at her sex. Then he lowered his head, and Danni gave a start as she felt his tongue begin lapping at the silky-smooth skin of her inner thigh.

He moved his mouth higher, his finger still working back and forth as he ran his tongue up her legs towards the centre of her desires. Danni was almost panting now, pressing her backside clear of the bed as she urged his fingers ever deeper inside her.

When his tongue found her clitoris, she cried aloud, the spasm of pleasure hitting her like an electric shock. He responded by removing his finger and, taking hold of her hips, burying his face between her thighs. He lapped and sucked at her hard little bud, taking it between her teeth and running his tongue back and forth over it.

She came with a cry. She couldn't help it. Never had she felt so aroused. Now, even as spasms of pleasure continued to course through her body, she realised how different sex could be with an experienced man.

Her orgasm went on for some time, her body rigid, her hips thrust upward against his face as she milked the pleasure from him. At last, though, she was coming down, lying back, her breasts rising and falling as she regained her breath.

11

'That was great,' she gasped.

'We've only just begun,' he said. 'Now it's time for you to taste your first cock.'

She stared at him. 'You want me to take you in my mouth?'

'Exactly.'

'I... I don't know how.'

'I'll show you.'

He took hold of her hands and pulled her to a sitting position.

'Undo my sash.'

Hesitantly, Danni reached out a hand and took hold of the sash of Peter's dressing-gown. She tugged at it gently and it came undone. The gown fell open, revealing that he was naked beneath. Danni's eyes were immediately drawn to his cock. It was long and thick, hanging down in front of a pair of heavy balls. He took hold of her hand and guided it to his groin, and she shivered slightly as her fingers closed about his shaft.

'Suck it.'

Slowly she leaned forward, lifting his cock to her lips. She could smell him now, a thick, musty aroma that aroused the basest of instincts within her, making her suddenly hungry to taste him. She took him into her mouth, sucking tentatively at him. He tasted salty, and she felt him twitch slightly as he began to stiffen.

Instinctively she reached for his balls, squeezing them in her palm as she continued to suck. He was becoming more rigid by the second now, and it thrilled her to see the effect she was having on him.

By the time he was fully erect she was fellating him hard, her head moving up and down on his shaft, coating it with a sheen of saliva. He grunted with pleasure as she did so, and she wondered if he was going to come in her mouth. She was surprised at her ambivalence at the idea. She would have expected it to revolt her, but she found herself anticipating the taste of his seed with some enthusiasm as

12

his arousal began to transmit itself to her.

As it happened, though, Peter had other plans. He suddenly withdrew his shining penis from her mouth.

'Turn round and lie over the bed,' he said.

Danni eagerly obeyed, kneeling on the carpet and leaning forward over the bedspread, spreading her legs as she did so.

'Now you're going to find out what it's like to do it doggy-fashion,' he said.

He ran a hand down over the soft flesh of her behind. Then she felt the warm, moist tip of his cock probing between her legs. Danni was fully aroused again now, and anxious for the sensation of an erect cock inside her. As she felt his pole nuzzling against the soft flesh of her slit, she pressed back at him, willing him to penetrate her.

'Ahhhh…!'

She cried aloud as he slid inside her, pressing hard so that his rampant knob slid all the way in, the lubrication inside her assisting his progress as he buried his cock to the hilt. Danni had never felt so filled. She had expected some pain, but all she felt was the most exquisite pleasure as he pressed his pubis against her backside.

He started to fuck her, his hips moving gently back and forth. At the same time he slid a finger underneath her and sought her clitoris, rubbing it with a circular motion as his cock moved in and out. Danni gripped the bedspread, her entire body alive with arousal as he took her. At last she understood what sex was all about, and what it felt to be fucked by a real man. She wondered why she had waited so long.

As his passion rose, so did Danni's, and their love-making became more frantic, he lunging against her with every stroke while she pressed back at him spreading her legs still wider, loving the friction of his swollen prick as it pumped back and forth.

All at once his grip on her tightened, his fingers digging

into the flesh of her thighs, his movements becoming suddenly jerky. Then he gave a gasp and she felt her vagina filled with his seed as his cock twitched violently within her.

Her second orgasm was better even than her first, shrill cries escaping her lips as she thrashed about beneath him. Every spurt sent new spasms of pleasure coursing through her as his hips crashed relentlessly against her small body.

Only when his thrusts slowed did Danni begin to come down, but still she kept her vagina clamped hard about his rod, as if afraid to lose a drop of the hot liquid that now filled her so deliciously. At last, though, there was no more, and he slumped against her, his heavy body almost crushing the air from her lungs.

He withdrew slowly, bringing a fresh moan from his young lover as she felt him slip from her. As he rose to his feet she rolled over to stare up at him, her soft skin criss-crossed with the marks of the eiderdown, her breasts rising and falling as she regained her breath. He smiled at her.

'Not bad for a beginner,' he said.

Chapter Two

Danni opened her eyes slowly, momentarily unsure of where she was. She blinked, trying to focus on the source of bright light in front of her. Slowly, as her vision adjusted, she saw the window of the hotel room and remembered. At the same time, memories of the night before began to come flooding back to her, and she sat up suddenly, looking across to the other side of the bed. It was empty, though the evidence that she had not been alone in the night was plain to see.

Tentatively, she slid a hand down between her thighs. She could still feel the stickiness of him there, confirmation that the previous night had not been a dream. She examined her conscience. Certainly she was shocked at the way she had behaved, but her main impression was of a night of pure pleasure, and, though she found herself blushing as she remembered her behaviour, she also remembered how alive she had felt in the hands of such an experienced lover.

After that first session they had showered together, washing each other's bodies under the warm spray. He had taken her again then and there, pushing her back against the wall of the shower cubicle and ramming his stiff cock into her while the water cascaded over their naked bodies. Then they had dried off and climbed onto the bed, where they spent ages exploring one another with their hands and mouths, he showing her what brought a man pleasure and schooling her in the ways of being a good lover. Later they made love once more before falling asleep together.

Danni lay on her back and thought of the way her body had responded to him. She could scarcely believe how her inhibitions had melted away under his tutoring, turning her from demure young English Miss into a willing and enthusiastic lover. She wondered again how she had gone so long without realising how much pleasure was to be gained from the physical contact of sex. She wondered too if she would have the courage to repeat the experience. The point was that Peter had made all the running, and she wasn't certain whether she would find such a forceful lover again.

Little did Danni know then that her life was about to change totally, and that the demure young beauty who had checked into the hotel on the previous day was soon to be lost forever.

She pulled back the sheets and rose from the bed. She padded across to the bathroom and turned on the shower. The water was wonderfully refreshing as it flowed over her, and she leaned back against the wall, gently rubbing her clitoris as she remembered her last shower, and her abandoned lovemaking in that small cubicle.

She washed herself thoroughly before stepping out onto the bathmat. Then she stopped, puzzled. There were no towels on the rail. There certainly had been the night before. Perhaps they had left them in the room.

She walked back into the hotel room, her feet leaving small wet prints on the carpet. She searched for the towels, but there were none. She would have to use her own.

She looked about for her rucksack. She was certain she had left it on a low table by the door, but it was nowhere to be seen. She looked under the bed and in the wardrobe, but without success.

Beginning to feel seriously worried, she began opening drawers. All were empty. Slowly the seriousness of her situation began to dawn on her. She was alone and naked in this strange hotel room with absolutely nothing. No clothes, no towel – not even a pair of panties.

All at once she gave a little cry of dismay. Her handbag was missing. She had placed it on the floor of the wardrobe when she'd arrived, but it was no longer there. With it had gone her passport, her traveller's cheques and all her money. But where could it have gone?

The truth began to dawn on her. She had been tricked! Peter was no more than a slimy con man who'd been after her possessions all along! He had worked his way into her confidence, then had taken what he wanted. Her face glowed as she thought how she had abandoned herself to him. For her, he had been a passionate lover, but for him the sex had been nothing more than a bonus as he had schemed to rob her.

But why take everything, even the towels? Surely they couldn't have much value? As she thought about the night before, though, she realised it wasn't the value that mattered to him, but the effect it would have on her. He must have known how disorienting it would be, and known also how reluctant she would be to raise the alarm, considering her situation. He was clearly a very devious man, and something of a sadist as well. Certainly he had left the youngster in a difficult and embarrassing position.

Danni wondered what she should do. She had to raise the alarm, she knew. But that would involve telling how she came to be naked in her room, with none of her possessions. Her face glowed with shame as she contemplated this. She knew, however, that she had no choice. She would have to tell somebody—

The sudden hammering on the door of her room made Danni start. She jumped to her feet, clutching her hands to her private parts in a reaction that betrayed her guilty feelings. Then the hammering came again.

'Open up in there!'

Danni's throat went dry. Who could it be?

So hard was the knocking that she feared the door might give way.

'Who... Who is it?' she asked, hesitantly.

'Come on! Open up this fuckin' door!'

'I can't,' she said, searching desperately about her for something to wear.

'Open up! Hotel Astra security!'

Danni feared the door wouldn't hold out much longer under such a violent onslaught. She grabbed hold of the bedsheet and tugged at it, pulling it from under the duvet. Then she wrapped it about her breasts and, clinging tightly to it with one hand, ran across to the door and opened it.

The man on the other side was tall and muscular. She recognised him as one of those standing by the entrance to the hotel the night before, presumably vetting the people entering. He strode into the room, pushing the youngster aside as he glanced quickly about him. He went into the bathroom, then came out and checked the closets. Then he confronted the trembling girl.

'Where is he?' he demanded.

'Where's who?' she asked.

'You know. Your pal from last night. Where the hell is he?'

'I don't know.'

He stepped close, towering over her.

'Listen young lady, don't play games. He's hiding somewhere. Now where?'

'Honestly I don't know. He's taken everything. Even my clothes. That's why I'm wearing this sheet.'

His eyes narrowed. 'But you know who he is. You arrived together.'

'I just hitched a lift with him, that's all. I'd never met him before.'

He paused, staring into her eyes.

'You'd better come downstairs. The boss wants a word with you.'

'But I can't. I've got no clothes.'

'Look,' he snarled. 'I haven't got time to argue. Either you get your ass downstairs now or I'll drag you down, clothes or no clothes.'

Danni made to protest again, but the look in his eye silenced her. Instead she sighed.

'All right.'

18

'This way.'

He took her arm and dragged her out into the corridor. She clutched at her sheet, trying desperately not to trip on the trailing ends as he pulled her along. He took her down the stairs, then along a passage to a door marked 'Private'. He knocked once and pushed her inside.

She found herself in a small office. Against the wall in front of her stood grey steel filing cabinets and there was a whiteboard on the wall. In one corner was a desk strewn with papers. A man was sitting behind it, a short balding man of about forty. He looked questioningly at Danni's escort.

'Well?'

'I think the bastard's given us the slip. She says she's just a hitchhiker. Got picked up by him. Says she doesn't know him beyond that.'

The man rose to his feet and crossed to where the forlorn beauty was standing. He studied her for a few moments with cold eyes.

'Of course you know him,' he said. 'He was in your room last night, wasn't he?'

'How did you know that?'

'It's my job to know what's going on in this hotel. This is the Hotel Astra, and I'm the manager. He was screwing you, wasn't he?'

'What business is that of yours?'

The man reached out suddenly and, taking hold of the sheet, pulled it from her. Danni made a grab for it, but in vain. With a cry, she wrapped her left arm across her breasts and slapped her right hand over her crotch.

'What you so shy about?' he mocked. 'According to you, you were fucked last night by a guy you don't even know. Why shouldn't we get a look too?'

'It wasn't like that.'

'He screwed you, didn't he?'

'Yes, but—'

19

'But nothing. Now where the hell did he go?'

'I don't know, I tell you.' There was an edge of desperation in Danni's voice now. 'He picked me up while I was hitchhiking yesterday. Said his name was Peter... Peter Bourne, that's it. He bought me dinner.'

'In return for a screw.'

'You make me sound like a prostitute,' she protested indignantly.

'That's what you look like to me, standing there with nothing on.'

'He stole my clothes. He stole my money... everything.'

'And that's not all. As well as ransacking his damned room, the bastard also broke into the bar last night and got away with the takings. Nearly five hundred dollars gone. What you gonna do about that?'

'What can I do?' Danni stared at the pair in desperation. 'I told you, he took my money too. He took everything.'

The balding man glared at her for a moment longer, then leaned against the edge of the desk. He ran his eyes up and down Danni's naked body, and she clutched her hands to herself still tighter, wishing she had at least some underwear.

'Well, I don't know,' he said wearily, rubbing his temples as though he had a nasty headache. 'I guess we'd better hand you over to the cops.'

'Hand me over to the police?'

'Sure. You're an accessory to a crime. You don't think we're going to let you go, now do you?'

'But please, I've done nothing wrong.'

'There's five hundred bucks missing. That's something wrong according to my book.'

At that moment there was a knock on the door.

'Yeah?' said the bald man.

The door opened and two men entered. When they caught sight of Danni they stopped, and her face glowed scarlet as their eyes scanned her naked body.

'Hakis, Zuko. Come on in and close the door. We don't

20

want the guests getting the wrong idea.'

The two men entered. Both were slim with Latin complexions. They both wore dark double-breasted suits, and sunglasses hid their eyes. Danni was instantly reminded of underworld gangsters she'd seen in films.

The one who had been referred to as Hakis spoke first. 'Who's the girl?' he asked.

'Bitch checked in with a guy last night. He spends all night screwing her, then hightails it with the contents of my cash register. She says she doesn't know him.'

The second man whistled. 'Sounds like you've been set up. What you gonna do?'

'She claims he took her stuff, Zuko. That's how come she's naked. I figure maybe I should just hand her over to the cops.'

'I guess so.'

'Look, forget the chick,' broke in the other man suddenly. 'You got the stuff?'

'Yeah. I got it.'

'Right. Zuko and I gotta get it delivered.'

The man behind the desk narrowed his eyes. 'You guys sure it'll be okay this time?'

'Sure. I mean, they'll never hit us a third time.'

'I dunno. I reckon they're getting inside info from somewhere. Maybe we should find another courier.'

'But who the hell could we trust?'

Danni listened to the conversation in silence, grateful that they had turned their attention from her for the moment. She had no idea of what they were speaking. She just wished they'd give her the sheet back.

All at once she realised that the room had gone quiet. She glanced up to see the two shady-looking men conversing quietly while glancing in her direction. Then the one called Zuko turned to the hotel manager.

'What about her?' he said, indicating Danni.

'What do you mean?'

21

'She could make the drop.'

'What, her?'

'Sure. Nobody knows who the hell she is. Bitch owes us a favour. She'd be perfect.'

The hotel manager scratched his head. 'I'm not so sure.'

But already the one called Hakis had turned to Danni.

'Take your hands away, girl, and show us what you've got.'

Danni looked at him in disbelief. 'I beg your pardon—!' She gave a shocked squeal of pain as Zuko brought his hand down hard on her backside, delivering a stinging blow and leaving a red palm-print on her pale flesh.

'Do as he says.'

Danni glanced fearfully from one face to another. This whole situation was getting seriously out of hand. Mentally she cursed the man who had got her into this mess. She glanced down at herself, wishing fervently that he had at least left her a pair of panties. Then the man raised his hand again and she knew she had no choice but to obey. Slowly, her cheeks flushed, she allowed her hands to fall to her sides, revealing her naked charms to the watching men.

There was silence for a moment as the four eyed her lovely young body. Then the one called Hakis spoke again.

'Hmm, not bad. Not bad at all. I reckon she'd make a pretty good whore.'

'Whore?' echoed Danni in alarm.

'Quiet,' ordered Hakis. He turned to the hotel manager. 'You reckon you could find some tart's clothes for her?'

Zuko nodded. 'Yeah, that'd be the perfect disguise around that part of town. Nobody's gonna notice one more whore.'

'I guess you're right.' The bald manager turned to his man, who had been standing quietly by, listening to the conversation. 'You reckon you could find something?'

'Sure. I'll check in the lost luggage room. We get all kinds of stuff left behind.'

'Good. Take these two with you and find something

22

suitable. I'll be with you in ten minutes.'

'You gonna look after her?'

'Yeah, I guess she owes me.'

The other three men grinned, then left, leaving Danni alone with the hotel manager. She was still standing with her hands by her sides, her face bright scarlet.

'Right,' he said, 'you've cost me a lot of money, and I want something in return.'

'I told you, I had nothing to do with it,' she protested.

'Except that you spent the night with that thieving bastard.'

Her colour deepened. 'I didn't know he was a crook.'

'Well, I reckon you can start paying your bill right now.'

'But how?'

He smiled and glanced down at the obvious bulge stretching the front of his trousers. 'I'm sure you can think of something appropriate,' he leered.

'What?'

'I think you understand me.'

'But… no, I can't.'

'Oh, I think you can, or I'll have you thrashed before you go out on your little errand. Believe me, that mark Zuko gave you is nothing compared to what I can do.'

'But I...'

'Just do as you're told. You're in a lot of trouble, girlie, and not keeping me happy will only make things a lot worse.'

Danni gazed into his face. There was no doubt about it; he was serious. But how could she do such a thing? After all, he was a complete stranger. But then again, so was that snake Bourne, and it hadn't stopped her sucking him. She glanced down at herself once more. Already she had bared all to this man. It was only a short step further to doing what he asked. Perhaps she should take the safest path after all.

'All right,' she said quietly.

'Now you're at last being sensible,' said the man. 'Come on then, we haven't got all morning.'

Danni took a pace forward and stood immediately in front

him. His eyes surveyed her bare breasts, and she realised with a shock that her nipples had stiffened for him. She would never have thought it possible, but to her shame the first stirrings of arousal were beginning within her. Somehow, the evening before had done more than just rouse her desires for a single night. It seemed also to have awakened something more fundamental in her nature; a latent sexuality that, until now, had been slumbering. As she dropped to her knees before the man, she suddenly realised that she was curious to taste his cock, and having no choice but to comply was fuelling her own excitement. Slowly she reached out a trembling hand and pulled down his zipper.

His penis was already semi-erect and, as she released it from his pants, she watched it stiffen still more before her eyes. She glanced up at his emotionless face.

'Go on,' he said firmly, 'you know what to do. Suck it.'

Slowly Danni leaned forward and took him into her mouth. He tasted somehow different from Bourne, and his cock was shorter. Still the scent and taste of him sent a tremor through her, and she began to suck harder as she warmed to her task.

Danni couldn't understand what was happening to her. Only the day before she would have laughed if anyone had suggested that she might fellate a man. Yet here she was, quite naked, kneeling in this dingy office, with a stranger's thick cock filling her mouth, working her head up and down with enthusiasm as she masturbated his shaft in her fist. It was as if her experience with Bourne had removed a block from her mind, freeing her to behave as she wished.

As she worked him harder, the man began to grunt with pleasure, his cock twitching violently under her fingers. Somehow this seemed to spur Danni on all the more as she sucked hard at him, her saliva escaping from her mouth and dribbling down into his thick mat of pubic hair. It was as if his excitement was transferring itself to her, and she milked him with vigour, her fist pumping back and forth as she devoured his stiff erection.

Without warning, a hot sticky fluid was invading her mouth. Her immediate instinct was to pull away, but he curled strong fingers into her hair and held her where she was, forcing her to devour his semen. It was the first time she had tasted a man's seed, and she gulped it down, swallowing hard as yet more leaked from his organ, the muscles of his groin contracting rhythmically with every spurt.

He held Danni until every last drop had been discharged into her mouth. Then he pushed her away. She sat back on her ankles, gazing up at him red-faced, a trickle of white fluid coating her chin.

He grinned down at her.

'I think you're going to make a good whore,' he said smugly.

Chapter Three

'Put those on, and be quick about it.'

Danni stared down at the garments Hakis had tossed onto the desk in front of her. They didn't seem much to the youngster. There was no underwear; just a small stretch top with a low neckline, and a black skirt.

She pulled the skirt about her hips. It came to just above her knees, and was a little too small, biting into her waist as she struggled to fasten it. There was a slit up the side that ran all the way to her waist, making it clear to even the most casual observer that she wore nothing underneath.

She pulled the top over her head. This, too, was small, and as she peeled it down over her breasts it clung tightly to her curves, outlining her firm orbs perfectly and leaving a deep expanse of cleavage on display. Her midriff was bare. There was a pair of high-heeled shoes on the floor and she slipped her feet into them. A mirror hung by the door, and she turned to look at herself.

Her cheeks reddened as she saw her reflection. If their intention had been to make her look like a tart, they had certainly succeeded. With the slit that ran up the side of the skirt, and the skimpy top, any man would have thought she was on the game. The shoes only served to make matters worse, accentuating the slenderness of her calves and her shapely ankles. Dressed as she was, she wouldn't normally dare show herself to her closest friends, yet she knew these men intended that she go out and walk the streets.

'Very nice.'

Hakis had moved behind her, and was admiring her figure. He placed his hands about her waist, running his fingers over the smooth flesh of her midriff. She tried to push them away, but he was very strong. He pulled her close and slid his hands up to her breasts, feeling their softness through the thin material. To Danni's embarrassment she felt her nipples harden once more as her vibrant young body responded to his touch, and she wondered again at the unexpected desires that suddenly seemed to be dominating her thoughts.

Hakis spun her round to face him.

'You're a sensitive little thing, aren't you?' he said. Then he took hold of her wrist, pulling her close until her face was only inches from his. 'Now listen, young lady,' he hissed. 'We're investing a lot in you this morning. You fuck up and you're in big trouble, understand?'

'No, I don't understand what you want of me,' she said, with more defiance than she really felt.

'We'll explain in the car,' he replied. 'Just make sure that, once we leave this office, you behave yourself. Zuko, show her.'

Zuko pulled his hand from his pocket. In it was a long, curved knife, the blade gleaming.

'Zuko's had a lot of practice with that thing,' said Hakis. 'Don't make him use it again. Now, you're not going to make any trouble, are you?'

Danni shook her head. It was clear to her that these were dangerous men, and that to resist them would be extremely foolish. Whatever it was they wanted of her, she would do.

Zuko opened the office door and motioned for her to go out. As she did so he fell in behind her, and she thought of the knife that was now so close to her liver. She walked down the corridor and out into the hotel lobby. There were a few people standing by the front desk, and all eyes turned as the beautiful youngster passed. She tried to ignore the glances and surreptitious remarks of those watching, her face glowing as she realised how obvious was her lack of underwear.

The two men took her outside to where a long black car was parked. Hakis climbed into the driver's seat while Zuko motioned Danni into the back, then got in beside her.

The car pulled away from the kerb and set off through the city streets. Danni sat in silence, gazing from her window, trying to make some sense of what was happening to her. By now she had expected to be on her travels once more. Instead, she was sitting in a car with a pair of mysterious thugs, one of whom possessed a frightful looking knife which he would doubtless use if provoked, and she was dressed like a common tart. She thought too of the incident in the manager's office. Had she really done what she did to that odious man? She could scarcely believe any it.

As they travelled on, she noticed that the area was becoming more and more squalid. The shops and hotels were giving way to derelict buildings, their fronts boarded up. On the street corners loafed gangs of young men, and everywhere was litter and graffiti and hungry looking strays.

Hakis pulled the car left onto a piece of derelict ground and stopped, turning off the engine. Then he turned round in his seat to look at Danni.

'Right, baby,' he growled. 'This is where you earn your keep. We've got a little delivery for you to make.'

'But why me?' asked Danni.

'Because you've got a face nobody knows,' said Zuko. 'We've had a little trouble delivering these packages. Our messengers keep getting waylaid. We need someone nobody knows. Then if they go for you, we know we've got a mole in the organisation.'

'Is it dangerous?' asked Danni.

She felt the steel of Zuko's knife pricking against her bare midriff from where it was concealed in his jacket pocket.

'It'll be a sight more dangerous for you if you don't do it,' he growled.

'Now,' said Hakis, 'the drop is in a bar about a mile from here. It's called Harry's Bar.'

'How do I find it?'

He pointed to an alley. 'Go down there, turn right at the

end. Then follow the street for six blocks. Harry's is on the right.'

As he was speaking, Zuko had levered open a hatch in the floor of the car. He pulled out a small shoulder-bag, not much bigger than a paperback book. He handed it to her.

'You take care of this now,' he said. 'That's if you know what's good for you.'

'What's in it?'

'Never you mind. Just take it to Harry's, and give it to the barman. He'll be expecting it.'

Hakis climbed out and opened the door beside her.

'Get out.'

Danni climbed from the car, then quickly turned back as a thought occurred to her.

'What if somebody propositions me?'

'What?'

'Well I'm supposed to be a prostitute, aren't I? What if somebody tries to pick me up?'

Hakis laughed. 'Then I guess you get screwed – but only once you've made the drop.'

'But, I—'

'Listen baby,' he snapped impatiently, 'you're supposed to be a whore, so you act like one.'

'You can't be serious.'

'Sure I am.'

Zuko pulled the knife from his pocket, and the blade flashed in the sunlight.

'Just take care of our property, that's all,' he growled. 'Now get moving... and remember, we'll be somewhere behind you and watching every move you make.'

29

Chapter Four

Danni's heart was pounding against her ribcage as she made
her way down the alley, the bag securely over her shoulder
and bouncing lightly against her hip as she walked. It was a
narrow, sinister place, the walls daubed with angry slogans.
Litter lay everywhere, and the stench of rotting waste was
almost overpowering. The two high-walled buildings
between which she walked blocked the sun, and the shade
chilled her flesh. She glanced back the way she had come.
The car was still parked in the sunshine, and she knew Hakis
and Zuko were watching her from behind the tinted windows,
and a shiver ran through her as she thought of that wicked
knife.

Ahead she could see the end of the alley, where occasional
cars zipped by. She glanced down, taking in the inadequacy
of her clothing. She wondered what people would think of
her. Her breasts were perfectly outlined by the thin top, her
nipples pressed so tight against the material that even the
smallest contour was visible. She knew she looked every
inch the tart she was supposed to be portraying.

And yet, once again, she found another quite unexpected
emotion beginning to creep into her mind as she considered
her appearance. It was an odd excitement at the blatant way
she was displaying herself. Danni knew she had a gorgeous
body, and had fantasised often about showing it off. A boy
she knew had once asked to photograph her nude and, though
she had refused, the idea had stayed with her since, and she
had often found herself unaccountably excited by the
thought. Now, as she contemplated the idea of being seen
so scantily dressed in a busy street, she felt once again the
odd, perverse thrill of arousal from deep within.

She reached the end of the alley and her footsteps faltered

momentarily. She knew Hakis and Zuko were still watching, so, taking a deep breath, she stepped out onto the street.

It was not the type of neighbourhood she would have visited by choice. Like the areas they had been driving through earlier, the street was strewn with litter. The few shops that were still in business were heavily barred at the front, and those that weren't had their windows boarded over and covered with fly-posters. There were a number of big old cars parked at the kerb, many of which looked as though they hadn't been driven for some time.

The people on the street were as dowdy as their surroundings. Mothers scurried by with ragged children in tow. Men stood in the shop entrances, their eyes hidden beneath cap peaks while, on the corners, groups of youths slouched, smoking and talking.

Danni hurried down the street, her high heels clicking against the pavement. She kept her head down, looking neither right nor left. As she passed one group of youths they shouted lewd comments at her, but she pretended not to hear, intent on getting to her destination as quickly as possible.

Now and then she passed genuine prostitutes, dressed in leather mini-skirts or thin frocks through which their underwear was visible. They stared at her with open hostility as she passed, making her quicken her step towards her destination.

She had gone four blocks now, and still the area was as squalid as ever. She stepped out as best she could, given the inadequacy of her skirt.

She first became aware of the man when, glancing in one of the rare shop windows, she glimpsed the reflection of a figure following her. She could make out little of him in the short time he was in her view, but she saw enough to know he was a heavily built figure, and that he was very close behind her.

She quickened her pace, listening hard for his tread, but

the sound of her own shoes drowned it out. Then she passed another window and her heart sank as she realised he was still there. She tried a new tactic, slowing down in the hope that he would pass her, but still he remained just behind. She clutched the bag tightly. If she lost that, there was no telling what Hakis and Zuko would do to her.

'Hey, baby, what's the problem?'

The voice came from close behind her, but still she didn't turn, keeping her eyes fixed straight ahead as she walked along. Then a hand descended on her shoulder.

'Listen babe, it's you I'm talking to.'

Aware that she could no longer ignore the man, Danni stopped and turned to face him. He was indeed large, with broad shoulders.

'What is it?' she asked. 'What do you want?'

'What d'ya think?' he asked. 'You're on the game, right? You're looking for business.'

'I... I'm on my way home,' she stammered stupidly.

'That's okay, I'll come with you.'

'No!'

'Then we'll go someplace else,' he persisted

'Look, I can't. Not just now—!'

He suddenly grabbed her wrist and twisted it painfully.

'Listen!' he hissed. 'You a whore or what?!'

She squirmed in his grasp. 'Please, you're hurting me.'

'Well?' he snapped, ignoring her discomfort.

'I am, but...'

'Then let's you and me go someplace and get it on. I don't give a shit where. I just wanna fuck you.'

She glanced about her. One of the gangs of youths was listening to the conversation.

'I can't take you to my place,' she said. 'My girlfriend's using it.'

'What the hell. We'll do it right here then.'

She looked at him incredulously. 'We can't do it here! People will see!'

He pulled her closer and, to her intense embarrassment, slipped a hand down inside her top, closing it over her breast. She tried to struggle free, but he was too strong for her, mauling her firm breast contemptuously.

'You gonna come along, or have I got to drag you?'

She tried to think straight; the man was obviously not taking no for an answer.

'Where can we go?' she asked quietly, trying to buy herself some time.

A lecherous smile spread across his face at her capitulation. 'Now that's more like it,' he leered. He relinquished his grip on her breast and backed her toward a narrow alley that ran off the main street. It was deserted and draped in chilly shadows, not unlike the one she had come down earlier. This one was, however, a dead end, with a high wall running across it. Danni glanced about anxiously. Surely he couldn't be suggesting they do anything there?

They reached the end of the alley. It widened out a little, with doorways on each side, and he took her to the left, pushing her up against an old, peeling door. In this position they were hidden from the street, but only just. She looked up at the man's unattractive face. He was staring down at her body, and all at once she realised the full import of what was happening. She, innocent little Danni Bright, was about to give herself for money in a dirty alleyway. She would sell her body to this burly stranger and would allow him to perform the most intimate act with her. It seemed barely credible, yet even as she stood, her back pressed against the rotting wood, the man was running a hand up the slit in her skirt, and she was doing nothing to stop him.

'How much?' he asked as his hand travelled higher up the smooth flesh of her thigh.

'Pardon?'

'You heard me. What's the charge? I don't want your pimp on my back.'

'Oh. I... er... Twenty dollars,' she stammered. She had

absolutely no idea what the going rate was, and had simply plucked the amount from the air.

'Twenty dollars?' He grinned and licked his whiskered chin salaciously. 'Okay, you gotta deal. Now get your skirt off.'

'Couldn't you just—'

'Get it off,' he hissed. 'Shit baby, you some kind of amateur or something?'

He stepped back, his eyes fixed on her. Danni glanced about. There was nobody in sight, though she knew that at any minute someone might walk up the alley. Reluctantly she reached for the catch at the side of the skirt and unhooked it.

The skirt came away, leaving her naked from the waist down. She blushed as the man's eyes fixed on the wispy blonde curls between her thighs.

'Very nice,' he murmured. 'Very nice indeed. Now show me your tits.'

Once again Danni hesitated, but she knew she must obey. Slowly she lifted the hem of the top, pulling it up and exposing the pale swellings of her breasts to him. He grinned, his eyes taking in her large brown teats which, to her embarrassment, were stiff and tingling.

He moved close. She could smell him; a mixture of sweat and tobacco smoke. Then his hand plunged between her thighs and she gasped as he nudged her feet apart with the scuffed toe of a shoe and slipped a rough finger into her.

Without warning an extraordinary thrill coursed through Danni's near-naked body. Despite her reluctance, the sensation of his finger probing her in so intimate a manner was suddenly very arousing indeed and, to her chagrin, she felt juices flowing deep within her as animal instincts took control. She knew he could sense her arousal, and he pressed her back, twisting his finger and watching as she squirmed, small moans escaping her moist lips.

'Shit baby, for a whore you're really hot for it,' he

34

murmured. 'You not been getting enough business or something?'

Danni said nothing, her eyes avoiding his, but her body said all as she pressed her wet crotch down onto his finger, the muscles of her sex tightening about his intruding digit.

He held her for a moment longer, then let go and stood back again. Danni remained where she was, her legs spread, pressed back against the door like some beautiful specimen pinned to a collector's board. Her breasts rose and fell as she breathed heavily. She scarcely believed she was behaving in such a disgraceful manner while people passed by not fifty metres away. And yet, far from concerning her, the idea was giving her a thrill that she wouldn't have thought possible only the day before. Somehow the thought of being seen like this, in broad daylight, was an extraordinary turn-on, and the more the stranger's eyes took in her charms the wetter she became.

His hands dropped to his waist and she watched in fascination as he unfastened his grubby jeans. He let them fall open and his cock sprang free, long and circumcised, the helmet shiny and smooth. Danni couldn't take her eyes off it as he ran his hand up and down the turgid shaft, his eyes still fixed on her.

He moved in again, his erection brushing against her bare stomach. He took hold of her under the arms and lifted until her feet were clear of the ground.

'Spread your legs, baby,' he said. 'Wrap them round my waist.'

Danni felt his thick member probing between her thighs, pressing insistently against her warm, soft flesh. She suddenly wanted him inside her, her inhibitions forgotten as the desire to be fucked overwhelmed her. She settled her thighs around his hips as she reached down and wrapping her fingers around his shaft. She guided him to her vagina, pressed his bulbous helmet against the damp, yielding flesh, then emitted a soft moan of pleasure as he stabbed with his hips and penetrated her.

He pressed her down onto his long pole, bringing fresh cries from her as she felt him slide ever deeper inside. He squeezed her lower and lower, until he was filling her wonderfully with his meaty erection.

He pressed her back into the doorway, the rough wood digging into her bare back. Then he began to fuck her, his hips thrusting forward with short jabbing movements, slamming her and the forgotten shoulder-bag against the door with every stroke.

The noise they made as they banged back and forth seemed tremendous to her ears, and she felt sure somebody would come and discover their shameful act. But the alley remained deserted, and slowly she became lost in the pure carnal pleasure of the moment, her arms about his neck, her legs wrapped round his hips as he fucked her young body with gusto.

He came quickly, almost too quickly for Danni, his cock pulsating as he pumped his seed deep into her vibrant body. It triggered a glorious orgasm in her. She threw her head back and cried aloud as her inner muscles tightened rhythmically about him, milking him, the sensation of his semen in her vagina taking her to knew heights of pleasure that even Bourne had failed to scale.

He went on humping against her until all his seed was spent, and she was a gasping, limp doll in his arms. Then he lifted her from his erection and deposited her on the step. She leant back against the door, panting for breath, careless and unashamed of her nudity. She glanced into his face, and he gave her a bemused grin.

'Shit, honey,' he exclaimed, 'I guess you needed that as much as me. You're some hot babe. Here.' He held out his hand.

Danni gazed at him for a moment, then realised he was giving her something. She took it from him and he turned and headed back up the alley, fastening his pants and whistling cheerfully.

She studied the note in her hand. It was a twenty-dollar bill.

Now she really was a whore.

Danni re-emerged onto the street, her skimpy clothing neatly back in place. The youths were still there, grinning and pointing, but she ignored them. She had lost enough time as it was. She had to be getting on with her mission.

For the next few blocks she went unmolested, making time as best she could, the bag still over her shoulder. Now and again a passer-by would look in her direction, or a comment would be made, but she paid no attention, her eyes fixed on the way she was going.

At last she caught sight of a flashing neon sign up ahead, bearing the words 'Harry's Bar'. She gave a sigh of relief. She didn't know what was in the bag, but she knew it must be valuable, and that she would only be comfortable once it was delivered.

She was less than a hundred yards from the bar when the car drew up next to her. At first she tried to ignore it, as she had all the others whose occupants had shown an interest in her, but it continued to crawl along beside her as she walked. She glanced sideways at it. It was a sleek, sporty saloon, with gleaming chrome work, quite out of keeping with the other, rather dilapidated vehicles she had seen in the street. She could feel the driver's eyes on her.

'Hey, you,' he called. She risked a glance at him. He wore a brightly coloured jacket and his wrists were adorned with heavy gold bracelets.

Danni's heart sank. Another pickup! She wished they hadn't made her look so obviously tarty. She was determined not to be diverted from her task again, so she kept on walking, staring straight ahead. To her relief the car accelerated suddenly, leaving her behind.

Then, to Danni's dismay, it stopped about fifty metres

ahead. She was even more surprised when she saw two women climb from its rear seats. They were both dressed tartily. If he already had those two in the car with him, why had he tried to stop her?

The two women positioned themselves side by side on the pavement, with the man behind them. Danni's footsteps faltered slightly as she approached them. They were staring right at her, and they looked none too friendly.

She made to pass them, but they moved across, blocking her way, so that she was obliged to come to a halt.

'Excuse me,' she said.

'This the one, girls?' It was the man behind them who spoke.

'That's her. Bitch turned a trick right in front of our eyes. Didn't even have the decency to do it indoors.'

The man moved in between the two prostitutes. 'This true?' he asked Danni.

'Look,' she replied, 'you're blocking the pavement. Please let me pass.'

She tried once more to move around them, but they side-stepped, preventing her from getting by.

'Please, what do you want?' she asked.

'We're asking you if you turned a trick back there – up that alley.'

'Why do you want to know?'

'Just answer the question,' said the man, icily. 'Blondie here tells me you took some guy up an alley. That true?'

Danni sighed; it seemed nothing in this city was allowed to be private. But despite her trepidation she knew it would be the safest ploy to maintain her act.

'I did some business, yes,' she said quietly, the blood rising in her cheeks at having to make such an admission.

'So, who's pimping for you?' he asked, his black eyes watching her closely.

'I – I don't understand.'

'It's a simple enough question,' he persisted. 'Who's your

38

pimp?'

'I... I don't have one.'

The man's black eyes narrowed. 'Listen baby, you're working my patch here, you know that?'

'No... I—'

'Well you do now. All the chicks round here work for me, ain't that right girls?'

'Yeah, that's right,' chorused the two.

'Now, let's see what you got,' he continued.

'I'm sorry?' Danni didn't quite understand his meaning.

'Show me how much the bastard paid you. Jeez, don't you talk English?'

'Oh.' Danni showed him the twenty-dollar bill crumpled in her fist. 'Just this.'

'What?' he sneered. 'You did it for twenty dollars? What the hell you think you're doing? You trying to do me out of my livelihood?'

Danni shook her head desperately. 'No, of course not.' She held out the bill. 'Here, take it. It's yours. I don't want it.'

'Damn right it's mine,' growled the man, snatching it from her. 'And what's in there?' he said, pointing to the tiny bag resting against her hip.

Danni froze, and clutched it ever tighter. 'Nothing,' she blurted, and waited for him to snatch that too.

Fortunately the man didn't pursue it. 'Get her in the fuckin' car. We got some serious talking to do.'

'I can't get in the car!' Danni protested.

'What you mean, you can't? Get in the goddamned car.'

'But, I'm going to Harry's Bar.'

'To poach some more of our business, eh?' sneered one of the women.

'No, I'm not.' Danni knew it was all going horribly wrong. 'I'm—'

'Too damn right you're not,' snapped the other. 'Come on, let's get the snotty bitch in the car.'

'No!' Danni tried to step back, but even as she protested the women moved quickly and grabbed her arms. She tried to struggle, but the pair were comfortably stronger than her. She looked about for help, but even those who had stopped to see what was happening seemed indifferent to her plight – or unwilling to risk helping in any way. Clearly the man and his girls had some clout on that street.

'But you don't understand,' she protested as they hustled her into the back of the car. 'I'm not a prostitute.'

'Oh no?' said one of the woman while chewing on her gum. 'Then how come you just sold yourself for twenty dollars?'

'No…' Danni pleaded. 'I… I was just playing a role. Somebody told me to. I had no other choice.'

'Some role play; getting fucked down an alley,' said the man. 'I guess we'd better give her a few lessons in what happens when someone muscles in on our patch, eh girls?'

'Yeah. Take her back to your place. We'll show her what's what.'

'No, please,' implored Danni, struggling to free her wrists. 'I have to get to Harry's bar.'

'All in good time, sister,' said one of the women. 'Right now you're coming with us.'

The pimp slammed the car into gear, and with a screech of tyres they were off down the road.

Danni watched in despair as the car swept past Harry's Bar and swung recklessly around a left turn. She glanced down at the bag clutched tightly in her hands. What would Hakis and Zuko say when she failed to deliver it? True it wasn't in any way her fault, but would they believe that? So far they had shown no sign at all of any sympathy toward her. Now she had failed them, and she had few illusions as to how they would react.

She glanced nervously at the two women who flanked her. One was a slim brunette with tightly permed hair. Her companion was a platinum blonde, and her roots showed darkly at the crown. Both wore thick make-up and both were dressed in brightly coloured mini-dresses that showed large expanses of thigh and deep cleavage. She knew she could expect little sympathy from the pair, and her heart sank at the way her life seemed to be spiralling downward in ever-decreasing circles.

They drove for about fifteen minutes through more rough, uninviting streets. The car took so many twists and turns that, by the time they finally pulled up outside a tenement block, Danni had completely lost her already uncertain bearings.

The brunette opened the door, and Danni was hauled unceremoniously from the car. They led her through a doorway into a musty corridor that smelled of stale urine, then up an unlit flight of steps. The pimp unlocked a door, and they ushered her inside.

The apartment was sparsely furnished, with posters on the grubby walls and a threadbare carpet on the floor. A bed in the corner gave a clue as to what it was used for. There was a door on the far side. Beyond was another room and, as she entered it, Danni stopped short, staring about her in amazement.

The room was furnished like none she had ever seen before. The decor was a drab purple that covered both walls and floor. There was another bed, but the rest of the furniture was totally unorthodox. There was a frame in the centre, consisting of a stout square of wood about seven feet high, with gleaming chains attached at each corner. Beside it was a sort of vaulting horse, similarly equipped with chains. There were a number of other devices, the purpose of which she could only guess at. On one wall was a rack bedecked with whips and canes, and another bearing chains and cuffs.

'How do you like our little torture chamber?' grinned the pimp. 'It's a real favourite with the customers.'

'It's a good place to show little upstarts like you what happens when you stray onto our territory,' said the blonde.

41

Danni stared at her with wide eyes, then at the equipment that filled the dank room.

'Listen,' she pleaded, 'it was a mistake. I didn't mean to invade your territory. You've taken my money, couldn't we just leave it at that?'

'You're damned right it was a mistake,' growled the pimp. 'Come on girls, let's get a look at little Miss Prim.'

The two whores grinned salaciously. Before Danni could protest, the blonde snatched her top and, with a single tug, tore it from her and slung it aside. Danni's hands flew up to her breasts, covering the nipples with her palms, but even as she did so the brunette grabbed her skirt, snapping the fastening as she tore it from her, leaving the youngster totally nude.

Once again Danni tried to cover herself, placing the shoulder-bag over her crotch while she hugged her breasts. But the brunette snatched it from her, carelessly tossed it aside as she had the ripped clothes, and Danni found herself being dragged towards the wooden frame.

She tried to struggle, but once again the strength of the two was too much for her and she had no chance. They worked quickly, clearly used to using the equipment. Danni's hands were pulled above her head and cold metal manacles closed about her wrists. Once these were in place the pair did the same with her legs, ignoring her desperate protests, closing the steel bands about her ankles and holding her fast. She was immobilised now, but still they hadn't finished. Taking hold of the chains, they hauled on them, pulling them tight and stretching Danni's lovely young body into the shape of an X.

Danni tugged at her bonds, but in vain. She was quite unable to move, her slender limbs pulled tight and already beginning to ache. On the wall directly opposite the frame was a mirror. With a groan of despair she closed her eyes against the sight of her own stretched and vulnerable body.

She was hit by a sense of absolute helplessness, the

intensity of which she had never felt before.

'Please,' she whispered. 'Please let me go.'

'Gag her,' said the pimp. 'We don't want to be disturbing the neighbours.'

The brunette pulled something from one of the racks. It was a black rubber ball with leather straps attached. She twisted Danni's hair, pulled her head back and forced the ball between her teeth. Then she snagged it tight behind Danni's head.

'Mmmff…' Speech was quite impossible with the gag in her mouth. All Danni could do was mumble incoherently.

'Good,' said the pimp approvingly. He stepped forward and slowly reached towards the trussed girl, his lifeless eyes glinting. Danni tried to draw back, but it was useless. His hand closed over her breast, and she closed her eyes again in defeat as he toyed with it, unhindered.

'Mmmff…' she moaned again.

'What's the matter, little missy?' taunted the man, 'don't you like guys touching your tits? Some whore you are,' he sniggered, and then turned to the other two. 'Now, let's teach her a little lesson.' He looked at the blonde. 'Do you wanna do the honours?'

'Sure,' she grinned. 'It'll be a pleasure.'

As Danni watched, she approached the rack and selected something from it. She brought it back and held it in front of the young captive's face. It was a cane, a long length of bamboo, not much thicker than a pencil. She flexed it between her hands while Danni looked on fearfully.

'I think you need a little reminder that this is *our* patch, just in case you were thinking of invading it again,' she said. 'A reminder you won't forget.'

'Mmmff!' Danni shook her head from side to side as a cold realisation crept over her. They were going to use the cane on her. They were going to beat her bare flesh, and there was absolutely nothing she could do about it. She stared despairingly at them, but they were stony-faced. Then the blonde moved behind her and lifted her arm.

'I'm going to enjoy this,' she said spitefully.

Swish! *Whack*!

She brought the cane down with tremendous force across Danni's bare backside, the wood cutting into the youngster's soft flesh. For a second she felt nothing, then a dreadful pain invaded her body that overshadowed all other senses, completely overwhelming her.

Swish! *Whack*!

The vicious woman brought the cane down again, striking the pale skin of Danni's backside just below the first blow, leaving a thin white mark that almost immediately began to darken to red. The naked youngster screamed into her gag as the pain hit her for the second time, the tears welling up in her beautiful eyes.

Swish! *Whack*!

Down it came with undiminished force, again swiping into her firm rump and leaving a fresh stripe across the smooth flesh. To Danni the pain was almost unbearable, yet she saw not a flicker of pity on the faces of her tormentors.

Swish! *Whack*!
Swish! *Whack*!
Swish! *Whack*!

The blows fell one after another, each one bringing excruciating agony to the young beauty as her body was rocked back and forth by the force of them. Her backside was on fire, the pain almost unimaginable, the tears rolling down her cheeks. Yet still the woman continued to beat her, apparently oblivious to her distress.

Swish! *Whack*!
Swish! *Whack*!
Swish! *Whack*!

Then, at last, it was over, and Danni hung in her chains, her naked body racked with sobs, her poor buttocks a mass of angry stripes. The blonde dropped the cane to the floor, stepped forward, and undid the gag. She pulled the ball from between Danni's teeth.

It was fully five minutes before Danni managed to bring herself into some semblance of control. When, at last, the mist cleared from her eyes, she gazed across at her reflection once more. Her face was red, and her skin glistened with a thin sheen of perspiration that covered her from head to toe. The stinging in her bottom was less intense now, but still she squirmed and whimpered.

The slimy pimp cupped her chin and pulled her face up to his.

'You understand now who's the boss on the street?'

'Yes,' she said quietly. 'I understand.' She had understood all along. It was just that he hadn't wanted to listen. He was only interested in controlling girls like her, and she knew now how he maintained it.

He moved a hand down between her legs, and she gave a sudden gasp as his fingers found her clitoris. With a shock she realised it was hard, and that even during the beating her juices had been flowing. In fact, now she thought about it, the caning had had a physical effect that she wouldn't have believed possible. It had actually aroused her, sexually. Now, as the pimp ran his finger back and forth over her clitoris, she found herself to be very turned on indeed.

Danni's mind was in turmoil. She didn't want to betray herself to the fiends, but her enforced nudity and her bondage were already exciting her more than she cared to admit. Now, as the pimp stimulated her with his finger, she felt her body responding to him in a way she simply couldn't control, and a small sigh escaped as her sex muscles contracted about his fingers.

'Shit,' he exclaimed, 'our little missy's horny as hell! Just look at her squirm.'

'Yeah,' agreed the brunette, 'I reckon you're right. She's hot for it. You want us to untie her?'

'Oh yeah. I like to sample the merchandise now and again – perk of the job,' he leered.

Danni stared at him, then at the two whores, as the import of what he was saying slowly sank in. He intended to fuck her. No permission had been asked, and none granted. It was as if he owned her. It was outrageous.

Yet, along with her indignation at his presumption, a further surge of arousal swept through her young body as she felt the women begin to slacken the chains. She could scarcely credit it, but she suddenly badly wanted to have sex. The beating, the bondage, and the humiliation all seemed to have released yet another aspect of the personality that had been deeply buried within her, a latent masochism she had never even dreamed existed, but which now threatened to overwhelm her.

She protested as they dragged her across to the bed, but her protests were half-hearted. The women eased her down onto her back, the soreness in her bottom returning and making her gasp as it came into contact with the rough blanket. As they nudged her legs apart she tried to resist, but a look from the blonde told her that was not such a good idea.

'You want us to chain her?' asked the brunette.

The pimp shook his head. 'Just give me a hand.'

The blonde sat at the top of the bed holding Danni's wrists above her head, while the brunette sank to her knees in front of the pimp. Danni watched, still not quite believing what was happening to her, as she pulled down his zip. She rummaged inside and pulled the pimp's cock into view. It was large, and stood stiffly from his pants. She took it hungrily into her eager mouth and began to suck. As she did so, Danni felt the blonde's free hand cup her breasts, and she gave a small whimper of perverse pleasure as the whore began to play with her stiff nipples.

The brunette sucked her boss expertly, her head bobbing back and forth, coating his helmet with a shiny sheen of saliva. The wet sounds of her working tongue and lips filled the squalid room. The pimp, meanwhile, had his eyes fixed

46

on the gorgeous English girl lying helplessly on the bed.

'Okay,' he wheezed excitedly, and pushed the whore away from him, 'that's enough.' Danni gazed up at him, biting her lip anxiously as the blonde continued to tease her aching teats.

'I think she wants it,' grinned the whore.

Danni shook her head. 'No... please leave me alone.'

But her body told a different story, and the pimp ignored the plea as, without bothering to remove his clothes, he clambered onto the sagging bed and knelt between her spread legs. The old springs creaked under the weight of the three.

The brunette licked his ear, fumbled for his erection, and guided the tip toward Danni's pulsating vagina. She gave a little cry as she felt him press against the entrance to her most private place. Then he was inside her, and for the second time that day Danni felt her body surrender to the advances of a stranger as she abandoned herself to her lust.

He fucked her with long, easy strokes, his mighty cock stimulating her wonderfully as it slid back and forth. Danni abandoned control of herself, allowing her hips to thrust up to match his strokes. The blonde released her wrists and Danni wrapped her arms about the pimp's neck, pulling him close until her breasts were pressed flat against his shirt as she cried aloud with undiluted pleasure.

When he came Danni responded with a shattering orgasm, her inner muscles squeezing his cock as his semen pumped into her. She cried aloud as her body writhed beneath his, her legs tightening about his hips as she sucked him still deeper within, revelling in the sensation of being filled by his seed.

At last she was still. The pimp rose, making her sigh as his cock slipped from her. He stood, staring down at the red-faced girl for a moment, then turned to his companions.

'Better get her cleaned up,' he said. 'I reckon she's gonna work for me from here on in.'

Danni emerged from the shower room still naked, and still

unable to believe what was happening to her. Two strangers had had sex with her, she had performed fellatio on another, and it was still barely midday! Her loss of innocence had been as sudden as it was unexpected. Yet despite the shame she felt at her lascivious behaviour, she had never felt more alive and, even now, her nudity was exciting her as she stood before the man and two women.

'You going to put her on our street?' asked the brunette.

'Sure,' said the pimp. 'She'll make me a tidy fortune.'

Danni shook her head. 'No,' she said. 'I'm not really a prostitute – you have to believe me.'

The pimp laughed. 'Oh, you're a whore all right,' he said. 'Only a whore would dress like that, pull a trick the way you did, then fuck like a bitch on heat straight afterwards.'

'But you don't understand,' protested the youngster, blushing at his crudity. 'Besides, those weren't my clothes.'

The brunette picked up the tattered remains of Danni's skirt and top. 'Well I sure hope the owner doesn't want them back,' she laughed.

'Listen,' implored Danni, 'you *must* let me go. I have to meet somebody. It's very important.'

The pimp's eyes narrowed. 'You ain't going no place, sister,' he said. 'Hey, get the stuff. That'll quieten her down.'

'It'll make her as meek as a lamb,' sniggered the brunette as she disappeared into the bathroom.

'What are you going to do to me?' asked Danni in alarm.

'Just give you something to make you feel good,' replied the pimp.

The brunette quickly returned, carrying a bowl with a syringe in it. Danni stared in horror.

'No.'

She shook her head in wide-eyed disbelief and backed towards the closed door. But the blonde was already behind her, and she grasped the youngster's arms, holding her tight so that, no matter how hard she struggled, there was no escape. The pimp took the syringe from the bowl and held it up.

'Don't worry,' he said with a twisted grin, 'you'll enjoy yourself. It's only afterwards it becomes unpleasant. And then we can always let you have some more.'

'No...' she said again, but felt powerless to resist as the brunette pulled her arm out straight. The pimp gripped Danni tightly just below the elbow, and she watched in dismay as the vein swelled under the pressure—

At that moment there was a frightening and rapid thumping on the front door of the apartment.

'What the fuck...!' The pimp wheeled around. 'Who the fucks that?! They'll break the bastard down if they keep that up!'

The noise continued relentlessly, the sound echoing about the tiny room. The pimp turned to his two whores.

'Who the hell *is* that?'

'I hate to think,' said the brunette. 'But you'd better answer it.'

The angry pimp put the syringe back in the bowl. 'You keep damned quiet,' he hissed at Danni, and gave her arm an extra squeeze that made her wince. 'I'll be back for you.'

He went through into the other room with his two girls following close behind, leaving Danni on her own. She crept to the doorway and listened as the banging continued.

'Who is it?' he shouted. 'What do you want?'

'Open this door!' It was a man's voice, and he sounded as angry as the pimp.

'What for? What do you want?' he repeated.

'You've got a girl in there. We want her.'

'Can't have her. She's working for me now.'

'The hell she is. She's got something we want.'

'What?'

'A package. She was delivering it for Hakis and Zuko, only we're going to get it first.'

'Who the hell are you?'

'This is Malone.'

Colour drained from the pimp's complexion. 'Malone?' he asked, in a much quieter, more respectful tone.

'Yeah, Malone. Now open this door or there'll be some real trouble. I want that package.'

Danni turned. There on the floor was the little bag. The slimy pimp had barely noticed it, being more intent on having her punished and then taking advantage of her vulnerability. Somehow, someone had got wind of the fact that she was delivering it, just as Hakis had said had happened before, and from the pimp's reaction the man – Malone – was not one to mess with. But if he got his hands on the contents of the bag she knew she would be in even deeper trouble than she was now.

The conversation between the pimp and the man outside the door continued, but Danni knew it was only a matter of time before the pimp either opened the door or stood back and watched it get battered down. She had to try to escape while there was still time.

She peered through the doorway. The pimp, the brunette and the blonde were concentrating firmly on the problem to hand. Nobody was paying her any attention. She had to take the chance while she could. Slowly she closed the door. Once it was shut she grabbed a chair and propped it against the handle. She knew it wouldn't keep them out for long, but it was better than nothing.

She grabbed the bag, then searched about for something to wear. The skirt and top were useless, so she hastily dragged a sheet from the bed. She wrapped it about her, then crossed to the window and glanced out. She was on the first floor, but she knew she had to risk it. She pulled at the handle, but it wouldn't move.

From the other room shouting was still going on. Then Danni heard the front door being unlatched and she knew time was running out. Even as she struggled frantically with the window she heard a shout that told her that they had seen the door to the room was closed. Instantly they were banging on it. As she watched, it bulged inwards and the chair moved slightly. She made a final desperate effort and, with a creak, the handle on the window moved. With a gasp of relief she pushed it open and leaned out.

Her heart sank. The drop was further than she had thought. She would almost certainly break an ankle if she jumped. The thumping on the door was becoming more frantic now as shoulders were put to it, and she knew the straining chair wouldn't hold them for very much longer. She anxiously glanced about for something to lower from the window – something to climb down – but could see nothing. Then she thought of the sheet. It was a large one, and would probably be long enough to nearly reach the pavement. Once on the ground she'd have to try and pull it down after her. She quickly unwrapped it from her body, leaving her naked once more. Then, with trembling fingers, she tied one corner round a radiator that stood beneath the window and threw the other end out of the window. Throwing the strap of the mysterious bag over her shoulder once again she jumped up onto the sill and looked down. Below was another of the ubiquitous alleys, and it was deserted. Grasping hold of the sheet, she leaned back and began the terrifying climb down. Even as she did so a splintering crash from above told her that the door had finally yielded to the onslaught.

She scrambled down as quickly as she was able, and was soon standing with trembling legs on the ground. She tugged at the sheet, but it held fast. Then the pimp's face appeared at the window.

'There she is!' he yelled, pointing. 'The bitch is trying to escape!'

He was pushed aside and another figure appeared. It was obviously Malone. He was an ugly man with long greasy hair and an angry scar dissecting his chin.

Then Danni saw the gun.

'Stop there!' he shouted, and made a threatening movement with the weapon. 'I'll use this if I have to!'

51

Despite the threat, Danni was driven by instinct. She turned and ducked and ran deeper into the alley, the shouted abuse of the two men ringing in her ears.

She came to a junction. To her right she could see cars passing. She glanced down at her naked body. She couldn't possibly go that way. She turned left, praying there would be nobody about, and set off at a run. Rounding a corner she was suddenly confronted by three young men playing with a basketball in the middle of a dank street. As she dashed past them they laughed and whistled and jeered.

Then she turned another corner and stopped short. In front of her was another busy street. There seemed nowhere to go, and she daren't go back and face her pursuers.

To her left was a high wall. There was a rotting door in it nearby, so she hurried to it and tried the latch. The door moved, and then creaked open, and Danni nipped inside. She looked around and found herself in an untidy yard. It was narrow and long, and led up to the rear of a scruffy building. In a near corner was an old shed. She quickly moved to it, hoping she might be able to get inside and conceal herself, but the door was bolted and padlocked. She was about to turn away when she noticed that the shed was slightly raised from the ground, presumably to preserve it from damp. Danni looked at the bag. If she could just get rid of it, that would be one less thing to worry about. She crouched down and felt beneath the shed. The ground was dry under there. Carefully, she pushed the bag as far underneath as she was able to. Satisfied that nobody would ever find it, she straightened up, and then considered her predicament.

It was not a particularly good one; lost and naked in the middle of a strange city, with no money and no friends. And to make matters worse, she was being pursued by all sorts of ruthless and angry villains. She had no doubt that Hakis and Zuko would have discovered by now that she hadn't made the delivery, and she knew they would be none too

52

happy with her.

She considered trying to contact the police, but quickly dismissed the idea. After all, although she had no idea what was in the bag she had little doubt it was illegal, and that would make her an accessory. Proving her innocence in the mess would not be easy. It looked as if she was on her own.

Her first priority must be to get some clothes. As she was, she was ridiculously conspicuous and extremely vulnerable. She had to find something to cover herself.

She made her way carefully up the yard, picking her way around the discarded junk and empty beer crates. Peering around one particularly rusty fridge, she studied the back of the building. It looked a little dilapidated, with ragged curtains hanging in the windows.

And then her heart leapt.

To her right, close to the building, was a rotary washing line, and billowing in the breeze were a number of white tablecloths.

It wasn't much, but at least one of the cloths would be enough to cover her nudity, thus solving the most immediate of her problems. She looked around the yard for a while, and decided she was completely alone. It was now or never.

Danni moved cautiously forward again. As she drew closer to the tall building she could see into one of the ground floor windows, and realised she was looking into the back of a bar. She could just make out illuminated advertising signs and beer pumps, as well as figures moving about. She hesitated. Anyone looking out would see her. At the moment, though, all heads seemed to be turned away from her. She had to take the chance. She edged forward once again.

The washing line was close to the window, and she felt horribly exposed as she crept closer. She reached for one of the tablecloths with trembling fingers – and then the crunch of a footstep made her freeze.

'Well, well, well,' said somebody with a gruff voice, 'what have we here then?'

53

Chapter Five

Fear knotted Danni's stomach as she swung round to face the speaker. There, behind her, were three men. The one who had spoken was tall and dark-skinned, with a shaven head. From one lobe dangled a bright golden earring, and his sleeveless vest revealed numerous tattoos on his muscular arms. His two companions were shorter, and were both dressed in casual shirts and blue jeans. All three were eyeing the naked young beauty with obvious interest.

Danni snatched at one of the cloths, pulling it from the line and hugging it around her shapely form. It was still damp, and her pink flesh could be seen through the translucent material. Three pairs of eyes blatantly surveyed every inch of the lovely morsel standing timidly before them. Panic welled up inside Danni, but she fought it down; she must remain calm and try to brazen her way out of this latest disaster.

'Hello guys,' she said. 'I was just borrowing one of these cloths.'

'Borrowing it, eh?' said the tall man. 'It sure looks like you need it.'

Danni blushed. 'I lost all my clothes,' she blurted stupidly.

'Sure, we can see that, can't we boys?'

His two companions nodded and mumbled in agreement. Danni eyed the three suspiciously.

'I... I'd better be going,' she said, edging away.

'Going? Going where? You can't go anywhere like that. Besides, that cloth doesn't belong to you.'

'I'd just be borrowing it,' she said. 'Until I get some proper clothes.'

'I don't think Ed would like that.'

'Who's Ed?'

'He owns this bar. Perhaps you'd better come on in and meet him.'

Danni looked at the man in alarm. 'Oh no,' she exclaimed, 'I couldn't go in there.'

'But you have to if you want to borrow that cloth.' He took a slow step nearer, as though stalking a timid animal. 'Come on, baby. Don't disappoint us now.'

Danni backed away, and staggered a little as her heel caught on a crate. 'No... I—'

The man lunged with surprising agility and snatched her arm, and before she could defend herself, Danni found herself being propelled towards the rear-entrance.

She desperately clutched the cloth to her breasts as they bundled her through the door. Inside the atmosphere was smoky and humid, and the strong aroma of male sweat filled her nostrils. There were about a dozen customers in the bar, all of them men, and heads turned on all sides as Danni stumbled in, propelled by six rough hands. 'Look, I think—' she tried to protest, but the tall man cut her off sharply.

'Hey, Ed,' he snapped, 'look what we found outside. This little thief was stealing one of the cloths from your line.'

The grubby man behind the bar was about fifty years old. He was small, with a pronounced paunch that spoke of too many years in the trade. His eyes narrowed as he took in Danni's slim form.

'Stealing?' he spat.

'I – I would have brought it back,' said Danni. 'Please, I just needed something to cover myself.'

'Shit Larry,' said a man close by. 'She's fucking naked under that cloth, ain't she?'

'Sure is,' grinned the tall man. 'Naked as the day she was born.'

As he confirmed the state of her undress, Danni heard chairs scraping back all around her, and the men began to move closer.

'Jeez you're right,' said another. 'I can see her arse. And

55

someone's been thrashing it, look!'

Danni swung round, pressing herself back against the bar, wincing slightly as she felt the hard wood against her tender behind.

The tall brute leaned even closer; she could smell his beer-stale breath.

'That right, baby? You get your arse thrashed?'

Danni lowered her gaze to the floor, and said nothing.

'Show us.'

She looked up at him. A nerve twitched in the corner of his eye; he was deadly serious. She glanced around at the other men. She was very nervous, but she dare not risk upsetting them. Perhaps if she complied they would help her. There seemed little else she could do.

She nibbled her lip. Then, slowly, she turned to face the bar, revealing her bare bottom to the men. At once there were whistles and shouts from those watching as they took in the pert globes and saw the criss-cross of angry stripes that decorated them. Danni remained stock-still, staring ahead at the large mirror behind the bar, her cheeks glowing. Then a rough hand touched one of her buttocks, and she gave a start.

'No,' she protested, instinctively pushing the hand away.

'Hey, easy,' said the tall man. 'I was just checking it out. Someone thrashed you good. Who was it?'

'It doesn't matter,' whispered Danni. 'Can I turn round now, please?'

'Sure you can. Listen, you look like you could use a drink. Hey, Ed, a beer for the lady.'

'No, it's all right. I have to be going.'

'You've got time for a beer, surely? Besides, you can't leave with Ed's cloth, can she Ed?'

The squat bar owner shook his head. 'Those damned things cost money.' He placed a bottle of beer on the bar beside Danni.

'Come on, baby, take a swig,' said the tall man.

. Danni glanced at the beer; there was no glass. Holding the cloth between her cleavage with one hand, she picked up the chilled bottle with the other and placed it to her lips. She took a sip. The beer was cold and refreshing, and she tipped her head slightly and savoured a second mouthful. Then she noticed that all eyes were upon her, and she realised what they were fantasising about as the glistening tip of the bottle lay between her moist lips. Blushing profusely, she stammered her thanks for the drink and put the bottle back on the bar.

'Nice technique,' grinned the tall man. 'Now, I think Ed wants his cloth back.'

Danni had been expecting, and dreading, this next move.

'The cloth – Ed wants it back.'

'But… it's all I've got on,' she protested, but with little hope of finding any compassion.

'That's okay, nobody here's going to mind.'

'But I can't. Please don't make me.'

'Listen, baby,' put in the bar owner, 'you took the damn cloth without asking. In my book that's stealing, and we don't like thieves around here.'

'Yeah,' called somebody. 'Take it off.'

Immediately every man in the oppressive bar seemed to swamp her and join in, urging her to remove the cloth. Danni didn't want to anger them; her position was precarious enough, and as the lewd urging grew louder she knew she really had no other choice but to do as they demanded.

'Okay,' she acquiesced quietly. 'I'll do what you want… if I have to.'

Slowly she lowered her hand, revealing her firm young breasts to the drooling men. She glanced down at them. She wasn't sure if it was the coldness of the damp cloth or something more fundamental, but her nipples were very hard, and she knew that fact was not lost on those watching. She felt the colour rise in her cheeks.

'And the rest,' urged someone. 'Show us the rest.'

Danni sighed resignedly and let the cloth fall away altogether.

The men mumbled their licentious approval as the young beauty stood quietly in defeat, her hands hanging by her sides, her charms on open display to everyone huddled around. The tall brute took the cloth from her limp fingers and threw it to the slavering bar owner, then he placed an arm about her waist.

'Now, that's better,' he said, his eyes fixed on Danni's erect nipples. 'Hey guys, aren't there any gentlemen here? Get the lady a stool.'

If Danni had hoped her ordeal would end there, she was quickly disappointed. It was clear that the men intended to enjoy the sight of her nudity for a while longer. With a sigh she accepted the stool and perched gingerly on it, once again receiving a reminder of the beating she had received such a short time before as the cold plastic of the seat came into contact with her bare bottom.

The next half hour was the most bizarre of Danni's young life. There she was, sitting at the bar of this male-only establishment, surrounded by ruffians drinking beers and passing lewd comments about her body and what they'd like to do with it. It was like a dream she sometimes had, where she was amongst a group of smartly dressed people, yet she herself had no clothes on. The difference, though, was that this was no dream, and the men who leered at her were very real indeed.

It was after she had finished her beer, and protested once again that she wanted some clothes, that the tall man made his next move.

'First you gotta dance for us,' he said.

'I beg your pardon?'

'You heard. We wanna see you dance.'

'Dance? What, right here? I can't.'

'Sure you can. A chick with a nice body like yours has got to be a good dancer. You can show us what you've got.'

'Haven't you already seen enough?' she asked despairingly.

'We like what we see,' he replied. 'Come on baby, we'll put something good on the juke-box, and you can dance on the bar.'

'But I can't dance.'

His face darkened slightly. 'Listen, either you dance or we get angry. You wouldn't like some more stripes across that pretty little arse of yours, now would you?'

Danni tried to argue, but the men were on their feet again and, despite her protests, she found herself being lifted bodily up onto the bar until she was standing above them, one hand clutched to her crotch, the other trying vainly to cover her breasts.

'Right,' the tall man continued, 'somebody put on some music. Something she can really shake her body to.'

Instantly the speakers at the back of the room struck up with a strong, rock number. It was loud, and filled the bar with a throbbing rhythm. Some of the men began to clap with the beat, while others banged their bottles on the tabletops, whooping their encouragement to poor Danni. She gazed down at them, an icy claw gripping and churning her stomach.

'Come on,' shouted someone. 'Get dancing.'

Slowly, reluctantly, Danni began to move in time with the pulsing music.

The truth was that Danni was an extremely good dancer. She had had some training when she was younger and had always been in demand during school dances, where she would sometimes dance alone while her friends watched, losing herself in the rhythm of the music, her natural inhibitions forgotten. But nothing had prepared her for this; standing above a group of lewd and inebriated men, completely naked, the only female in the room. She knew she had to do it though, or risk their wrath, so she tried as best she could not to think of the sight she made, and concentrated on the music. She ground her hips from side to side, moving languidly, her eyes closed as she lost herself to the beat.

'Move your hands!' came a gruff instruction from the audience.

'Yeah, show us the lot,' commanded another.

Danni opened her eyes and gazed down at them again. She was still covering her breasts and sex with her hands, but as their shouted demands grew more intense she knew she would have to obey them. Reluctantly she let her hands fall away. Standing as she was, up on the bar, she knew she was giving them a perfect view of her exposed sex, and an unexpected and inexplicable shiver of excitement gripped her young body.

The beat intensified, and she found herself losing herself in the music, just as had happened in her younger days. She let her hips and breasts sway seductively from side to side, knowing full well what effect she would be having on the ogling mass of drunks, and thrilling to the naughty realisation. Gradually she became aware of her own simmering arousal. She could barely comprehend the gorgeous sensation, but suddenly there was something unbelievably wicked and sensual about exhibiting her body in such a wanton manner. She remembered the mirror, and couldn't resist turning to watch herself as she twisted and swayed. She saw a beautiful young girl, her body slim and sexy, writhing sensuously, apparently unconcerned by such lewd behaviour.

She turned to face the gawking men once more. She was now extremely turned on indeed. Almost unconsciously her hands crept up her torso, stroking and teasing. She cupped her breasts, lifting and caressing them. The sensation of her own touch was wonderful, and she began to stimulate her nipples, taking them between finger and thumb and teasing the aching buds to hardness, bringing a fresh murmur of appreciation and encouragement from those watching.

She peered down through lowered eyelashes. She had their total attention now, and she loved it. Jean fronts bulged their silent homage to her performance. Never before had she felt so turned on. Some perverse side of her nature was beginning to take command of her once more as the latent exhibitionist within drifted to the surface. She felt a surge of warmth in her crotch as she imagined the sight she must make.

The sensation when she touched her clitoris was electric. A gasp escaped her moist lips as she began her intimate caresses. Danni rarely masturbated, but now her enforced nudity, the earthy rhythm of the music, and the appreciative audience, stripped her of all inhibitions, and she began to rub herself, her fingers moving back and forth over her pulsing bud as her body trembled with arousal. Her dance was no more; she was standing with her feet apart, one hand squeezing and caressing her delectable breasts while the other teased her labia. And the more abandoned her behaviour became, the more her juices coated her fingers and the creamy flesh of her thighs.

Danni was out of control; lost in the heavenly delights of self-stimulation, scarcely hearing the comments of those watching as she pleasured herself with enthusiasm. Her fingers pumped in and out, faster and faster, the tension building until she wanted to scream with sheer lust.

She came with a cry, a glorious orgasm sweeping through her trembling body. Her fingers moved still faster, extracting every ounce of pleasure that could be extracted.

As her lust began to slowly ebb she dropped forward onto her knees, her head thrown back, her mouth open as she breathed deeply, and her breasts rising and falling as she gradually calmed and gathered her senses.

Danni looked around at the smirking men, still barely able to believe what she had just done. Now that the passion of the moment had drained away, the stark reality was almost impossible to accept. How could she have possibly behaved in such a disgraceful way for all those slavering men?

Yet, as she felt the wetness that coated her fingers, she had to accept that she had behaved in such a disgraceful way. But, she also had to accept that she had just experienced the most extraordinary orgasm, brought about as much by the way the rude audience had watched her as by the ministrations of her fingers. If she had had any doubts about the exhibitionist within, they had to be utterly dispelled now. Innocent young Danni Bright had become a sensual, sexual being with desires she had never dreamed possible.

A rough hand closed around her breast, and she looked up to see the tall man stroking her, his large fingers teasing her still swollen nipples. She drew back slightly, but he continued his mauling, grinning broadly as he did so. She turned to the wheezing bar owner, unable to miss the telltale bulge beneath his grubby apron.

'Is there somewhere I could clean up?' she asked.

'There's the kitchen out back,' he blurted, prodding his thumb towards an opening behind the bar. 'There's a sink in there.'

Danni tried to climb down from the bar, but the tall man gripped her arm.

'Where d'you think you're going?' he said. 'We're not done with you yet.'

'I just need to clean up a bit,' she complained. 'Please stop squeezing my arm, you're hurting me.'

He held onto her for a moment longer, and then relented, releasing his crushing grip and allowing her to drop down beside Ed. The bar owner licked his fat lips, clearly relishing being in such close proximity to the young beauty, and Danni quickly slipped away from him and through to the back.

As she washed, she wasn't surprised to hear someone come into the kitchen. She was even less surprised to see it was the bar owner. He moved close behind her, and she felt his fingers trace the smooth skin of her shoulders. She shuddered at the clammy touch, but dared not rebuff him.

'That was quite some dance,' he drooled.

Danni blushed, but said nothing.

'You danced there like you'd been doing it all your life. You danced like a professional.'

'I... I used to enjoy dancing,' she said. 'But I've never danced like that before. I've never danced naked.'

'A girl can make good money dancing naked in this city.'

'I don't think so – it's not the sort of thing I do.'

'No?'

Danni closed her eyes and said nothing as she felt something firm nudge between her buttocks. His touch made her skin crawl, but she knew it would be extremely unwise to let her revulsion show.

'Well, you've got to do something.' His breath was heavily laden with a sickly-sweet cocktail of garlic and tobacco. It ruffled the soft hair at her temple as he spoke.

'What do you mean?'

'I got a call a few minutes before you turned up here. Word is that people are looking for you... Word is they're very important people.'

Danni thought her legs were going to give way. 'Im – important people?'

'Oh yeah. How long you been in this city?'

'I only arrived yesterday.'

'That figures. This city's run by two rival gangs – the Dirangos and the Killarneys. Both have been trying for years to take control of the other's territory. Word is that the Dirangos gave some English chick a package to deliver, but it never got there, and now both gangs are after her. Now that English chick wouldn't be you, would it?'

'I...' Danni wanted to deny her part in the episode, but the redness in her cheeks betrayed her.

The sleazy bar owner smiled and nodded knowingly at her silent admission. 'And what did you do with the package?'

Danni thought quickly. At the end of the day, whatever was in that bag was the one thing that just might save her.

63

For the time being she had to protect its hiding place.

'I – I lost it,' she stammered, and cringed at how unconvincing she sounded. She could feel his beady eyes boring into her, and for a moment she feared he wouldn't believe her. He shook his head.

'You lost it.'

'Yes… I dropped it somewhere.'

'Really?' He didn't sound convinced.

'Yes.'

'Well, in that case you're in even bigger trouble than before,' he said. 'It won't be long until word gets out about the English girl who's putting on a show in my bar. Then they'll track you down.'

'But please, what can I do?'

He ran rough fingers over her cheek. She tried to pull away, but there was nowhere to go, pinned against the sink as she was.

'Perhaps I can help you.'

'How – how would you do that?'

The clammy touch slid down the elegant sweep of her slender neck, crept under her arm, and cupped her naked breast. She wanted to push it away, but dare not. Instead she stood quietly as he stroked her protruding nipple with his thumb, trying to suppress the treacherous feeling that the intimacy of his touch was evoking within her.

'I'm not just the barman here,' he said. 'I own this bar, along with a few others.'

'I know,' said Danni, though she couldn't understand why this should be relevant to her situation.

'I got a good friend, runs a club on the other side of the city. A place where guys go to relax. She could use a new girl there.'

'Doing what?'

'A little bit of dancing. A little bit of entertaining.' As he spoke he turned her slightly and squeezed her breast, staring into her eyes. 'A little bit of something else.'

'Something else?'

'Yeah, keeping the customers satisfied, as it were.'

'You mean...'

'You know what I mean.'

Danni shook her head. 'I couldn't... I—'

'It'd be the perfect hiding place until the heat dies down.'

'No. No, sorry, I just couldn't—'

'Please yourself.' He stepped back a little. 'I guess you'd better go back to the bar, then. The boys are preparing one of the pool tables, and they're drawing lots to see who's going to fuck you on it first.'

'What?'

'What did you expect after your little performance? You're about to get gang-banged by a bunch of pretty rough guys. Now get back out there and be ready to spread your legs.'

'No, please,' panic gripped her. 'I can't!'

The sleaze grinned slyly. 'You know the alternative.' He was still toying with her breast, his stubby fingers sending small shocks of pleasure through her as they pinched and rolled her sensitive nipples.

'What about them?' she said, meaning the drunken rabble in the bar. 'They'll come in here after me.'

'There's a door leads out the back,' he replied. 'I'll take you out and hide you, then tell them you ran off. When things have settled down, I'll come and get you.'

Danni hesitated. How could she be sure she could trust this horrible little man? Yet the alternative, being thrown to the waiting mob, didn't bear thinking about. What option did she have but to trust him, if she wasn't to go out there and submit to them?

'All right,' she said. 'I'll do what you say.'

'Now you're talking sense at last,' he said. 'Come with me.'

'Couldn't I get something to wear?'

'No time for that. Come on.' And, grabbing Danni's hand, he dragged her towards the rear door.

Chapter Six

Danni shivered slightly on the metal floor, though it wasn't cold that chilled her. In fact, the temperature in the back of the van in which she huddled was oppressively high, and but for the fact that she was naked, she would have been very hot indeed. No, the shiver was one of apprehension as she waited to discover what would befall her next.

She had no idea how long she had been in the smelly vehicle. The bar owner had bundled her out of the kitchen back door, and led her through an archway in the wall that surrounded the garden. He had wasted no time in unlocking the rear doors of the rusty van, and thrusting the young beauty inside. Then, to her dismay, he produced a crumpled tie from his pocket, with an evil glint of intent in his eyes.

'What are you going to do with that?' she asked, already fearing the worst.

'Just a bit of insurance, honey,' he replied. 'I wouldn't want to come back and find the lovely bird has flown.'

'But—'

'But nothing. Hold out your arms. Unless you'd prefer to go back to the bar, that is. I'm sure they're still waiting for you.'

Danni had stared at him for a moment in disbelief, then her shoulders had slumped in resignation. As far as she could see, this man was her only salvation. It was a choice of obeying him, or giving herself up to the mercy of the men waiting in the bar, or the thugs who were tracking her. Slowly she stretched her arms towards him.

'Good girl,' he said, and swiftly tied one end around her left wrist. He then pulled her arms behind her and she felt him thread it through part of the van's bodywork, before wrapping it around her right wrist and knotting it tightly.

66

She tried to move her arms, but they were trapped behind her back and she was trussed and helpless. The chill ran through her as she realised the control the squalid little man now exercised over her. He must have seen her consternation, for a triumphant smile flickered across his features.

'Don't worry, baby,' he said. 'Just behave yourself and you'll be okay.' He reached for her breasts again, his fingers lingering on the warm, soft flesh. Danni looked away, avoiding the gloating in his hungry eyes, but she knew her nipples were responding; hardening at once as he stroked them.

'You're gonna do really well for me,' he murmured. Then he turned and climbed from the van, locking the doors behind him.

Things were looking extremely bleak; rapidly turning from bad to worse. Danni wondered what the men in the bar said when the owner had returned without her. She guessed they had been none too pleased to discover she had escaped. She thought of them 'preparing' the pool table and eagerly awaiting her return. She imagined herself stretched out across the hard surface, wrists and ankles held wide apart as they took it in turns to screw her, thrusting their stiff cocks into her open vagina. The image made her shiver all the more.

She wished she had been left with a little more mobility. Her crouched position was very uncomfortable. She tried to stretch, but in the confined space and with her wrists bound she could gain little relief. She pondered her recent performance on the bar, and felt totally ashamed...

And yet, as she waited, alone and filled with anticipation of what was to come, she couldn't suppress the excitement that was beginning to build in the pit of her stomach. She thought of the establishment she was being taken to, and what would be expected of her there. It seemed barely possible that she should have found herself in this predicament. How could she possibly survive as a club dancer? Yet when she again thought back to what had happened in the bar, she realised that she was capable of more than she had ever thought possible. Even her most erotic dreams had not matched that incident for sheer wantonness. But that hadn't been a dream – it had been real, and as she remembered her disgraceful behaviour another tremor ran through her and she felt a familiar moistness deep inside her sex.

She shook her head. Surely what had happened to her was cruel and wrong. How then, could she explain her orgasm in the bar, or those she had enjoyed with the pimp and the stranger in the alley? Even now, she realised that the current bondage was quite simply thrilling her to the core. What was happening to her? What had become of the demure English girl she had been only the day before, and from where had this sudden appetite for raw sex come? She tried to blot from her thoughts the erotic images that were beginning to dominate them, but all she could think about was her vulnerability and the imminent return of the horrible bar owner, when he would no doubt do with her as he wished.

Almost immediately Danni heard someone shuffling around outside and the key turn in the lock. Her stomach muscles tightened in anticipation. She watched as the van door creaked slowly open, and then the sunlight swamped her cramped prison and framed the bar owner's rotund form. Danni blinked against the sudden brightness as he clambered inside and closed the door behind him. As he did so the vehicle rattled and shook into life, and she realised that someone was in the cab and had started the engine.

The bar owner's beady eyes crawled over every inch of Danni's exposed body. Her cheeks glowed with the humiliation of being inspected like a piece of meat, but she said nothing.

'The guys weren't too pleased that you'd gone,' he smiled. 'I guess your little act made them think you were game for anything.'

Danni said nothing.

'Still, they calmed down in the end, after a few more drinks. And now I've got you all to myself.'

'I... I thought you were taking me somewhere safe,' she said.

'Sure I am. Harry's up front at the moment. He's gonna drive. Meanwhile you and me are going to get better acquainted.'

Danni had known he would be back to take advantage of her. And despite her dislike of the dirty little man, if she were honest with herself, the thought of his return had been fuelling her arousal from the moment he'd left her tied and helpless. Now, as he reached for her breasts once more, she was unable to suppress a gasp as her flesh finally received the stimulation she had been eagerly anticipating during her naked sojourn.

At that moment there was a grinding of gears, and with a groan of complaint the vehicle lurched forward.

'It's a long drive,' leered the bar owner, licking his fat lips. 'But I guess we can amuse ourselves on the way.' He held her ankles and pulled until she was sitting with her legs out straight. He then placed a hand on her stomach, and it slowly slid lower.

'Please...' she whimpered quietly. But he ignored her, his fingers stroking the silky down between her smooth thighs, and then sliding lower still, toward the very centre of her desires.

'Ohhh...' she sighed, and a sudden jolt shook her petite frame as his rough fingers found her clitoris. She blushed with shame as she realised how wet she already was; her lustful daydreams now betrayed to her vile captor.

'Hey, you're horny again, you sexy little bitch,' he beamed.

Danni said nothing, but her breath shortened as he began to maul her, and her thighs inched slightly wider apart, allowing him even better access to her charms. He smirked as he saw her natural reaction.

'You're going to be real good in your new job,' he said.

69

'And I reckon you'll like it a whole lot.'

'Please don't do that to me,' she begged, but she knew that the way her body was responding was giving a completely different message, and she couldn't suppress a soft moan of delight as a finger slid into the humid depths of her sex.

'You like the bondage, too, don't you?' he went on, ignoring her weak pleas. 'You're quite a find, you little English beauty. Just wait until the club members get a load of you.'

'What… what is this job, exactly?' she managed to stammer.

'You'll find out soon enough. Meanwhile you and me are gonna have us some fun.'

She peeped at him; he had an annoying air of smug confidence as he prodded and probed her in the most intimate manner. She despised the overweight little man. She should scream; but would anybody hear her over the sounds of the traffic, before he silenced her with his hands or, even worse, some sort of gag. She should try to escape this unjust imprisonment; but struggling would clearly be useless with her hands tied the way they were. And then worse – far worse – were the delicious sensations his clumsy fumblings were inducing. Despite her shame she didn't want him to stop, and the more he worked his fingers back and forth inside her, the more aroused she was becoming – and the less inclined she felt to escape.

Then without warning his ministrations ceased, drawing a sigh of frustration from the confused youngster. He supported himself against the battered side of the van as it pitched unsteadily round a corner. He eyed her up and down, and the realisation of her wanton pose fuelled her vexation. She immediately tried to close her legs, but he suddenly slapped her inner thigh, dealing a stinging blow to her smooth flesh and bringing a cry of surprise and pain from her lips.

'Keep your legs apart, baby,' he ordered. 'I got something

here to put between them.'

She nibbled her lip. 'You've no right to treat me like this,' she protested.

'I rescued you from the bar didn't I? And I'm going to find you a job. I reckon I've got every right. Otherwise I could always call up the guys looking for you and tell them where you are.'

'You wouldn't.'

'Wouldn't I?'

Danni knew it was hopeless, and despite her dislike for the man, she was *very* turned on. Perhaps if she just closed her eyes…

'Please,' she whispered, 'don't hurt me.'

The prurient bar owner grinned in victory. 'That's the last thing I'm gonna do.'

Without tearing his eyes from his delicious prize he threw off the apron and undid his belt with excited fingers. In no time his trousers were rucked around his ankles, and he knelt in the most undignified manner, trying to keep his balance as the rattling vehicle swayed and turned. Despite her anxiety, Danni found her eyes drawn to his cock, which speared up from between his hairy thighs, thick and hard. It was uncircumcised, and the foreskin was rolled back beneath the swollen glans. It twitched threateningly as he took it in his fist.

He crept close, shuffling between her thighs. Without another word he spread the lips of her sex, revealing the glistening wetness within. Then he manoeuvred his bursting glans against her and began to press. She gave a small cry as he penetrated her, his thick cock easing inside as his weight bore down on the helpless young beauty. For Danni, the sensation was extraordinary; a mixture of shame at her own lascivious behaviour and pure relief after the frustration of her prolonged bondage. She moaned her delight as his cock forged deeper and deeper. Even the excruciating discomfort of having her arms squashed against the unyielding side of the van could not detract from her soaring ecstasy.

The squat bar owner lay heavily on her, his forehead buried on her shoulder and his only movement the staccato stabbing of his hips as he rutted against her. He grunted like a pig and slobbered against her throat and the warm upper-slopes of her soft breasts. His wiry chest-hair agitated her aching nipples.

Danni was cramped and squashed, and the tie tugged painfully on her wrists and cut into her flesh, but somehow the pain and the bondage only added to her intense excitement. His movements gradually became more and more erratic as he thrust his hefty erection into her, banging her head and shoulders back against the metallic wall and making her firm breasts shudder with every ferocious stroke. Danni was beyond caring; abandoned to her own overpowering lust, her breath coming in hoarse pants as she felt yet another orgasm building inexorably.

They came simultaneously. Danni contracted and rippled her vaginal muscles about his cock as he discharged his semen into her. Her body bucked in its bondage, waves of pure pleasure coursing through it with every exuberant lunge of his hips. Even as his ungainly movements faltered and slowed she continued to clutch him close with her legs, milking every drop of his seed until there was no more, and he finally slumped, his hot face lolling in her cleavage and his cock still embedded in her deep and velvety warmth.

'Like I said,' he mumbled breathlessly into her luscious young flesh, 'you're going to be just fine.'

By the time the van came to a halt he was relatively decent again, his soft and now unimpressive penis tucked away safely in his trousers. Danni was still tied to the bulkhead, and the suddenness of their arrival wrenched her back to reality. As the back doors opened new anxieties assailed her.

She had no idea where she was, or to what extent she could trust the nasty little man. The one thing she was sure of, though, was that she was a marked woman, and that it was essential she keep out of the clutches of the two gangs that were seeking her.

She thought of the bag. At one point she had considered telling him about it, and asking him to hide it somewhere inside his bar. But she had decided against such a move. That package represented her one bargaining chip should she ever fall into the hands of the men who sought her, and it was unlikely that anyone would find it where it was. Better that she say nothing about its whereabouts.

The bar owner swung the rear doors open with a crash. Danni gazed out, but all she could see was a bare brick wall. He climbed out, and at the same time she heard the driver's door slam. There followed a brief and mumbled conversation, none of which Danni could make out. Then he appeared again, this time accompanied by a handsome young man with dark curly hair and blue eyes. The newcomer eyed Danni with undisguised interest as the two got into the van, and she shrunk under the realisation that he probably had a very good idea as to what she had been up to during the journey.

One wrist was released and the tie unthreaded from its anchorage point, and then she was quickly tied again, her hands still behind her back.

'Is that really necessary?' she asked quietly.

'Just a precaution. Come on, come and see your new home.'

Each man took an arm and pulled her out into the daylight. Her stiff body ached. The van was parked in an enclosed area behind a rather scruffy looking building. It was about five stories high. The tall surrounding buildings encroached on one another, obscuring most of the sky and casting chilly shadows. She looked nervously about, aware that from any of the overlooking windows any amount of observers could look down and see her nakedness.

The bar owner led her around the side of the van and up to

a small red door set in the back of the building. He opened it and pushed her inside. As he did so she heard the van start up again and drive away. Danni found herself in a narrow corridor with no windows so that, when the door was closed behind them, the only light came from a single naked bulb that hung from the ceiling. The wooden floor was uncarpeted, the walls dirty and neglected. Danni's heart sank as she was pushed along to the end, where another closed door awaited them.

They went through and up a narrow flight of stairs that showed the same degree of neglect as the corridor had. To Danni it felt very strange to be naked in such a bare, dingy place, and the tie that bound her wrists made her feel doubly uncomfortable. She wondered what she would do if they encountered anybody.

At the top of the stairs was another passageway, with doors yearning a lick of paint lining either side. The bar owner stopped her in front of one which bore a sign that indicated the manager of this building operated from within, knocked once, and without awaiting a response he opened it and pushed her inside.

The office was scruffy but functional, with an old threadbare carpet on the floor and a desk in one corner. The only decoration was a couple of girlie calendars on the wall from which naked girls smiled out. Behind the desk sat a woman. She appeared to be in her early thirties, and wore a red, low-cut dress that showed off a deep cleavage and full bosom. She eyed Danni with an expression of suspicion.

'What the hell's this, Ed?'

'Someone I think you could use, Lucy.'

'I suspect you've been using her already,' said the woman pointedly, as she studied Danni with the expert air of a farmer at a livestock auction.

'Yeah, well, we might of amused ourselves a little on the way over, eh honey?'

Danni blushed at the matter-of-fact manner in which they

discussed her, wishing she had something with which to cover her nudity.

The woman cocked her head slightly to one side, an eyebrow raised quizzically. 'You got her wrists tied back there, Ed? She kinky or something?'

He sniggered and licked his lips salaciously. 'You know, I think she might just be. But I did that as a precaution. I'll free her if you want.'

The woman rose to her feet without giving a response as to whether he should or whether he shouldn't. She was a good deal taller than Danni, and the high heels she wore made her even more so. She had a shapely figure, with a large bust and broad hips. Her dress was very short, revealing long, slender legs encased in black stockings. She was too beautiful for such dank surroundings, though there was a hardness about her expression and a coldness in her eyes that Danni found intimidating. Her long hair was platinum blonde, and she tossed it back confidently as she inspected Danni's delicious form.

'What's your name?' she snapped.

'Da – Danielle,' she stammered instantly, finding herself almost overawed by the woman. 'But my friends call me Danni.'

'Are you in some kind of trouble… Danni?'

Danni shook her head, aware that the bar owner knew different and waiting for him to expose her untruth.

'Are you on drugs?'

'No. Nothing like that. I've never taken drugs of any kind.'

'You have a nice accent,' purred the woman, reaching out to stroke her cheek with soft fingertips. 'You're English?'

Danni shivered at the nice touch, and nodded.

'She's on the level, Lucy,' put in Ed, and Danni suspected he didn't want the woman to know of her serious predicament. 'She just needs to lay low for a while, that's all. What's with all the questions?'

'I've got to be careful who I take around here,' said the

woman, without taking her sparkling eyes off Danni. 'You know that, Ed.'

'She's a good kid. She'll be a major asset, believe me.'

'Can you dance?'

'A little,' replied Danni.

'Can she dance!' enthused the bar owner. 'You should have seen her back at the bar!'

The woman gently lifted Danni's chin with one manicured finger. 'Do you know what kind of a place I run here?'

'No... I'm not sure.'

'Well, in the front bar it's lap dancing. You get to keep a G-string on, and the customers show their appreciation by slipping banknotes in your garter.'

'I don't think this one will want to work in the front—' blurted the bar owner, before hastily checking his comment and cursing under his breath.

'Ah ha...! So she is in some kind of trouble?'

'Well... er...' he bumbled. 'Let's just say there are some people she doesn't want to meet.' He laughed nervously. 'Nothing for you to worry about.'

'I don't doubt that.' The woman was still scrutinising Danni, apparently making her mind up over something. 'Very well,' she eventually said, 'if you're going to use the back bars you'll have to work that little bit harder. The customers expect more of you there. Do you get my meaning?'

Danni shook her head, although she did have a fair idea of the woman's meaning.

'Well for a start, you lose the G-string. And sometimes the garter too. But the men still need somewhere to slip the banknotes.'

Danni stared at her confusedly for a moment, and then the meaning of her words hit home.

'There are other services they'll expect, as well. Especially if you like having that pretty arse of yours thrashed. They'll pay good money to do that.'

Danni shook her head. 'I – I don't think I could do it,' she stammered.

The bar owner leant closer and hissed anxiously in her ear. 'Listen doll, you've got no other choice. What are you going to do, go back on the streets as you are? This place will give you the chance to lay low for a while as well as earn some money. In a couple of months you'll be back on your feet.'

Such was his intensity, it was clear to Danni that he would somehow benefit if she stayed and worked for the woman. 'But those things you'd want me to do...'

'Oh please!' he snapped, 'don't act all coy now! I know what you can do, remember?'

Danni blushed at the truth of his cruel words. 'I – I'm not sure—'

'Look,' the woman interrupted impatiently, 'I'm not going to force you into anything. You can leave right now if you want to. But if you stay, I'll see you keep half of what you earn and give you a roof over your head.'

'Well—'

'But if you *do* stay it'll be for a minimum two weeks; I have to at least recoup my expenditure. And you'll do exactly what I say. So what's it to be? It's up to you.'

Danni hesitated. She considered what was being demanded of her. Under any normal circumstances she would have dismissed the whole thing at once. After all, she was a decent girl wasn't she? Properly brought up? Yet her reflection spoke otherwise, and she knew the alternative to working in this place was even worse. Here, at least, she could earn some money and was offered some hope. To go back onto the streets and to fall into the hands of the Dirangos or the Killarneys was unthinkable. Even if she did hand over the package, she still risked incurring their anger. At least staying there would give her a little time to think.

There was something else praying on her mind, though. It was something she scarcely dared admit, even to herself. The idea of what was being asked of her, the dancing, the

77

attention of the men, even the prospect of the beatings, was exciting her more than she could have imagined. Even now, after more sexual encounters in one day than in her life to date, she could feel the warmth returning to her sex as she contemplated her fate in the club.

Trembling, she looked the woman in the eye.

'I... I'd like to stay, please,' she whispered.

Chapter Seven

The music in the bar was so loud Danni found it amazing that anyone could hear themselves think. It blasted from speakers in every corner of the room, a throbbing beat that seemed to envelop the entire body in a pulsating cocoon. Still, the customers seemed able to make conversation, shouting into each other's ears and laughing raucously at their stories and jokes.

Danni looked about the room. It was quite a large area with a bar at one end, where a man in a white jacket was serving drinks. There were about thirty customers, all men, sitting in twos and threes at the tables and sipping their drinks. Here and there, waitresses flitted about. They wore tiny black outfits with plunging necklines and skirts so short the smallest movement revealed their brief underwear. Opposite the bar was a stage upon which a lone, bikini-clad girl was dancing with an expression of boredom on her face.

Danni was surveying the scene from above the area where the drinkers sat. She was in a small security room, and the window offered a perfect view of the goings-on below. Now, as she watched the scantily-clad women move about the room, she felt a twinge of apprehension at the thought that she too would soon be down amongst the drinkers.

It was more than twenty-four hours since Ed had delivered her to the Hot Laps Club. After her interview with Lucy, Ed had gone, and she'd been left alone in a small room for more than an hour, her wrists still tied; apparently Ed considered the loss of an old tie well worth the fun he'd had. Eventually a girl appeared. She chewed gum lazily and introduced herself as Zoe, and she spoke with a round southern accent that Danni found difficult to understand.

She had led Danni upstairs to a bathroom. There the

wrinkled tie was removed and she was allowed to shower. She was greatly relieved to wash away the day's grime and the evidence of the men who'd had their way with her, but she was a little unsettled by the way Zoe eagerly watched her ablutions. Once she'd dried herself she was taken back downstairs and into another part of the building.

The decor there was quite different from what she'd seen earlier. A deep burgundy carpet covered the floor of the hallway she was led along, and the walls were hung with gaudy red wallpaper. Doors of polished wood lined the passageway, and all of them where closed.

'What is this place?' she asked.

Zoe grinned, but said nothing.

She was shown into a small bedroom. A taciturn black woman immediately brought a tray of food and then left again. Danni ate ravenously, suddenly aware of just how hungry she was.

'You'd better get some sleep now,' Zoe said when the food had been demolished. 'You'll be very busy tomorrow.'

She made Danni lie on the bed, and then snapped a handcuff around one wrist and attached the other cuff to the bed frame. Danni protested, but was ignored. And when Zoe left the room and the door closed behind her, Danni heard the key turn in the lock.

So exhausted was she after such a bizarre adventure that she slept through until late the next morning, waking to see the sunlight streaming in through the small window. She managed to lever herself up far enough to peer out. Below were the litter-strewn streets that were so characteristic of the city. Danni was on the second floor and, even had she not been shackled to the bed, she knew there was no escape that way. She seemed to be a prisoner in the place. But at least it was tolerably comfortable, and it afforded a roof over her head.

The black woman brought meals to her room at midday

and in the evening. This and brief accompanied visits to the ablutions were the only punctuation in an otherwise featureless day. For the rest of the time Danni was obliged to sit on her bed, one hand still shackled to the post, and contemplate the mess she was in.

It was evening when Lucy came. She wore a long, gold dress that clung beautifully to her curves. She freed Danni's wrist and took her to a dressing room, where she sat her down at a make-up table. Danni's naturally beautiful features needed little enhancing with the cosmetics provided, but she applied some mascara and lipstick and brushed her hair out.

The costume Lucy gave her was very skimpy indeed, consisting of a diminutive silver bikini top that lifted her breasts and enhanced her cleavage, and a pair of matching and equally tiny silver panties.

And now Danni was in the security room. Lucy had told her to watch the other girls and the way they behaved with the men, and she had done so, observing how they reacted when the men fondled their thighs or slipped their hands up their skirts. It appeared they were fair game for such liberties, simply laughing as they twisted away. In one or two cases she saw large tips change hands, and now and then a piece of paper was passed to one or other of the girls. Danni could only guess at the content of the notes.

Danni spotted Lucy entering the club. The woman looked gorgeous in her long gown, and she was clearly familiar with many of the customers, moving about the tables and chatting and laughing easily with them.

Danni noticed two men sitting at a table near the stage, trying to get Lucy's attention. At last they succeeded in calling her over, and a conversation ensued. One of the waitresses was summoned to the table, and Danni saw a banknote change hands. Then, to her surprise, the girl began to undo the buttons that ran down the front of her dress. As the garment fell open Danni saw the girl wore only a brief

G-string beneath. Then she thought about what she'd been told the day before, and realised she was about to witness lap-dancing for the first time.

For a moment the music in the bar stopped. Then a new tune started, a throbbing disco number, and the girl broke into her dance.

Danni watched in fascination as the waitress gyrated to the music. She was a tall and willowy blonde, with long legs and extremely large breasts that shook with every movement she made, bringing shouts of delight from those watching.

Danni remembered her own performance in that seedy bar the day before. She had been dancing for the whole room, but this girl was clearly concentrating on the table in front of her, moving closer and closer to the men, who had pushed the table aside to allow her access to them.

There was no doubt that the girl was experienced at the dancing, swaying back and forth, teasing the men as she gyrated before them, and then pulled back just as they reached for her. Danni found herself strangely drawn to the girl's antics, watching closely as she enticed the drooling men with her beautiful body. Even from where she sat, Danni could see her nipples were erect, and she wondered if she was as aroused as she looked.

One of the men produced another banknote from his pocket and waved it at the near-nude beauty. The girl moved forward. She spread her legs and straddled the man's knees, her lovely breasts swaying back and forth only inches from his face. The man tucked the note into her garter. This time the girl didn't pull away. She sank a little lower and rubbed her crotch lightly over the man's knee. Danni watched her expression. She really looked as if she was enjoying it, her face a picture of lust as she began pressing down harder against the man's leg. The young English girl wondered at the sensation she must be feeling through the thin G-string. Already the outline of her cleft was easily visible, and Danni fancied that she could detect a darkening of the material as the wetness leaked from her vagina.

Now it was the other man's turn to slip a note into the dancer's garter, and she transferred her attention to him, squatting over his lap and grinding her sex down onto his leg, her expression intense as she closed her eyes and nibbled her lip. There was no doubt in Danni's mind now that the girl was very aroused indeed, and she slipped a finger into her own panties as she watched the show progress.

The men reached into their pockets once again, and the girl shifted from one to the other as they stuffed yet more money into her garter. The G-string was beginning to ride up into her cunt now, the wetness evident to all as her sex lips wrapped about it. She seemed lost in a world of her own, her head thrown back, her long locks swaying as she thrust her breasts forward.

Danni wondered at the men's restraint in not touching her body, but she guessed that such a move would result in their expulsion from the establishment. Then she thought of what Lucy had told her about the back bars, and a shudder ran through her as she contemplated what lay in store.

The music was building to a climax now, and as it did the dancer slid manicured fingers inside her G-string. She stood up, her fingers moving back and forth beneath the material. Then she cried aloud as an orgasm shook her lovely frame, her breasts quivering in response to the sensual convulsions of her body. At the same moment the music reached a crescendo, and her head dropped forward, her hair obscuring her face.

For a few seconds the tableau below Danni was frozen. Then the girl seemed to recover her senses, scooping up her dress from the floor and running for the exit, while the men whistled and shouted their appreciation.

Danni withdrew her fingers from inside her panties, amazed at how wet she was. At the same moment the door behind her opened. She swung round to see Lucy standing there.

'Come on, young lady,' she said. 'You've got your first customers.'

From her position behind the bar Danni eyed the two men nervously. They were sitting at a table in the corner, eating a meal and talking quietly to one another. As Danni watched, Lucy went across to them and they looked up. They clearly hadn't noticed Danni and the club manager entering through the discreet door at the back of the bar, but they smiled upon recognising the woman.

The three conversed for a few moments, and Danni saw the men look in her direction. A small thrill tingled down her spine as she took in the pair of diners. They were both in their forties and had the air of businessmen. Both wore expensive looking suits with conservative ties. One was a large man with dark hair flecked with grey at the temples and combed back. His companion was balding, of stockier build and wore a shiny gold watch and an identity bracelet. Neither was in any sense Danni's ideal man, but still the thought of what might be to come excited her in an odd way.

Lucy returned to where Danni was standing.

'Open a bottle of the claret,' she said, indicating a rack of wines, and then the two men, 'and serve those gentlemen. Remember, they're customers and they're paying well. Do exactly what they say.' Then she was gone, leaving the nervous youngster alone in the bar.

Danni selected a bottle of claret and took it across to the men. She presented it to the large man, who nodded his approval. As she leaned over to fill each man's glass she was acutely aware of their eyes on her bosom. The brief top she wore hid very little, and she felt her cheeks colouring at the frankness of their gazes.

For the next half hour or so Danni was preoccupied with keeping the men's glasses filled and serving them with liqueurs and brandy. A waitress appeared every now and again to clear the crockery or deliver a new course. When the waitress served them their coffee, the men moved through to a private room, and silently indicated that Danni should follow.

The room was sparsely furnished, but cosy. The two men sat in large armchairs and continued to chat, apparently oblivious to the young beauty who stood quietly by. All the time she waited, Danni's mind was conjuring up the most erotic thoughts. She couldn't blot from her thoughts the image of the girl lap-dancing.

By the time the balding man finally beckoned to her, Danni was feeling very anxious indeed. With the pair sitting she felt awkward and conspicuous, and the skimpiness of her costume increased her unease. She stood, hands by her side, as they eyed her up and down.

'What's your name?' asked the balding man.

'Danielle, sir.'

'I haven't seen you here before, Danielle.'

'No sir. This is my first night.'

'Your first night?' Their eyes sparkled and they looked pleased. 'And are you ready to please us?'

'Y-yes sir,' she stammered. 'I… I am ready to please in whatever way I can.' She had been told how to respond by Lucy; any other response would not be tolerated.

'You have lovely breasts, Danielle.'

'Th-thank you, sir.'

'But I see you are blushing,' the man said smugly. 'Surely this doesn't embarrass you?'

'I'm sorry, sir.'

'On the contrary, your modesty is charming. It makes the whole experience all the more pleasurable. Please remove your top.'

The words were spoken casually, with no change in expression, yet they brought a tight knot to Danni's stomach, and she knew the colour in her cheeks deepened as he gave the order.

She reached nervously behind her back for the catch on the bra. She unhooked it, keeping one hand clamped over the cups so it remained in place. Then, slowly, she let it fall away, revealing her perfect young breasts to the watching pair.

'Very nice.' This time it was the larger man who spoke. 'Play with them.'

'Sir?'

'Play with your tits. Stimulate your nipples. Come on, Danielle, surely you've played with yourself before?'

Trembling slightly, Danni reached up and placed her hands over the soft globes of her breasts. She began to move them in circles, stimulating the nipples so they hardened to solid little peaks, the brown flesh puckering under her touch. She wasn't certain what was required of her, so she allowed her instincts to take over, squeezing her breasts together then raising them, as if offering them to the watching men. Then, on an impulse, she raised her right breast and, craning down, licked her nipple. It was the most extraordinary sensation, sending a spasm of pleasure through her body and bringing a sudden surge of wetness to her already damp crotch. She glanced through lowered eyelashes as she licked, and the expressions on the men's faces told her they could sense how aroused she was becoming.

'Dance for us, Danielle,' ordered the large man. 'Show us how you can move that sexy body of yours.'

'Yes sir. If that's what you want, sir.'

She began to dance. At first her movements were mechanical and stilted, such was her nervousness and inexperience. Gradually, though, she started to involve herself in the melody of the music coming through from the bar, and her dancing became more fluid.

She moved closer to the men. On the wall behind them was a huge mirror, and she watched herself gyrating, her breasts quivering with every subtle movement.

She danced for about five minutes, gradually shedding her inhibitions as she lost herself in the rhythm of the tune. She was acutely aware of the men's lecherous eyes upon her, but somehow, as had happened in the bar the previous day, the exposure seemed to spur her on, and the more she danced the sexier she felt.

The men shifted in their chairs and were clearly appreciating the naïvely sensual performance. The larger of the two crooked a finger, beckoning her closer still. She obeyed, leaning forward, her firm breasts swaying deliciously before him.

'Take your pants off,' he ordered. 'Show us your snatch, you gorgeous little bitch.'

Danni cringed as the full shameful enormity of her behaviour hit home. Yesterday she had danced naked because she'd had no choice. Today she was doing it for money. Yesterday she had been trying to save herself. Today she was on the verge of becoming a whore.

She reached slowly down for the waistband of her panties. There was nobody else in the room, but she saw the security camera high up on one wall, and knew someone would be watching her performance. She turned her back on the two men, suddenly feeling shy, and slowly pulled her panties down.

As she uncovered her bottom she heard the men's smutty exclamations and remembered for the first time the stripes of the cane that still decorated her behind. At that moment she wanted to pull them up again and run from the room. But where could she go? She was as trapped then as she had been when the cuffs were on her. So, fighting against her natural modesty, she let the panties slip down to her ankles.

She straightened, and stood for a moment with her back still to the men. Then, with a deep breath, she turned to face them, giving them a full-frontal view of her naked body.

For a moment she stood perfectly still, watching their lecherous smiles as they absorbed every detail of her. Then the balding man snapped his fingers, and she remembered the music. She began to move again, swaying her hips and breasts in a manner she knew would please her small audience of two.

The balding man reached into his pocket and pulled something out. He held it up, and Danni saw it was a banknote. He folded it lengthways, then beckoned her forward. Slowly, her heart pounding, Danni moved towards him. As she came close he dropped his eyes to her crotch, and she knew what she must do. She spread her legs, straddling his knees, and stood there, her hips still swaying back and forth. He touched her sex, bringing a gasp from her and sending a shiver through her shapely form. Gently, he prised her sex lips apart with his fingers, then began sliding the note into her vagina.

Danni bit her lip as she felt the intimacy of his touch. It scarcely seemed credible to her that she was standing before two immaculately dressed men, her legs spread while one of them penetrated her so intimately. Yet, above and beyond the shame, she was experiencing a sensation of intense arousal, and the moans that came from deep within were moans of lust as the heat in her belly increased with every second.

He slid the note all the way in and his fingers lingered for a moment, toying with the little bud of her clitoris. He watched the expression on her face as she fought to control her emotions. Then he withdrew and she instinctively squatted lower and ground her sex against his thigh, savouring the delicious feel of the coarse material of his suit between her legs. Danni closed her eyes and worked herself back and forth on him, her whole body gripped by desire.

A hand touched her left breast, squeezing it gently, and she opened her eyes to see the other man now holding some money. She could scarcely bring herself to move from her position, but she knew she must. Raising herself from the first man's lap, she stepped back and moved to one side so she was facing the larger man. Then she moved forward once more, spreading her thighs and pressing her pubis forward in an unambiguous gesture of invitation.

Like his companion, the man took his time, clearly enjoying the way she reacted, her control slipping away as a second note was pressed into her glistening sex. As he pushed it in, his fingers slid in with it, and Danni gasped aloud as her sex convulsed, the walls of her vagina closing about the intruding digit. When he finally withdrew she needed no further encouragement, immediately squatting down over his lap and beginning to pleasure herself against his knee.

She came without warning. One moment she had been simply rubbing herself back and forth against him, the next she was crying out as a sudden orgasm shook her lovely young body, her breasts oscillating as she ground herself down still harder against him. The man made no move, simply grinning broadly as he watched her come, her juices leaving a dark patch on the leg of his trousers.

It was some time before Danni regained control. When she did, she rose to her feet, her cheeks bright red as she realised that, for the second time in two days, she had masturbated to orgasm in front of complete strangers. This time, though, the ordeal wasn't over. No sooner had she regained her breath, than the balding man pulled her to him.

'Suck me,' he ordered.

'S-sir?'

'You heard me. Suck my cock. It's about time you concentrated on us instead of yourself.'

Danni stared down at his crotch. She could see the large bulge waiting for her. Now she was expected to finish the job. Once again she glanced momentarily at the camera. Then she dropped to her knees.

She ran her hands over the man's crotch, feeling the hardness beneath the material. She leaned forward, her lovely breasts dangling enticingly as she reached for his fly. She pulled down his zipper, then slipped her hand inside. He was wearing cotton briefs, and she could feel the girth and heat of his penis through them. She moved her fingers higher and dragged down the waistband. His cock sprang free before her eyes, long and extremely hard. She wrapped her hands about it, pulling back his foreskin and uncovering his glans. It was shiny with his secretions, a small transparent bead sitting on the tip. Fascinated, she moved her fingers down to the base and cupped his large balls, squeezing the tight sac and feeling them move as his cock stiffened still further.

She leaned even closer, and her senses were swamped by his male scent. Then she opened her mouth and took him inside, tasting his arousal as she licked at his throbbing tool.

She began to suck him, her lips tight about his shaft while she moved her head up and down, allowing him to slide in and out of her mouth. There was something indefinably exciting about fellating him in this way; bent naked over his lap, her stiff nipples brushing against his legs as she went down on him. She sucked harder, caressing his balls as she did so, loving the convulsions that ran through his tool at regular intervals, proof positive of the effect her ministrations were having on him.

Without warning he grabbed her hair and pulled her up. His glistening cock slipped from between her lips as she gazed quizzically up at him.

He nodded across the room. She turned her head and her eyes widened. The larger man had moved from his armchair to a low sofa, and was now totally naked, his sturdy legs lolling apart and his cock sprouting thickly from his groin. He was running his fingers gently up and down his shaft, and as the wide-eyed beauty looked across he beckoned to her.

Danni rose and turned to him. As she moved across the small space she could feel his eyes upon her, his fist still languidly pumping his foreskin up and down.

This time she didn't need any instructions. She dropped to her knees in front of him, her eyes taking in his body. He had a muscular frame, his chest covered with thick, black hair. His cock was even longer than his companion's, spearing up from a dense mat of pubic hair, his heavy balls hanging beneath. As Danni leaned forward he gripped her breasts, cupping them and sending short shocks of excitement through her as her nipples chafed against his palms.

She took him into her mouth, another spasm of lust shaking her as once again she smelt and tasted his maleness. She began to suck with an enthusiasm matching that shown to his partner, her fingers closing about his shaft as she set to work with her tongue. Behind her she could hear a rustle of clothing, and she knew his companion was undressing, but for the moment her attention was on the cock thrusting up into her mouth, forcing her jaws wide apart as his arousal increased.

Danni knew she would have to satisfy both men, though the idea was an extraordinary one. What sort of a slut had she become, she wondered, to contemplate performing so intimate an act with two men in quick succession? But even Danni wasn't prepared for what happened next. The fingers that ran up the inside of her thigh took her completely by surprise, and she gave a little cry, muffled by her mouthful of stiff cock, as she felt them slide upwards toward the burning heat of her sex.

She tried to turn her head, but the man in whose lap it was buried held her down, his hips thrusting up at her as he fucked her face with relish. Then the fingers were tracing her wet labia, and a violent tremor shook her young frame as he found her clitoris and began to tease it.

Then she felt another sensation deep in her vagina, a sensation that caused a new flow of juices within her. At first she wasn't certain what it was. Then she remembered the banknotes that had invaded her so intimately. The man

91

was slowly pulling them out, each tug sending new spasms of arousal through her. He took his time, clearly enjoying her humiliation. When at last both soggy notes were out, Danni was positively gasping with lust, her lips clamped tightly about the cock in her mouth as she sucked it hungrily.

Even then she wasn't expecting the insistent glans that nuzzled up against the soft opening to her vagina, and another muffled cry escaped as she finally understood. They were going to take her at the same time; one in her mouth, and one from behind. Danni, in her innocence, had never dreamed of accommodating two men simultaneously, yet that was clearly what they intended, and there was no question of denying them.

For a second she resisted, tensing in an attempt to rebuff the approach. But he was not to be denied. His fingers prised apart her nether lips, and the wetness within gave him all the assistance he needed to sink his rampant cock deep into her vagina.

He thrust urgently, grinding his hips forward and shunting her petite form back and forth. At the same time his companion increased the intensity of his own assault, feeding his erection deeper and deeper into her mouth until she was almost choking.

Suddenly Danni's resistance evaporated as she was completely overcome by the eroticism of the situation. It was all so obscene – it was delicious. As the two strangers used her body for their own gratification she abandoned herself, submitting totally to them, the power of her own desire blotting all other thoughts from her mind.

When the man in her mouth came, it almost took her by surprise. One second she was sucking him avidly, and the next her mouth was filling with his hot, creamy seed. He came so copiously a little seeped from the corner of her stretched lips, trickled down her chin, and onto her slender throat. So intent was she on savouring as much as possible that, when the balding man erupted she was hardly aware it was happening. Moments later her body was shaken by another delicious orgasm, her inner muscles milking the shaft that was filling her so deliciously as she bucked and writhed between her two lovers.

The orgasm went on and on. Danni's senses were overcome with lustful pleasure. It was the most glorious orgasm of her life and, when at last the two men pushed her aside, she was totally drained. She lay back on the carpet, an expression of sublime rapture on her face.

It was only when she opened her eyes and saw the men pulling on their clothes that the full impact of what she was doing hit her.

In just two days, Danni had graduated from innocent traveller to full-time whore.

Chapter Eight

As Danni waited for Zoe in the small bare room she was unable to keep her eyes from the mirror on the wall opposite. Indeed, in the harsh light from the single bulb hanging overhead there was little else to look at, and she certainly made an extraordinary sight.

What she wore could scarcely be called clothes. Her breasts were covered by what was no more than a rag. This had been wrapped around her and tied below one armpit. The material was threadbare and riddled with holes. Knotted around her hips was a similar piece of cloth. It was larger, but still only just covered her bottom, and when she moved the slit at the side showed the full length of her shapely thigh. She was barefoot, making her appear even more petite than usual as she stood, contemplating her image.

To be so scantily dressed was bad enough, but the addition of the bondage made things much worse. Her wrists were lashed together behind her back with strong twine. Her elbows were bound too, rendering her arms completely useless and forcing her shoulders back and thrusting her vulnerable breasts forward. A cloth had been stuffed into her mouth and another bound around it and knotted beneath her hair, effectively gagging her.

As she waited, she wondered what new indignities lay in store for her.

Danni had been at the club for nearly three weeks now. During those weeks she had learned a great deal about her own desires and those of the men who frequented the establishment. Each night she had been taken to one or other of the rooms, where she was obliged to perform for the customers. Usually it was a man or a pair of men, and they would make her dance naked for them. Some would be content to just watch, but most took full advantage, using her in a variety of innovative positions and scenarios. Some had her two or three times during the course of the evening, keeping her for hours at a time and using her at their leisure.

Danni anticipated every session with a heavy heart, knowing she would be obliged to do whatever was asked of her, and that she would be allowed no concession to modesty. What shamed her most, though, was the way her body always responded to the treatment. Throughout her ordeals she would be intensely aroused, and the countless orgasms she enjoyed were genuine, shaking her nubile frame with lust as she responded to whatever treatment she was obliged to endure.

During daylight hours she was kept as a virtual prisoner in the club. She knew this was partly for her own protection, but she knew too that it was designed to underline her submission to Lucy and the patrons of the club. They gave her no clothes beyond the costumes she wore in the evening, and these were taken away during the day for laundering, so that she was obliged to remain in her room much of the time. When she did emerge, all she had to wear were transparent shawls supplied by Lucy that she would wrap about her. These hid almost nothing of her curvaceous body, and the sniggers and remarks of the club staff soon sent her back to her room.

Tonight, though, things were different. Zoe had taken her from her room early on, and had brought her to the bare room, where she made her don the ragged garments. Then she had bound and gagged her, brushing aside the English girl's questions as she rendered her helpless. Now, as she waited, her heart pounding with a mixture of fear and excitement, Danni could only wonder at what would unfold.

She heard a footfall outside the room. She stiffened, a shiver running through her as she heard the key turning in the lock. The door opened, and Zoe stood before her.

Danni's jaw dropped. The American girl was also wearing

an unusual outfit, but it was very different from her own. Her shapely torso was squeezed into a black leather garment cut high at the sides and low at the front. A wide belt accentuated her wispy waist. She wore matching gloves that reached her elbows, and her legs were encased in fishnet hold-up stockings that left an expanse of creamy thigh which drew the eye to the tiny triangle of black leather that tantalisingly covered her delicate mound. She wore a pair of black stilettos on her neat feet, and in her hand she held a cruel-looking horsewhip.

Zoe was not alone. Another girl entered wearing an identical outfit. Danni knew her as Vanessa, a raven-haired beauty whom she'd only occasionally encountered during her stay at the club. Danni had never spoken to her, but she was aware that she found her predicament amusing, and she had seen her and Zoe discussing her while she was awaiting her duties on more than one occasion. Now, as she warily eyed the two women in their dominatrix outfits, she felt a knot of fear and anticipation form in the pit of her stomach.

'Right then, little slave,' Zoe drawled, 'your master is waiting for you. Come along.'

She stepped forward and Danni spied something in her other hand. It was a leather collar, dotted with silver studs. Knowing resistance was hopeless, Danni allowed Zoe to buckle it around her throat. Then Vanessa handed Zoe a long silver chain, like a dog's lead, and she fastened it to a ring that hung from the front of the collar.

Zoe tested it, tugging sharply and making Danni stagger forward. 'She'll do,' she said with a smug grin. 'Come on Vanessa, they'll be waiting for us.'

She pulled on the lead again, and Danni was obliged to follow her out of the room and along the corridor, with Vanessa close behind.

As they led her up flights of narrow stairs, Danni felt her apprehension increase. But with it came another feeling; one that was becoming all too familiar to the young beauty.

Somehow the inadequacy of her costume, along with the twine that rendered her so helpless, were beginning to excite her anew. What was it about her that made her react so to such cruel and unnatural treatment? Surely any normal girl would be overcome by fear and disgust and would be fighting to escape. Yet, not only was she going meekly along with the abuse, but she was also becoming more and more aroused by the second. Even the humiliation of the collar and the sight of the whip that Zoe carried were simply increasing the heat in her belly as she was taken up to whomever she was destined to entertain for the night.

They reached the part of the club where the private rooms were. Zoe led her charge past the ones she normally occupied, and on to the far end of the corridor. They stopped outside a closed door and Zoe knocked. A woman's voice called for them to enter.

Zoe opened the door and pulled the bound girl into the mysterious room. The lead was removed, and the two glamorous escorts positioned themselves on either side of their young captive.

Danni felt vulnerable between the two women, their superior stature enhanced by the height of the heels they wore. There was a strong light shining directly into her eyes and she blinked and squinted as she tried to discern her surroundings. Gradually she became aware of two shadowy figures sitting together on some sort of sofa. She sensed one of them was Lucy, and the other was a man.

'Stand up straight, slave,' ordered Vanessa. 'Hold your head up and spread your legs.'

Danni did as she was told, holding her body erect, her breasts pressing forward. Zoe rapped her on the thigh with the whip, making her shuffle her feet even further apart, and then turned to the two dark figures.

'The slave is ready to greet her master,' she said.

The man rose and stepped into the pool of light. He was tall, and as he moved closer Danni felt very insignificant indeed. He looked to be in his fifties and was powerfully built, with broad shoulders and a rugged face. His hair was silver, and he sported a neat moustache. His suit appeared to be of fine cloth and expensively tailored.

He walked around her, his eyes taking in every luscious detail of her near nude body. Having concluded his inspection he nodded, clearly satisfied.

'Very nice, Lucy,' he said appreciatively. 'Very nice indeed.'

'The slave is here for punishment,' said Vanessa. 'What is the master's wish?'

The man's eyes never left the trembling girl. 'Remove the gag,' he said smoothly.

Zoe moved behind Danni and expedited the order. It was a great relief for the captive girl, and she worked her jaw up and down, trying to ease the aching muscles.

'What have you to say for yourself, young lady?' asked the man.

'I... nothing, sir,' she said meekly, somewhat confused by the question.

The whip hissed as Zoe swept it down viciously across Danni's thighs, making cry out with pain and shock.

'Nothing master!' she corrected.

'Nothing master!' Danni blurted, biting her lip as the pain seared through her.

'Strip her,' he said, without emotion.

She stared at the man and instinctively tried to back away. But Zoe and Vanessa held her easily. There was nowhere to go, and nothing she could do as the two reached for the skimpy rags that were her only protection from the man's gaze.

It took little effort to rip them away. Danni was naked, her full breasts jutting forward, her nipples protruding; traitorous and shameful evidence of the excitement that had been building ever since her wrists had been tied.

Once again the man took his time, inspecting the lovely

young body that was now fully revealed to him. Danni felt the colour rise in her cheeks as he walked around her again, his eyes fixed on her smooth flesh. She tugged at her bonds, wishing fervently that there were some means by which she could cover herself, but there was no chance, so she gave up and stood quietly, her head hung in shame.

He placed a finger under her chin and lifted her face to his. His unshakeable stare drilled deep into her eyes, and Danni swooned beneath his powerful aura. There was no cruelty in his expression, just a look of intense interest.

'Do you know what we're going to do to you?' he asked, with the same air of immovable confidence.

'You – you're going to w-whip me, master?'

He smiled and nodded. 'We are. And are you afraid?'

'Yes, master,' she confirmed. 'I am afraid.'

'Well don't be. It's good that a young woman accepts a sound whipping occasionally. It reminds her of the eroticism of submission. You are, I know, a very sensuous young lady.'

'I—'

'Lucy tells me you have an insatiable sexual appetite. Stronger than any girl she's had here before. That's something I wish to witness.'

Danni blushed again as his words evoked an inexplicable thrill deep within her soul. There was something dangerously attractive about the man, something that made her want to submit to his darkest desires. As she looked up into his abstruse face she felt a new surge of simmering excitement.

'You enjoy the bondage and the humiliation it brings, don't you?'

Danni wasn't surprised by his perceptiveness. She dropped her eyes, too ashamed to answer.

'Well, today we're adding a new dimension to that,' he went on. 'The dimension of pain. But there will be pleasure too. In fact, I shall see to it that the pain and the pleasure mingle, so that the distinction between them will become blurred. Lucy has the very device to do that.' He turned to the madame. 'Are we ready?'

'Whenever you like,' the woman replied.

'Good.' He looked back at the naked, trembling youngster. 'You will receive ten strokes. Do you accept your punishment?'

Danni felt a new tightness in her stomach. Her mouth was dry. She could barely utter her answer.

'Yes… master.'

He turned to her two guards. 'See to it,' he said, with an awful finality.

Danni was pushed to one side by the two dominatrix. At the same time a spotlight came on and illuminated a frame that stood close to one wall. It was triangular in shape, tapering to a point at the top and opening out to four legs, each around three feet apart. It was about seven feet tall, with rings set at the top and on the front legs close to the floor. Just below waist height a wooden border ran around in which a series of holes had been bored.

While Vanessa was freeing Danni's wrists, Zoe opened a bag that sat beside the frame and pulled out more lengths of twine. Danni had little time to enjoy the release, for Zoe immediately pulled her hands out in front of her and bound her wrists once more. Once fastened, the ends were looped through the ring at the top of the frame and pulled tight, forcing the hapless youngster up onto tiptoe as the ties were made fast. At the same time Vanessa bound her ankles, nudged them apart, and fastened them to the rings in the frame's legs.

By the time they had finished, Danni was quite unable to move, her lovely body stretched taut, her breasts protruding through the gap in the frame, the smooth curves of her backside perfectly presented for the punishment to follow. To make things even worse a mirror had been placed in front of her, so she had no option but to watch her reflection and to ponder the total helplessness of her situation.

The man came forward from the shadows, and she was

reminded once more of his quiet authority as he examined her bonds. Still he did not touch her, although she secretly longed for him to. There was something about him that made her want to submit to him and, had he wanted her there and then, she would have made no objection.

He stood close and once more captivated her gaze.

'I promised you pleasure as well as pain, my little English beauty,' he said. 'With the pleasure will come further humiliation, but I believe you will respond positively to that. I will not have you gagged again. I will enjoy hearing your pleas and deciding which are for pain and which are for pleasure.'

He nodded to Zoe, who reached into the bag once again. Danni craned round to see what was happening, and her eyes widened as she saw the object the leather-clad woman was holding.

It was a phallus. It was a perfectly shaped model of a penis. It was made of a black, rubbery substance, each vein picked out perfectly, the bulbous end thick and shiny. Zoe turned it in her hands, running her fingers up and down its length as she might a real erection. Danni shivered as she watched the woman handle it so reverently.

Zoe moved until her leather-moulded breasts caressed Danni's stretched back, and held the object in front of the poor girl's face. It seemed to be solid, but when it was turned Danni saw it was hollow, a hole running up the centre about half an inch in diameter. Zoe turned it once again and pressed it against the captive's lips.

'Suck it,' she ordered.

Danni resisted for a second, then opened her mouth and allowed it inside. It was large, larger than any real cock she had ever experienced, and it stretched her lips as Zoe fed it deeper. It tasted of rubber, the smell filling Danni's senses as she instinctively began to suck. Zoe moved it back and forth a few times, just as a man would with a genuine erection. Then she pulled it out again.

It was wet and shiny with the youngster's saliva. Zoe smiled. 'That should help it slide in,' she drawled, and dropped to her knees. Danni felt a hand stroke her inner thighs, the sensation sending tremors through her tensed frame as the fingers worked higher. She gasped aloud as they touched her moist labia and prised her lips apart.

'Is she wet?' asked the man.

'Just look,' replied Zoe.

She held up her fingers and Danni saw in the mirror that they were glistening with her juices. Once again she felt her colour rise as the occupants of the room were shown the proof of her arousal. Then she felt the fingers on her sex again, and the pressure of the phallus as it was eased up between her nether lips.

Danni's backside writhed as Zoe twisted and pushed, pressing the thick object up into her vagina. In the mirror Danni could watch the whole exercise, the black object contrasting sharply with the pale flesh of her thighs and the succulence of her sex.

Danni groaned, certain that she could take not another inch of the dildo. Yet still Zoe continued pushing, filling Danni until only the base of the monstrous thing was still visible.

But Zoe still hadn't finished. She beckoned to Vanessa, and Danni saw that the other girl held some kind of long metal bolt in her hand. She slipped it through a hole in the border of wood that ran around the frame at just about the level of Danni's crotch. Then, as the trussed captive watched in horror, she inserted the end into a hollow cavity in the phallus and pushed the bolt all the way home, fixing the thing to the frame in such a way that it speared up at an angle as it disappeared into Danni's body.

She could scarcely believe the fiendishness of the device, holding her fast, her arms stretched above her, her legs spread wide, while the obscene black device penetrated her fully in the most intimate manner possible.

Zoe stood back and the man stepped forward once more, checking the security of Danni's bonds.

'Good,' he said at last. 'Start the punishment.'

Zoe took the whip from her companion and flexed it in her hands. Danni felt her heart sink as she watched in the mirror. The girl took a couple of practice swings, making the whip whistle through the air. Then she took up a position behind Danni and tapped the leather against the smooth, white flesh of her behind. She pulled back her arm.

Swish! Whack!

She brought the whip down with all her force, the thin length cracking into Danni's bottom and sending an intense pain surging through her. Danni screamed, appalled by the way the whip hurt. But already Zoe was dealing a second blow.

Swish! Whack!

She brought the weapon down again, cutting agonisingly into Danni's unprotected flesh and wrenching an even louder scream from her as another stripe was laid across her behind. She clenched her fists, her eyes welling with tears as she braced herself for another stroke.

Swish! Whack!

This time the whip came up under her bottom, making the firm flesh quiver as it struck home and throwing Danni's hips forward against the frame. As the blow struck the dildo thrust suddenly deeper into her, bringing the most exquisite sensations, even as she cried out from the pain. For a fleeting second she remembered what the man had said about the mingling of pain with pleasure. Then the whip fell again.

Swish! Whack!

Danni sagged and whimpered as the vicious leather bit yet again. But the phallus pressed, releasing a surge of undiluted pleasure.

Swish! Whack!
Swish! Whack!
Swish! Whack!

The blows were relentless, leaving angry stripe after angry stripe across the wailing girl's clenched buttocks. Yet it was the dildo that was filling her thoughts, her screams turning to gasps as it continued to ram into her with every stroke of the whip. She knew what the man had meant now. Pain and pleasure filled her equally, until she was barely able to tell one from the other, her sex milking the false cock that filled her so deliciously.

Swish! Whack!
Swish! Whack!

Only one more blow to come now, and Danni was almost delirious. Her hips ground down on the wood as she struggled against her bonds, intent only on pleasuring herself.

Swish! Whack!

The final blow thwacked into her unprotected buttocks with undiminished force, wrenching the loudest cry yet from her lungs. Still she tried desperately to press the phallus deeper, but without the impetus of the whip she couldn't, and she whimpered with frustration as her burning bottom writhed back and forth.

The man was near again.

'Was I right?' he asked. 'Do you understand the joys of pleasure and pain?'

'Y-yes, master,' she sniffled.

'And do you now want relief?'

Her head and shoulders sagged. 'Yes please... master,' she whispered.

'Very good. Proceed.'

Danni lifted her weary head and looked into the mirror. What she saw through fluttering and moistened eyelashes made her gasp.

Another man had emerged from the shadows!

She'd not known he was there. Had he been lurking there, watching the whole of her humiliating punishment? He was naked, and his muscled and oiled body shone in the light. As Danni held her breath and watched, Vanessa dropped to her knees before him and balanced his penis on her palm as though it was priceless. It was already erect, a result, Danni guessed, of witnessing her ordeal. Now, as Vanessa took it wistfully between her lips, she could see the fierce passion in his eyes.

Danni felt a hand on her sore bottom and winced as Zoe pulled her stinging buttocks apart. Then came another new sensation. Something cool and smooth was dabbed onto her very private opening. The relentless reflection told her that Zoe had a pot of jelly-like substance in her hand, and was applying it to her rear. She pressed, and Danni stiffened and sighed with confusion as a straightened finger slid in to the first knuckle.

Vanessa rose, and Danni's eyes were drawn again to the silent man's bobbing erection as he moved towards her. Her poor head was spinning. Why had Zoe been so rude with her bottom? And why the jelly? Danni didn't understand, but then she felt Zoe pull her buttocks apart once more, and as Vanessa guided the pulsing stalk of rigid flesh between them realisation suddenly dawned.

He was going to penetrate her bottom!

So shocked was she, she could do no more than emit a feeble whimper of protest. She tried to clamp her buttocks together, but it was too late. His stiff cock was too powerful and pressed against its target, which was newly lubricated and rendered helpless to resist any invasion by the jelly ointment.

'Relax,' Zoe murmured in her ear. 'You can't stop this, so just let it happen.'

It wasn't easy; Danni's instincts were telling her to repel the intruder. But she knew Zoe was right – it was pointless to resist. She held her breath and relaxed as best she could.

Danni whimpered as the silent man remorselessly penetrated her, his thick cock sinking into her tight rear passage. The confusing sensation initially took her breath away, but as he shoved himself in, deeper and deeper, Danni

105

was reminded of the dildo that was still buried in her vagina. Every shunt by the man caused the thick phallus to move deliciously within her, so that once again she found herself pushing any discomfort to the back of her mind as the pleasure took over.

He moulded her buttocks around his buried cock with strong hands and stabbed his hips back and forth, thrusting her straining body against the creaking wooden frame. Every new thrust and grind sent waves of lascivious pleasure through her. She gazed dreamily at the bizarre reflection in the mirror, and a new surge of lust gripped her. Strong arms enfolded her perspiring body and large hands closed over her yearning breasts. The man stared back at her, no emotion registering on his face, as his groin slapped rhythmically against her bottom and matched the rhythmic squelching of the artificial penis stretching her clutching vagina. Danni bit her lip and shuddered as she thought of those silent observers watching her lewd performance.

Then she heard the man hiss in her ear and felt him stiffen, his hands squeezing so that her soft breasts bulged between his fingers as his thrusts turned to urgent jabs. His cock swelled even further, and then Danni felt the extraordinary sensation as he erupted deep in her bottom. The feel of his orgasm was too much for her. She came with a scream, her sex pulsating as it contracted about the hard rubber pole that filled it. The orgasm was long and loud as she finally let herself go, her naked body writhing as best it could in the bondage while she rode out her pleasure on the long, black phallus.

By the time the man withdrew Danni could take no more. She hung limp and exhausted from the frame. She barely noticed the twine being unfastened, her limbs too weak to hold her as she slumped into the arms of the two women. She was vaguely aware of being carried across to the couch, then she closed her eyes and sweet oblivion engulfed her.

Danni opened her eyes and stared up at the face hovering above her. For a moment there was no recognition. Then she realised it was Lucy. The glamorous woman was speaking in a soothing tone and holding something for her. Danni blinked, and then realised she was being offered a glass of water. She took it, and immediately spilled some onto the carpet as her hands trembled. She guided the glass carefully to her lips and sipped from it. The water was ice cold and refreshing, and she drank it down gratefully, draining the glass before handing it back. Then she propped herself up on one elbow and gazed about.

She was still in the room where they had whipped her, but one spotlight had been switched off and the horrible frame was once again draped in shadow. The sting of that punishment had faded to a throb, but she was still aware of its potency. She was on the couch, and watching her from two armchairs were Lucy and the urbane man who'd had her punished. There was no sign of Zoe and Vanessa, or of the younger man who had...

'Feeling better now?' asked Lucy with syrupy empathy.

'I... yes, I think so,' mumbled Danni, gingerly feeling her smarting buttocks.

'You did very well,' smiled the madame. 'I've rarely seen a girl react with such passion, particularly considering it was the first time you've...' her amused eyes drifted to where Danni's hand softly caressed her punished bottom, '...been buggered. It was your first time, wasn't it?'

Danni lowered her eyes and nodded.

'And that immense orgasm was genuine too, wasn't it?'

The exhausted girl nodded again.

'You were right, Lucy,' said the man, studying the girl carefully, 'she really is something special.'

Lucy looked extremely pleased with herself. 'I told you so. I think she's just what you're looking for.'

'I think you could be right.'

Danni stared from one to the other. 'What's going on?'

she asked warily, a new panic slowly churning her stomach. She looked at the man with a courage she didn't feel. 'How am I "just what you're looking for"?'

Lucy tore her eyes from the delicious morsel spread before her for the first time and turned to her male associate. 'I think we should tell her,' she said.

'Tell... tell me what?' Danni didn't like the way things were heading.

'Well, my dear friend here has a proposition for you,' Lucy said. 'A proposition which I think you should consider very carefully.'

Danni looked questioningly at the man.

'This is Charles Wright,' Lucy continued, indicating the man with her hand. 'Mr Wright is looking for a young lady to perform a service for him, and he's more than a little interested in you.'

Danni listened to the words in silence. She wasn't sure how to reply. It was such a bizarre situation to be formerly introduced to a man who had just instigated her whipping and bizarre seduction, while lying naked before him. Somehow a handshake seemed rather inappropriate.

'Before Mr Wright puts his proposal to you, I think you should know that your position here might not be as secure as we'd hoped,' added Lucy.

An icy finger of dread traced its way up Danni's spine. 'W-what do you mean?' she stammered.

'This business with the Dirangos and the Killarneys is more serious than we thought.'

Danni sat up. 'What?'

'I don't know what you did to upset them, and I'm not going to ask,' the madame went on. 'All I know is that there have been men from both gangs hanging around here and asking some awkward questions, and it's making me nervous.'

'But you said I'd be safe here,' Danni protested, her heart sinking. 'That's why I'm doing all this.' She turned to Wright.

'I'm not this type of girl really,' she pleaded. 'It's just that I had no choice.'

'I know we said we'd shelter you,' put in Lucy. 'And that's precisely why we're having this conversation. I could have betrayed you more than a week ago if I'd wanted. You've got to remember that I'm taking a risk here too.'

Danni's shoulders sagged. 'I know,' she said quietly. 'But you do ask an awful lot of me.'

'Only because I know you'll deliver, honey. There's not many girls I'd put through what you experienced tonight. Now, I want you to listen to what Mr Wright has to say.'

Danni felt utterly empty and alone, but she looked up at the man, and was once again struck by the intensity of his gaze. There was something oddly attractive about him that she couldn't quite fathom. And she knew, whatever the proposition, she would find it very hard to refuse even if she had a choice – which it seemed she didn't.

'All right,' she said. 'What are you suggesting?'

'Lucy feels you should get out of the city for a while,' he said, with confident ease. 'As she told you, those thugs are very keen to find you, and even in a city of this size it's not easy to hide. Particularly if you're young and beautiful and speak with a different accent.'

'Ed's already received a number of unpleasant visits,' added Lucy, 'and although he's said nothing so far, they're obviously pretty sure you're here. It's only a matter of time before they start getting heavy here, too.'

Danni felt sick. 'I've got to get away then.'

'And that's what Mr Wright is here for.'

'Can you help me?' she asked him beseechingly. 'What would I have to do?'

'You'd have to work for me.'

'Doing what?'

'Let me explain,' said Wright, avoiding the question for a moment, and savouring the desperation in her voice. 'I have a place about ten miles out of town. It's a private house with a large estate. There's just me and the servants, and my houseguests. I'd like you to come and live there for a while. Naturally you'd be paid.'

Danni was finding it difficult to absorb his words; her mind kept returning to those bullies chasing her. 'But I don't understand,' she said, shaking her head as though to clear it. 'Why would you want to pay me to live in your house?'

'Because you'd be providing a service for me.'

Danni eyed him suspiciously. 'What kind of a service?' she asked guardedly.

For a second Wright looked slightly embarrassed. Then he said, 'For many years I've had a kind of fantasy about a woman,' he said. 'A woman who was totally promiscuous, who would give herself to any man who asked, in any way he asked. In short, a complete slut.'

'And you think I'm a slut?' Danni felt outraged, despite the evidence of her recent activities at the club.

'I didn't say that. But I think you could play my slut for me.'

'I'm not sure I understand.'

'Well, this woman became so real to me that I began to talk about her to my friends. I pretended she was a distant cousin, and I used to tell them what she'd get up to. I guess it gave me a kind of kick too. Trouble is, I painted such a good picture they all want to meet her, so now I've got to find her.'

'This is the strangest thing I've ever heard,' gasped Danni.

'Strange or not, I've got to find my promiscuous cousin. And I kind of think I might have found her.'

'But why me? Surely there are plenty of girls in this town who'd fill your needs?'

'That's what I thought, but there aren't. I've been searching for weeks. Most whores are trash. They put on an act for you, but they're all lousy actresses. There's no joy fucking a woman who fakes her orgasms, and believe me I can tell when they do.'

Danni shook her head again. 'I don't think I'm the one you're looking for. I'm really very shy. I'm only doing this because I have no choice.'

'That's what makes you absolutely perfect,' said Wright. 'You have that shy, innocent air about you. But I've had the pleasure of witnessing another side to your nature – remember?' Danni blushed. 'And an irresistible side it is, too.' He smiled, as if savouring the vision of her tied to the frame. 'Oh yes,' he concluded, 'you're exactly the girl I've been looking for.'

'He's right you know,' added Lucy. 'I've watched you closely. I know you never fake it.'

Danni could have curled up and died at the way they discussed her. 'Even so,' she said meekly, 'I don't think—'

'Listen,' Wright interrupted, 'do it for me for one month. After that I'll help you get home, that's a promise.'

'And you'd be much safer there than in this club,' put in Lucy.

Danni looked from one to the other, her mind in a whirl. It was true that, despite the fact she hated the idea of what she did at the club, the reality was quite different. She had never before felt so alive and fulfilled as she had in recent weeks. But could she really give herself in the way this man wanted her to? And what would her friends at home think if they found out? Then again, she mused, what would they think of what she was doing now?

She glanced down at herself. She had almost forgotten her nudity, so accustomed was she becoming to being in such a state. Perhaps she could play the person Wright wanted her to. Besides, what choice did she have? Staying there would almost certainly result in those dangerous thugs finding her... and then what would happen? She shuddered at the thought.

'Just for a month?' she asked quietly.

'One month,' Wright confirmed. 'Then you'll be free to do as you wish.'

'And you'll tell me exactly what you want of me?'

'Naturally.'

Danni took a deep breath. 'All right,' she said. 'I'll do it.'

Chapter Nine

Danni stood at her bedroom window, staring out at the grounds below. There was no doubt that Wright was extremely rich. The grounds were huge, stretching down to woods and parkland. In the distance she could see a gardener labouring with an overloaded wheelbarrow.

She turned and wandered about the room. Wright had, true to his word, provided her with a sumptuous apartment with a king-sized bed and plenty of living space. The adjoining bathroom was large and well appointed and, with hi-fi, television and a drinks cabinet, there was little she could want for.

She crossed to the wardrobe and opened it. The racks inside were hung with a variety of outfits. She pulled a dress from its hanger and examined it. It was bright red and very short. She ran her fingers over the fine stitching, feeling the quality of the material. Then she replaced it in the wardrobe, precisely where she had found it. Each outfit bore a number emblazoned on the hanger, and as she gazed upon them she wondered what she would be wearing that afternoon.

She had arrived at Wright's mansion the night before. He had travelled with her in the back of his sumptuous limousine. She'd expected him to seduce her during the journey out to the country – checking on the quality of his goods – but he hadn't laid a finger on her. He had simply explained her position and responsibilities in greater detail.

'You will be my cousin Judith,' he had explained. 'You will call me Charles. Have you got that?'

'You're Charles, I'm Judith.'

'Good. Now, Judith is a girl with few inhibitions. All my friends have heard tales about her promiscuity. She loves to play around, and she doesn't care who she plays around with

– or who's watching. All right?'

'Yes, Charles.' As she listened to his instructions a tremor of anticipation shook the delicious youngster. Would she really be able to sustain such an act? Could she keep up such a performance for as long as was required? She tried to concentrate on what Wright was saying.

'You will have your own room, which will be yours alone to use. Your seductions will take place elsewhere. There are cameras concealed all over the house, so I shall be able to film and monitor your activities if I wish.'

'F-film them?'

'Certainly. I wish to be able to enjoy the more exciting episodes over and over again, as well as showing them to my friends. I trust you have no objections?'

'I... who would see them?'

'Anyone I choose.'

'I see.'

'For the most part I expect you to take the initiative with those friends of mine you encounter. The rules are simple: you will never refuse anyone who wishes to have some fun with you, and you will do precisely what is demanded.'

'Anything?'

'Within reason, yes. They will be permitted to dress you, strip you, tie you and beat you if the whim takes them. And you must participate with enthusiasm.'

'I must?'

Wright nodded. 'I may express disapproval at your actions, but you are to pay no attention to anything I say to you in public.'

Danni weighed these words in her mind. In ordering her to disobey him in public, he was ensuring that all her behaviour would be seen as on her own initiative. It was a clever ploy, she mused. To be seen as acting under his orders would have implied that she was reluctant. However, this way she would be seen as the slut he intended her to be.

'I have provided a wardrobe of suitable clothes,' he went

114

on. 'You will be told what to wear at any one time. You will wear what is on the hanger and nothing else, apart from footwear, which will be similarly numbered.'

'Can I go where I like?'

'Within the grounds of the house, yes. Sometimes you will be required to be in certain places, in which case you will be told. Occasionally you may be taken away from the house, but the rules will still apply.'

'Will I be assigned to particular partners?'

'Generally you will be free to please whomever wants you. Occasionally, though, you will become the property of specific guests, in which case they will control what you do and with whom. Now, do you have any more questions?'

Danni shook her head. 'You've made it all very clear,' she said.

'Good.'

He had not spoken to her again during the journey. When they arrived at the front of his mansion he had simply gone inside and left her alone. Moments later a pretty young maid of about Danni's own age had appeared. She said nothing, simply motioning for Danni to follow her.

Danni had been very uncertain indeed, padding along behind the swaying skirt of the maid. Occasionally they passed other servants who stopped to stare at her, and she had been relieved when they finally reached the room. The maid showed her around, and then left her alone. She showered, and then climbed between the crisp sheets on the huge bed and fell asleep almost immediately.

The maid entered with a tray of breakfast almost the instant Danni awoke. The food was delicious, and as soon as the last piece of toast and jam had been devoured the maid reappeared with a letter which she handed to Danni, before picking up the tray and leaving once more.

Danni tore open the envelope. It contained a single piece of paper, and she read the words on it with some anticipation:

Come to the swimming pool at two to have a swim and to meet Mr Reynolds. Outfit seventeen.

Danni turned away from the wardrobe and looked nervously at her watch. It was ten minutes to two. She knew it was time to go, but she hesitated. What on earth had she let herself in for?

She paused before the full-length mirror positioned opposite the bed and examined her reflection. Hanger seventeen had held only a very short robe, tied at the waist by a sash. It was made of sheer, almost transparent material so that the dark circles of her areolae and the light triangle of hair between her thighs were faintly visible. There had been no swimming costume. The shoes were open leather sandals with a high heel. Under normal circumstances she would have considered the outfit too revealing even to wear about her room. Now, as she turned toward the door, her heart was hammering at the prospect of walking down to the pool in such a state of near undress.

She stepped from the room, and suddenly realised she had no idea where the pool was. To her left and right the hallway looked identical. She hesitated for a moment, temporarily unsure of what to do. Then, for want of a better plan, she turned left and set off.

The house was huge, with a myriad of passages and stairways, but she found her way down to the ground floor without too much difficulty. A maid was polishing silver at a table and she asked her the way, blushing as the girl stared at her quite inadequate outfit.

The pool was set at the back of the house on a wide terrace with a bar at one end. There were half a dozen people, both men and women, basking in the sunshine on reclining chairs, and Danni felt her stomach knot as she made her way towards them, her shoes seeming to make an unnaturally loud clacking sound on the paving stones. As she approached, faces turned in her direction and she saw eyes widen at the

116

inadequacy of her gown. Remembering her part, though, she kept her head high and her expression calm.

On the far side, close to the bar, she could see Wright lying on a sun lounger beside another man on a similar lounger. Both wore shorts and T-shirt, and Wright beckoned to her as she approached.

'Ah, Judith, this is Mr Reynolds,' he said, indicating the other man. 'We've been doing some business this morning, but now we're taking a rest. Please, join us. John, this is my cousin, Judith.'

The man nodded without speaking, and Danni could see his eyes were fixed on her body, the robe quite unable to hide the fact that she wore nothing underneath. He seemed to be of a similar age to his host, but rather overweight with a pronounced paunch. His hair was receding too. He wasn't exactly Danni's idea of a perfect partner, but she tried to ignore that, concentrating instead on the bulge that was beginning to show beneath his shorts.

Wright ordered more drinks from a hovering member of the staff and then looked back up at Danni from behind his sunglasses. Danni resisted the temptation to use her hands to hide herself, instead placing one hand on her hip and letting the other dangle at her side.

'But Judith,' said Wright, in mock amazement, 'you're not wearing a swimming costume.'

'No, I didn't bring one.' She tried to reply as she thought her new character would. 'It doesn't matter does it?'

'Well, everyone else is wearing one,' he said. 'Couldn't you borrow one?'

'Oh, don't be such a prude, Charles,' she replied. 'I'm sure Mr Reynolds has no objection, do you?'

The man shook his head dumbly.

'You see? Now, I'm going for a swim.'

Danni looked at Wright for a moment, her eyebrows slightly raised as she tried to gauge his reaction to her performance so far. He nodded, a gesture so small that only

117

Danni would have detected it. Taking a deep breath she reached for the sash about her waist and undid the bow. Then, trembling slightly with shame, she let it fall open, revealing her curvaceous body. She shrugged the garment off and let it flutter to the ground. From behind she heard a low whistle, and knew somebody had seen the stripes on her buttocks from the previous night's whipping. She paused for a moment, posing for them. Outwardly she knew she appeared totally calm, but inside she was in a state of high tension, and she wondered if anybody could detect the way she was shaking. Then she turned towards the pool.

'Judith, dear, what on earth happened to your bottom?' asked Wright.

Danni stopped and glanced coyly over her shoulder. 'Somebody whipped it, Charles,' she said.

'Who?'

'A woman called Zoe. It was just a bit of fun.'

He shook his head in mock surprise as she made her way to the edge of the pool. She wanted to hurry, and to immerse her body as quickly as possible, so as to hide herself from the staring eyes. But she knew she must play her part, so she sauntered along, pausing at the poolside to kick off her shoes. Then she dived gracefully into the water, allowing its coolness to envelop her as she swam to the other end.

She remained in the water for about ten minutes, swimming back and forth, thoroughly enjoying the sensation of being nude in the pool. Two men joined her, and she was careful to put on a show for them, since she knew Wright would be watching. She drifted on her back, her lovely breasts breaking the lapping surface, her nipples hardened by the cold. She managed to brush them against one of the men, the feel of his bare flesh against hers sending a thrill through her. But she was slightly concerned that they might proposition her, as she knew her task was to entertain Mr Reynolds, so she decided she had better get out before things went too far.

She hauled herself from the water and made her way back to the reclining men, once again taking her time. She knew the colour in her cheeks was bright, but she tried to remain calm as if her behaviour, strolling nude amongst these strangers, was totally normal.

She reached Wright and his companion and stood between them, sipping her drink. She was careful to keep her legs slightly apart and to angle herself slightly towards Reynolds so he was presented with a close view of her wispy pubes. Her body was dripping with water, but it was the wetness inside her vagina that was concentrating her mind, as she suddenly realised that her behaviour was beginning to excite her. Once again she was surprised by the recalcitrant behaviour of her body. This couldn't really be turning her on, could it? After all, she was simply acting a part. She wasn't really a flirty exhibitionist – was she?

One of the staff placed a lounger between Reynolds and Wright, and invited her to recline upon it. The two men made conversation across her, but she knew that both only had eyes for her. Their obvious interest in her was increasing her arousal by the second, and she felt her nipples stiffen, more from the contemplation of what was to come than from the gentle breeze that danced across them. She had a strange urge to pinch the twin buds, but she daren't. Instead she stretched herself languidly and closed her eyes, letting her bare flesh soak up the warmth of the sun.

She must have dozed off for a short time, for when she opened her eyes again the sun had moved a little and Wright was standing over her, silhouetted darkly against the bright blue sky.

'I have to go inside and make a call, Judith,' he said. 'Perhaps you'll look after Mr Reynolds. He'd very much like to see some of the grounds.'

Danni propped herself up onto one elbow, her breasts falling forward as she did so. She glanced across at Reynolds, who was clearly still captivated by the curvaceous young vision lying beside him. Although he did absolutely nothing for her, she beamed her warmest, sexiest smile at him. 'Of course I will,' she said with as much enthusiasm as she could muster, slipping her shoes, rising gracefully to her feet, and offering him her hand. 'Would you like to come with me, Mr Reynolds,' she offered, with genuine innocence.

Deliberately misunderstanding her invitation he sniggered and licked his lips as he lumbered to his feet. 'You bet I would!' he wheezed unhealthily.

'Aren't you going to put your wrap on, Judith?' asked Wright.

Danni sensed the suggestion implicit in the question. She had been going to wear the garment, inadequate though it was, but now she shook her head. 'I'd prefer to go just like this. Mr Reynolds doesn't mind,' she forced herself to give the guest another suggestive grin, 'do you, Mr Reynolds?'

The man shook his head, his eyes not leaving her breasts.

Danni took his hand and they set off across the terrace towards the lawns, with the other sun worshippers staring after them.

'Actually, I don't know my way around my cousin's garden either,' Danni rambled, not really knowing what she should say to the man. 'But we can explore together, can't we?'

Danni was nervous and not looking forward to entertaining Mr Reynolds. Her blatant flirting in front of the other guests was quite alien to her, and she was angry for getting into a stupid situation where she had no choice but to do as she was told for as long as it amused her new owner. For as long as he demanded she had to play a part. She was now Judith, and she had to become the playful little wanton that Judith was supposed to be.

They crossed the lawns and walked away from the house towards a wooded copse about a quarter of a mile away. As they walked Danni babbled nervously, commenting on a flower here or a tree there. She could see two gardeners ahead tending a flowerbed, and at the sight of the naked beauty approaching they stopped work and leaned on their tools, staring blatantly at her charms and muttering quietly to each other.

Reynolds said little as they strolled, and Danni knew he was more interested in her swaying breasts than her inane observations. A furtive glance down at the bulge distending his shorts clearly indicated the extent of the effect she was having upon him. Summoning every ounce of determination and pushing her increasing angst to the back of her mind, she disengaged her hand from his and slipped her arm as far around his corpulent waist as she could. And when he did the same to her and crushed her to him she placed her hand over his and moved it down from her hip to her bottom.

Suddenly Danni experienced a tiny and inexplicable spark of arousal. The feel of his body so close to hers, his clumsy hand squeezing her bare buttocks, and the fact that she had no choice but to please the stranger, was beginning to excite her more than she could have imagined possible. Somehow it didn't matter that he wasn't young or attractive. In fact, in a way, his age and appearance made the prospect of having to seduce him curiously tantalising. His advantage over her in years was not, she sensed, matched by an advantage over even her relative inexperience with the opposite sex. He was definitely feeling uncomfortable in the presence of a younger and available girl.

They passed beneath the shade of the trees, Danni still clamped to his side, his shirt brushing her nipple and making it stand out all the more. As the gently whispering trees enveloped them and the house disappeared from view she knew the time had come. She stopped and pulled him round to face her.

'Do you like me?' she asked, cocking her head to one side and pouting.

'I... yes, of course,' he mumbled lamely.

She reached out and closed her fingers over his crotch. 'You're awfully hard,' she whispered innocently. 'What's caused that, then?'

'It's you.' He chuckled uncomfortably. 'That's what you do to me.'

'I do?' she gasped with mock naïvety. 'Would you like me to cover myself up? I could go back and get my robe, if it would help.'

'No. No... please, you don't have to do that,' he stammered, dabbing at the tiny beads of sweat that burst onto his generous forehead.

'But we'll have to do something about this,' she purred, squeezing him again, feeling increasingly sexy. 'Would you like me to make you a little more comfortable?'

'Bloody hell,' he panted.

Danni smiled with more confidence than she felt, then dropped quietly to her knees. Her hand was shaking as she reached for elasticated waistband. She pulled down, the material snagged for a second on his erection, she could feel his heat and smell his masculine arousal, and than she freed the shorts and his cock sprang up before her eyes.

'My, my,' she exclaimed, 'you are excited, Mr Reynolds.'

'Bloody hell,' he muttered again, disbelief in his voice.

Danni gazed at the column of flesh pulsing rhythmically before her flushed face. It was short and thick, the circumcised glans swollen and bulbous. She ran her fingers up and down its length a couple of times, making him gasp. Then she leaned forward and took him into her mouth.

He grunted as she tightened her lips about him, and for a moment she thought he might come too quickly. But he didn't, and she sucked noisily, enjoying the taste of his arousal, her head moving back and forth as she slipped her hand into his shorts and cupped his balls.

To her surprise, and disappointment, he suddenly entwined his fingers in her hair and pulled her back off his erection. She peeped up at him, fearful that she'd done something wrong. 'What's the matter,' she asked. 'Aren't I doing it right?'

'You're doing wonderfully,' he gasped. 'But I don't want to come in your mouth.'

Danni waited to hear what he did want, her hand lazily milking his length.

'I... I want to fuck you,' he stammered like a shy schoolboy. It was as though he had absolved himself of some pent-up guilt or emotion, for he suddenly became more commanding. He pulled Danni to her feet and guided her over to a tree that lent at an acute angle. He turned her and pushed her down over the wide trunk. The bark was rough against her bare flesh, but the discomfort sent a new tremor of excitement down her spine.

As his large bulk closed in on her she caught a movement over his shoulder. Someone was hiding and watching them. She realised it was the two gardeners, and was about to protest and warn her companion when she remembered she was Judith, and Judith wouldn't care, no matter how many dirty old perverts spied on her.

'I'm all yours,' she whispered to Reynolds, while staring at the two lechers.

He paused for a moment, staring at her, his eyes travelling over the soft swellings of her breasts, then dropping down to her sex, so moist and invitingly opened for him.

As his bulbous glans brushed against her swollen clitoris she let out a gasp of delight. The realisation of just how turned on she was made her swoon and clutch his shoulders to pull him closer.

He penetrated her easily. Danni moaned aloud as he pressed himself home, his erection stretching and filling her sex and sending shards of desire spearing through her.

He began bucking against her at once with eager thrusts that confirmed his own extreme arousal. Despite the discomfort of the rough tree, Danni responded, jabbing her hips against his, matching his every thrust as she abandoned herself totally to her lustful desires.

His hands clamped around her breasts, kneading and

123

pawing them with artless enthusiasm. Danni revelled in the crude treatment she was receiving, treatment that was somehow enhanced by being sandwiched between his sweating and grunting mass and the unyielding trunk.

He came quickly, slobbering kisses all over her flushed face as he did, his cock twitching as he pumped his seed deep into her vagina. Despite his grossly inept techniques, Danni responded with her own shattering climax, unable to suppress the cries of delight as her tension was at last released. She pressed her hips forward, urging him ever deeper as his balls continued to fill her, his grunts turning to gasps at the sensation of her inner muscles milking his shaft. Through misty vision Danni could still see the gardeners, their eyes wide at what they were witnessing, and the thought of their gazes upon her gave new impetus to her enjoyment as she imagined how stiff their cocks must be.

Reynolds went on thrusting until he was utterly spent, then collapsed, crushing the breath from her lungs as he smothered her against the tree.

'Damn, you're one dirty little bitch, Judith,' he panted against her shoulder.

'I know,' she replied, as she gazed over his shoulder at where the gardeners had been.

Chapter Ten

As the week progressed, Danni learned more and more about what it felt like to be Judith. Wright had numerous houseguests at his mansion, and it soon became clear to her that word had begun to get around about her lascivious behaviour. Every day saw new people arriving, some staying for just a few hours, others using the numerous guestrooms in the mansion.

After the first encounter by the poolside, Wright saw to it that she was placed in a number of situations where men took advantage of her. For the first two or three days her encounters, like that with Reynolds, were entirely contrived by him, setting her up with a man and then leaving her to be seduced. After that, though, his tactics changed, so that the initiative was given back to her. The first of these was on the fourth afternoon, when he had ordered her to join a group of men playing croquet on the front lawn. She had been allowed only a blouse and a short, tight skirt, and the bending involved in playing the game had soon revealed to her fellow players that she wore no underwear. She had been partnered with a good-looking young man, and had immediately fallen into Judith's character, flirting with him outrageously. Before long he was surreptitiously groping her, and no sooner had the game ended than he took her to his room. The rest of the afternoon had been spent enjoying some of the best sex she could remember.

This episode set the scene for the rest of the week. Danni, wearing the sexiest of outfits, would single out a man from whatever group she was with and would invariably end up having some form of sex with him. She was careful not to pick only young and handsome men, and was often pleasantly surprised by the prowess and sexual ingenuity of the older ones, so that her own lustful desires were always satisfied.

For Danni herself, the life she was forced to lead was one she found hard to reconcile. Every morning she awoke feeling ashamed and embarrassed by her behaviour on the previous day, and, when she donned some of the outfits Wright had prepared for her, her heart would sink as she contemplated what was to come. Yet, once she had overcome her natural modesty, she found herself revelling in the sexual encounters that followed, and would often come two or three times in a session; wonderful, shattering orgasms that would leave her gasping for breath.

It was early in the second week that the first change in her routine occurred, and she had her first opportunity to leave the mansion.

For once Wright didn't engineer the episode. After an enjoyable dinner she had retired with the guests to a saloon, where they had sipped their coffee and chatted. There were five of them, three men, including Wright, as well as Danni and a woman called Tonia.

Tonia, Danni had come to realise, was a frequent visitor to Wright's mansion. Indeed, she had been one of the people beside the pool when Danni had taken Reynolds off to the woods. The young English girl had often been aware of the woman's presence after that and had, on more than one occasion, been embarrassed by her glances as Danni was taken upstairs by one of her many lovers. Tonia was about twenty-five years old, tall and dark, with deep green eyes and high cheekbones. Like Danni she was often the centre of attention of the male guests, but unlike the youngster she kept them at arms length, and Danni had never seen any evidence that she had so much as allowed a kiss to any of her suitors. This made Danni especially embarrassed when in the woman's presence, since her own promiscuity was obvious to all, particularly when she dressed so revealingly.

Whether it had been Wright's intention to leave Danni

alone with Tonia she never knew. It was certainly not his
initiative. One of the young men had asked to see some
paintings that Wright owned, and the other man had gone
along with them, leaving the two females alone. Danni had
felt somewhat uncomfortable sitting with the woman. She
was wearing a long black evening dress that was slit to the
hip on one side, and had a neckline that plunged and
highlighted her cleavage. Tonia's dress was much more
modest, though tight, so that her curves were beautifully
accentuated.

For a while the pair chatted politely, though Danni was
more than conscious of the interest Tonia was taking in her,
enquiring in some depth about her relationship to Wright
and the length of her stay. It was about ten minutes after the
men had left that the conversation took a different and
unexpected turn.

'How many men have fucked you since you've been
staying here?' asked Tonia.

The question and choice of phrase took Danni completely
by surprise. 'I beg your pardon?' she said, a little indignantly.

'How many men have had you?' persisted the composed
woman. 'To my knowledge it's at least five, but I suspect
it's actually more. Would I be right?'

'I – I think that's a rather personal question… isn't it?'

'Sure. But we Americans like to be forthright. Not like
you British. You're so pompous and reserved.' She smiled
with an avaricious glint in her eyes. 'Although in your case
I'm not so sure.'

Danni shifted awkwardly, feeling acutely embarrassed
under the unfair scrutiny of the relentless woman. She felt
she had to say something to justify herself, but she didn't
quite know what. 'I – I just like men…' she blurted, without
really thinking, '…that's all.'

'And do you like women?'

'Women?' Danni wrung her fingers in her lap. 'W-what
do you mean?'

'Do you fuck with women?'

Danni blushed again at the woman's cruel bluntness. 'I – I don't know what you mean. I—'

'Never mind,' Tonia interrupted, putting the bumbling girl out of her misery. She smiled warmly and took the pressure off by shifting the subject just a little. 'Those are some outfits you wear, though,' she said. 'They don't leave very much to the imagination.'

'I suppose I like men to look at me.'

'So I see. And to do more than just look, from what I've seen.'

Danni said nothing, finding it difficult to maintain the role of Judith in front of the woman.

Tonia leaned forward and placed a hand on Danni's knee. 'Listen baby, I'm having a little party tomorrow night at my place. Would you like to come?'

Danni stared at her. Tonia's presence unsettled her greatly. The last thing she wanted was to place herself in the woman's power. But she wasn't Danni at the moment, she was Judith, and she had to react in the way Judith would.

'What kind of a party?' she asked guardedly.

'Just a few friends coming round for some drinks and a little fun. You'd enjoy it.'

'I'll have to make sure Charles hasn't any other plans.'

'It's not Charles I'm inviting, it's you. And I'm sure my guests would be amused by your presence.'

'How do you mean, amused?'

'Don't be so defensive, Judith,' Tonia remonstrated. 'You have to admit that the men are hopelessly attracted to you. All I'm saying is that my friends would be too.'

'I don't know...'

'You're not afraid are you? After all, you've never shown any reluctance before.'

Danni realised that Tonia was playing a game with her, and was momentarily tempted to get up and walk out. But she knew she couldn't. She had to consider what Judith would do.

At that moment Wright reappeared with his two companions.

'I'm sorry about that,' he apologised to the female's. 'What were you two chatting about?'

'I've invited Judith to my party tomorrow night,' said Tonia brightly.

Danni looked up at him. 'Is that all right?' she asked, hoping he would say no.

'Of course it is, my dear, although I hope you'll behave yourself.' He turned to the two men. 'I'm afraid Judith sometimes gets carried away, especially in male company. Don't you my dear?'

'I'm just enjoying life while I'm young.'

One of the men sat beside her and placed a hand on her knee. 'Tell me how you enjoy yourself, Judith,' he leered, and Danni knew she wouldn't sleep alone that night as she felt his fingers crawl furtively up her thigh.

Chapter Eleven

Danni sat in the back of the limousine as it purred through the streets, her heart heavy with anticipation of what was to come. The idea of an evening at Tonia's house was one that filled her with trepidation. There was something about the woman that made her very nervous indeed. The American had an air of confidence about her that Danni lacked. What really bothered the youngster, though, was the way she herself was forced to act, and the reaction of Tonia to her promiscuity. The woman's own behaviour, as compared to her own, always seemed to give her the moral high ground.

Above all, though, Danni knew her own confidence would be eroded by the way Wright had made her dress for that evening. Dress was hardly the word, she mused; she was practically naked.

She had been allowed no top as such. All she had found on the hanger was a long white silk scarf. This she had draped about her neck so that the two ends hung down over her breasts. It really was quite inadequate. She also wore the briefest of bikini bottoms, not much more than a G-string, also in white. The skimpy garment was very tight, so much so that it outlined her sex lips perfectly, and the near transparent material left her pubis almost completely exposed. Worse still, she'd had to trim her downy hair in order to ensure that the tiny triangle covered it. White stockings with lacy, elasticated tops encased her shapely legs. Her shoes were shiny white with high heels and pointed toes. All in all it was an outrageous outfit, that she would have been embarrassed to wear even in the privacy of the bedroom, yet here she was on her way to a party attended by people she didn't even know.

The car slowed and pulled into a driveway. The house

was a large one, though by no means comparable with Wright's. As they drew to a smooth halt at the entrance a man stepped forward and opened Danni's door. She peered out, suddenly feeling the panic rising as she realised that the time had come to reveal her outfit.

'Miss?' The chauffeur had turned in his seat and the tinted screen that separated him from his passenger buzzed expensively as it lowered. 'This is the place, miss.'

Danni took a deep breath, then stepped from the car. As she bent forward the scarf fell away from her breasts, momentarily uncovering them completely. She hastily grabbed the ends, straightening up and draping them over her nipples once more.

There were a few steps up to the front door, which was being majestically held open by a liveried servant. If Danni's outfit shocked him he didn't show it. Maybe, she reflected hopefully, she would not be the only one so attired.

As she reached the door, Danni turned to watch Wright's limo drive away. It occurred to her that she had made no arrangements about being collected, and she felt a momentary sense of isolation as she realised she was alone, with no means of escape. Just then another car drew up and she turned and entered the house, anxious not to be seen by the people in the vehicle.

She found herself in a large hallway. In front of her were grand double doors. They were open, and there posed the elegant Tonia. Beyond her, Danni could see people milling around and gossiping and laughing politely. Any hopes she might have had that her appearance would not be out of place were immediately and violently dashed. Every woman within sight wore a beautiful gown, and the men wore dark and immaculately tailored suits. Danni glanced down at her own barely covered figure, and wished desperately that she was more adequately covered.

As she approached Tonia, the lovely hostess theatrically stretched out a hand.

'Ah, Judith, you came,' she beamed. 'But what happened to your clothes? Were you mugged or something on the way?' She threw her head back and tittered gaily at her wit.

'No, I—'

'Well don't just stand there, my dear – people will see you. Quick, you'd better come upstairs and I'll find you something more suitable to wear.'

'I… I don't need anything,' Danni struggled to say what she knew Wright would expect her to say, her face reddening.

'But what do you mean?' Tonia looked genuinely taken aback. 'You're practically naked.'

'I wore these deliberately. Don't you like them?' She dropped her hands to her sides and gallantly returning Tonia's stare.

'What an extraordinary girl you are!' the woman enthused with a knowing glint in her eye. 'You're outrageous! Look at the way the servants are staring!'

Danni was relieved that she'd apparently behaved – so far – in the correct manner. She was certain that Wright would have gauged Tonia's reaction before selecting the minuscule outfit. She wondered for a second if she and Wright had planned this whole thing together. Somehow she didn't think so. Tonia had, from the start, struck her as a woman with a mind of her own. She had seen Danni's behaviour at the mansion, and was clearly quite capable of arranging this herself. 'You didn't mention what I should wear,' she said, feeling a need to defend herself.

'No I didn't,' Tonia's eyes were crawling appreciatively over her young guest as she spoke, 'but you obviously knew there would be other guests here.'

Danni nodded.

'And don't you mind that they stare at you?'

Danni hung her head. Of course she minded. She had never been so embarrassed in her life. But she was Judith for the night.

Tonia smiled again, and Danni hesitated for a moment,

132

and then followed her into the room as she turned and gracefully joined her guests. There were about twenty people there, both couples and single men and women, and the gay babble died as though someone had turned off a recording, and all eyes turned in Danni's direction.

Tonia took her to a group of eight or nine who were standing beside the large fireplace.

'This is Judith,' she announced to them. 'Judith is Charles Wright's cousin from England. She's staying with him for a short while.'

One of the women in the group, a stern-looking headmistress type glanced at Danni with some distaste. 'And is that how they dress for parties in England?' she sneered.

'I didn't know dress was formal tonight,' replied Danni, wondering why Wright should want to expose her to such humiliation.

'Formal? You look as though you thought it was optional,' returned the woman, and there was a murmur of sycophantic agreement from the little gathering.

'Judith is a little bit of a – how shall I put it – flighty young thing, I'm afraid,' said Tonia. 'If I'd known she was going to show up like this I'd have warned you all.'

'Can't you give her something to put on?' asked the woman.

'I guess I could. Judith, why not go up and borrow one of my dresses?' Tonia offered again. 'You're more than welcome to.'

Danni wished she could say yes. She longed to hide herself from the disapproving eyes all about her. But she dared not.

'No, thank you,' she said. 'I want to stay as I am.'

'You see what I mean?' said Tonia to her friends. 'She's a lost cause, I'm afraid. Now, darling,' she turned back to Danni, 'what would you like to drink?'

A waiter brought Danni her requested gin and tonic and she sipped it uncomfortably. Conversation in the group returned to normal, though she contributed only

133

monosyllables, preferring to remain quietly on the edge. Meanwhile Tonia moved off to mingle amongst the rest of her guests.

Danni glanced about at the assembled people. There was a wide mix of ages, from men and women past middle age to others not much older than her. She eyed some of the younger females, envious of their dresses, and still acutely aware of the inadequacy of her own attire. She adjusted the scarf in a vain attempt to cover her jutting breasts, and nodded as the man beside her passed a remark that she didn't really take in.

Suddenly Tonia was at her side once more. 'Judith,' she said, 'there's a couple of young men over there who are dying to meet you. Come along with me.'

She took Danni by the arm and led her across the room. The two were standing by one of the large Georgian windows. Tonia introduced them. Bart was tall with thick curly hair and an infectious grin. His companion, Gary, was shorter and tubbier. Neither of them was particularly good-looking.

'This is Judith,' said Tonia.

Danni nodded bashfully. She noticed that some of the men were risking the wrath of their womenfolk by stealing furtive glances at her near-nudity.

There was a slightly awkward pause, and then Tonia said, 'Well, I can see you three are going to get along just fine. I'll leave you to get better acquainted.'

Danni barely heard the two men as they jostled verbally for her attentions, too distracted was she by her reflection in one of the many mirrors reminding her that this was no ordinary social gathering. Despite her embarrassment, though, she knew she had to stay in the character of Judith, and she concentrated on responding to their flirting as best she could.

When Bart asked if she'd like to see the gardens Danni sensed his ulterior motive at once. She knew the intention was to get her away from the rest of the guests, and under normal circumstances she would definitely have thought twice. But she was Judith, and Judith dressed outrageously and never turned down a proposition from a man. She was also keen to escape the judgemental scrutiny of the gossiping throng.

'That would be nice,' she lied. 'Shall we go?'

The two men took a hand each and led the young beauty out through a pair of double doors on the far side of the room. The doors opened onto a patio, and beyond that was the garden. They strolled down a path, still holding her hands. At the end there was an ornamental pond, with lily pads floating on its surface. They paused there, and Gary wandered down to the edge while Bart remained with Danni.

He slipped an arm around her waist, and she knew it would be best to do or say nothing that could be interpreted as an objection. He turned her and cupped her cheek in his hand, staring into her eyes. Then he let his fingers trace down the side of her throat, brush the scarf aside and close over her breast. Danni said nothing, but she knew that the way her nipple protruded so proudly told him the effect his caresses were having. He leaned down and placed his lips over hers. For a second she resisted, then his tongue penetrated her mouth and she gave herself up to the kiss, intertwining her tongue with his and closing her eyes as his closeness threatened to overwhelm her.

He kissed her passionately, and she fairly melted into his arms, loving the way his fingers explored her breasts, the heat suddenly beginning to rise within her. For a second she wondered at her wantonness. She had met this man less than ten minutes before, and now she was letting him caress her in the most intimate manner, as if they were long time lovers. But he had aroused her passions now, and she knew she would do whatever he demanded.

Suddenly she felt hands at her waist. Someone – Gary – hooked his fingers into the waistband of her tiny panties.

She tried to protest, but Bart's mouth clamped still tighter over her own and his arms wrapped about her, holding her firmly. She struggled, but he was too strong for her, and there was nothing she could do to prevent Gary dragging the briefs down her thighs until they dropped to her ankles. Moments later his hands were sliding up between her thighs and seeking her sex.

Danni moaned as he slid his fingers into her. The pair were allowing no concessions whatsoever. They wanted her, and they intended to take her. Bart's embrace was powerful, crushing her close while his friend caressed her intimately, his fingers teasing her clitoris and sending wave after wave of pure pleasure through her trembling body.

Bart broke off his kiss, staring down at her pretty face, and she knew he could see the lust in her eyes. He mauled her breasts once more, kneading them between his fingers.

'You… you mustn't,' she murmured. But even as she spoke Gary gripped her arms, dragging her backwards and down onto the grass. Once again the young beauty put up a struggle, but it was useless against the two determined and randy men. In no time she found herself lying back on the lawn with Bart pressing her shoulders down.

Gary pulled the scarf from her neck and tossed it aside.

'Spread your legs, baby,' he cajoled.

Danni realised at once the futility of arguing. In truth, she knew any resistance would only be a token gesture. She was too aroused now not to go the full way with the pair and, as she watched Bart unzip his neat trousers, a tremor of eager lust ran through her body. It was with an urgency that shamed her that she worked her panties off one foot with the other and then kicked them aside.

Bart took her first. The coupling was completely without ceremony. He simply lowered his trousers a little, pulled out his rampant cock, dropped to his knees between her thighs, and lunged into her. Danni whimpered and dug her nails into his shoulders as he rutted on top of her, thrusting her hips up at him and urging him deeper. She struggled to breathe as his considerable weight bore down on her petite frame. She could barely credit her own wantonness as her body responded to him, her vaginal muscles caressing his thick shaft even as it violated her. Moments later she abandoned herself totally to him as he began to fuck her with gusto.

He took her with a series of animalistic grunts, pinning her to the ground as he thrust again and again. The last vestiges of Danni's resistance had evaporated. She was consumed by the sensation of his cock as it ploughed back and forth inside her, every stroke sending her to new heights of ecstasy, so that she cried aloud, oblivious to whoever might hear.

His thrusts became more urgent, his hips pounding down against her own, and she knew he would soon come. Over his shoulder she could see Gary slowly masturbating as he watched the debauched scene before him.

As happened so often, it was the feel of a man erupting deep into her vagina that triggered Danni's climax. The orgasm was as delicious as it was violent, her perspiring body shaken to the core as he spent. Then he was pulling away as his friend took his place.

Gary screwed her in the same impersonal manner as Bart had. But Danni didn't care. The more she experienced the pleasures of sex, the more she came to see that it was a purely physical thing for her. Perhaps she really was a whore, she wasn't sure. All she really knew was that when men took her the way these two had she was more aroused than by the wooing of any lover.

Gary came quickly, pumping his seed into the lovely writhing girl beneath him and bringing her to another glorious climax. By the time he withdrew Danni was panting with exhaustion, her aching breasts rising and falling as she gazed up at the two men.

They both tucked their deflating specimens back into their

trousers and straightened their clothing. Then they took her hands and pulled her to her feet. Danni stood before them, suddenly embarrassed at her nudity, feeling pale and vulnerable in the strange garden. She picked up her scarf and slipped it around her neck once more, then looked about for her panties. She couldn't see them anywhere.

She turned to the men for some help.

Bart grinned. 'I guess you were a little too eager to kick them off,' he said. 'There they are.'

Danni followed the direction of his pointing finger, and gasped her dismay. There, floating lazily on the surface of the pond, were her panties.

'Oh no,' she whispered. 'What can I do?'

'You could try fishing them out with a stick,' suggested Bart.

Danni glared at him for a moment, and then realised it was her only choice, and began searching the water's edge. She quickly found a long stick and reached out with it. It was just too short.

'Try holding onto that tree,' said Gary, clearly just as amused as his friend by Danni's predicament.

The tree was a small one, and it was growing right at the edge of the pond. Danni wrapped one arm around it and leaned out over the gently lapping water, stretching to reach her bobbing panties, the stick held at arm's length. She dipped the tip into the water and tried to bring it up under the waterlogged material. For a second she seemed to have them hooked, and she lifted the stick. But the stupid garment slipped from it, and Danni squealed with frustration as her panties suddenly sank below the surface. She poked about frantically with the stick, but in vain. All she managed to do was to stir up a muddy cloud that swallowed her panties, and she guessed they must have got snagged in something near the bottom.

She hauled herself back and turned to find the two selfish men had left her alone. Then she heard a voice calling from the house; it was Tonia.

'Come on inside, Judith,' she called. 'We're about to sit down to eat...'

Danni crouched in the bushes, wondering what on earth she could do next. Her panties were beyond retrieval, that was for sure. If she had been embarrassed by her lack of clothing before, that was as nothing to how she felt now. How could she possibly return to the party naked from the waist down? Yet where else could she go? She was trapped at the bottom of the garden, and her hostess was calling to her. She glanced about for something she could use to cover herself, but saw nothing even remotely suitable.

'Judith, are you out there?' called Tonia.

Danni knew there was no mileage in hiding. 'I'm just down here... by the pond.'

Tonia suddenly rounded a large shrub and came face to face with the English girl. 'Oh,' she exclaimed, clearly bemused by Danni's increasingly bizarre state of undress, 'there you are.' Danni cringed as the older woman took in her state of nudity.

'What have you done with your knickers?' she asked.

'I...' Danni felt so stupid, 'I lost them.'

'You lost them?' Tonia couldn't keep the grin from turning up the corners of her sensuous mouth. 'And where did you lose them?'

'In – in the pond...' she bowed her head like a shamed schoolgirl. 'They sank.'

'But why did you take them off?'

'I didn't. Gary did.'

'Gary took your knickers off?'

Danni nodded.

'And did he screw you?'

Danni hesitated, struggling to keep up the pretence of being the brazen Judith, and then she nodded again.

'My God, you don't waste much time, do you Judith?

You've barely met him and already he's sampled your charms. So what was Bart doing all this time?'

'H-he screwed me too.'

'Both of them screwed you? Here, in my garden?'

Danni dropped her gaze. 'Yes,' she said humbly.

Tonia shook her head. 'It's true what they said about you, Judith,' she said. 'You really are a loose young lady.'

Danni wanted to protest, but she remembered her brief. She was Judith, and Judith was, indeed, a young lady of dubious morals. She steeled herself. 'I can do what I want,' she said defiantly. 'It's none of your business.'

'No, I suppose it's not,' said Tonia. 'Oh well, you'd better come back up to the house. We're about to eat.'

'But I can't come up like this!'

'Why not?' mocked Tonia. 'Since when did you start to list modesty amongst your qualities?'

More and more Danni was hating being thought of badly. 'Can't you lend me some panties?'

'Not if you're going to lose them again. Besides, what's the point? The first guy you talk to will have you charmed out of them in five seconds flat.'

'But—'

'I'll tell you what I'll do,' interrupted Tonia, clearly enjoying Danni's chagrin. 'You wait at the door and I'll get your napkin from the table. Once you're sitting down nobody will notice. Come with me.'

She turned and headed towards the house. Danni didn't want to go back, but she seemed to have no choice. Even if she could find another way out of the garden that didn't involve going through the house, where could she go? She was dependent on these people, and she knew it. Slowly, reluctantly, she followed behind Tonia.

When she reached the house there was nobody in sight apart from a servant collecting empty glasses.

'Wait here,' said Tonia. 'I'll be back in a moment.'

She left Danni alone with the man. He stopped his work

when he saw her mouthwatering condition, and stared blatantly at her. Embarrassed, Danni placed a hand over her crotch in an attempt to cover her nudity. The servant stood, his eyes fixed on her for a moment, then he continued with his duties without a word.

A couple of minutes passed, and then Tonia reappeared holding a large white napkin. She gave it to Danni. 'Here,' she said, 'cover yourself with that and come on. I'll take you in the back way. Your seat is right by the door, so you shouldn't attract too much attention.'

Danni held the napkin against her tummy so that it hung down just to her thighs. Then she followed Tonia through a door and down a hall. They passed through the kitchen, and Danni avoided the staffs' eyes as they took in the curves of her bare behind. Then they went along another hall and stopped at a closed door.

'Your seat is straight through here,' said Tonia. 'Now hurry up, everyone's waiting to start.'

Danni pushed open the door. At once the hubbub of conversation assailed her ears and she found herself looking into a room full of the guests, all seated about a long table. There was an empty chair near to where she stood. Nobody seemed to have noticed her arrival, so she slipped quietly onto the vacant chair, maintaining what little modesty she had left with the starched napkin and hoping no one had noticed her lack of panties. She adjusted the scarf to cover her breasts as best she could.

There was a glass of white wine in front of her and she savoured a long and much needed drink. Her heart was thumping and her throat was dry. As she put the glass down her hand was shaking.

It was a few minutes before she calmed down enough to begin to take an interest in her surroundings. She was sitting at the table with about thirty other people. Many were chatting together, but she was only too aware of the number of eyes on her, and she tugged nervously at the scarf ends in

141

a vain attempt to regain some decency.

She glanced to her right and left. Both her immediate neighbours were male. To her right was an older man, and the most noticeable thing about him was a bushy moustache. He had an air of confidence as he chatted to a woman on his right.

The man on Danni's left was younger, with cropped hair and glasses. He seemed strangely uncomfortable at her presence, casting surreptitious sidelong glances at her near-naked condition. But his expression was more one of distaste than of lust. Still, she noticed that he could barely take his eyes off her, furtively eyeing her up at every opportunity.

The first course arrived. Normally she would have been starving by now, but her nerves had destroyed her appetite. She picked at the food, not really enjoying it, so that a good deal remained on her plate when it was cleared away.

It was while she was waiting for the next course that she felt a hand on her knee. The sudden contact made her jump, and she darted a glance to her right. The older man was still chatting affably with the woman, yet it could only be his hand that was squeezing the smooth denier of her stockings, stroking her leg and sending small shivers down her spine.

Danni's first reaction was to remove the hand. But then she remembered that it was not hers, but Judith's leg the man was feeling, and Judith would react in a completely different way to such an approach. She took a sip of the very nice wine, trying to remain outwardly passive as the hand crept further up towards her stocking top.

When the fingers found the silky smooth flesh of her thigh she gave a little gasp, her flesh tingling under the touch. He stroked her there, moving his fingers back and forth, and she had to nibble her lip to stop herself making a sound. She glanced anxiously about. The rest of the guests were chatting away normally. Even the man on her right was showing no sign that anything was amiss, despite the way his fingers squeezed her so intimately.

The hand moved higher still, and Danni knew he was seeking her sex. What would he think when he discovered she was wearing nothing there? Her face glowed at the thought, yet still she made no move to stop him as his fingers crawled closer and closer to their goal. She was shaking slightly now, becoming more and more aroused as she anticipated his touch. She felt her nipples stiffen under their inadequate covering as the fingers neared their journey's end.

'Oh!' She stifled the cry as best she could, but still a few heads turned in her direction as he found her clitoris. He ran a digit over the erect bud, and she inhaled sharply as a delicious spasm of pleasure ran through her. She threw the man another glance. His conversation had faltered for a second as he discovered that she was naked below the waist, and now, for the first time, he turned to look at her.

'Please be careful,' she whispered as his fingers slid between the lips of her sex. 'You'll make me come if you don't stop doing that.'

He smiled paternally. 'What happened to your knickers, my little angel?' he asked, dabbing his lips with a crisp napkin so that nobody but the object of his desire could hear what he said.

'I lost them,' she blurted under her breath. 'I... Oh!'

Another cry escaped her lips as he delved deeper into her moist vagina, twisting his fingers as he did so.

'You like that, don't you?' he smiled pleasantly, giving the impression to anyone watching that he was discussing nothing more interesting than the weather with the young beauty.

'I... yes, I do. But you mustn't do any more.' Danni was trying hard to maintain the poise that a girl like Judith might under such circumstances. 'It's very naughty,' she whispered, forcing a smile like his.

'But I like naughty young ladies,' he replied. 'If you put your hand in my lap you'll find out just how much I like naughty young ladies.'

'I beg your pardon?' Danni was sure the whole room could hear their disgraceful conversation, but judging by the lack of anyone taking any notice she knew they could not.

'You heard me, my little angel,' he coaxed. 'Go on, put your hand in my lap. Nobody will see. They're all too wrapped up in their own insignificant little worlds.'

Danni stared at him for a second. He was clearly serious. He pressed his clever fingers deeper, and she found herself spreading her legs a little to accommodate him. Slowly she slipped her hand beneath the table.

She immediately felt his cock twitch. The front of his trousers was lifting like a tent, and she gingerly ran her fingers over the bulge, squeezing it gently as she did so.'

'See how hard you've made me, you sexy little tease?' he breathed quietly. 'I think you should do something about that, now don't you?'

Danni wanted to tell him to get lost; he was taking far too great a liberty with her. But she was Judith now, and Judith would react quite differently.

'What do you want me to do?' she asked, trying to control the way her muscles were rhythmically contracting about his probing fingers.

'How about a nice wank.' The crudity of his words were in stark contrast to the smiling and well mannered façade presented to the other guests.

'But aren't you afraid someone will see?' she gasped, hoping he wasn't serious.

'And who's going to see?' he said, his tone becoming just a little sterner. 'Come on, Judith, don't play games with me; you could find yourself out of your depth.'

Danni sensed he was not a man to annoy, and so she moved her hand around his lap and felt for the zip. It stubbornly refused to negotiate the immense bulge stretching it, but after a couple of tugs it conceded, and then she reached inside and eased his awakening column of flesh from the warm

144

nest of his underpants.

Trying to keep her arm as still as possible, so as not to attract any attention to what her hand might be doing, she ran her fingertips down the rigid length, tracing its gnarled contours. It was soon as stiff as a ramrod, spearing straight up from his groin, thick and hot. She wrapped her fingers around it and started to masturbate him as ordered, noting the expression of pleasure on his face.

She glanced to her left. The bespectacled man was watching her, and she knew he could tell what she was doing. His eyes were fixed on her slightly moving forearm where it disappeared beneath the tablecloth, and try as she might, there was no disguising what she was up to.

'That's very nice,' whispered the older man. 'But the trouble is, I don't want to come all over my suit.'

'You – you could use your napkin,' she suggested, wishing the floor would open up and swallow her.

He grinned. 'No… I have a much better idea, my little angel. You could use your mouth.'

'I…' poor Danni was stunned. 'I could do what?'

'You could use your mouth,' he repeated casually. 'Come on, they'll be serving the next course soon.'

She didn't know what to do. 'P-people will k-know,' she stammered, struggling to keep her voice down.

'No they won't,' he said, totally assured. 'Nobody's taking any notice of what we're up to. Get on with it, Judith.' Again he flashed her an unspoken warning that it would be unwise to disobey.

Danni glanced about. He was right; apart from the quiet man on her left, everybody else seemed to be far too enwrapped in himself or herself to be paying any attention to what she was doing. Even so, she made a pretence of breaking her bread roll, and drop it theatrically onto the floor.

With a deep breath she slipped down under the table, gasping a little as the man's fingers slid out of her wet vagina. She knew her other companion would see what she was

145

doing, but that couldn't be helped. She manoeuvred herself between the man's legs and grasped his cock once more. Then she leaned forward, beneath the cover of the tablecloth, and took him between her lips.

She began to fellate the man. At once her senses were enveloped with the taste and scent of him, and she momentarily forgot her extraordinary situation, intent only on pleasuring the stranger. As she sucked he reached under the table, brushed her scarf aside, and massaged her sensitive breasts.

He came suddenly, his rampant cock spitting into her mouth. She kept her lips sealed tightly around the pulsing flesh until she had swallowed every drop of his seed, then she tucked him back into his trousers and slid back up onto her chair.

One or two eyes looked in her direction as she emerged with the roll and rearranged the scarf to cover her breasts. But aside from the man whose semen she had just swallowed, only the man to her left knew what had happened, and he was staring straight ahead, saying nothing, his nose raised indignantly. She sensed he was near bursting with rage at being subjected to her lascivious activities.

She turned to the older man for some sort of moral support, only to find him deep in conversation again with the woman to his right, as if nothing at all had happened.

By the time the meal came to an end, Danni had regained a little of her self-confidence and had begun to fall back into Judith's character. A couple of the guests sitting opposite her had engaged her in conversation, and she had responded happily. The man with the glasses continued to ignore her, but she could live with that.

Before long she was feeling almost at ease, though her lack of underwear continued to prey on her mind.

As the staff began to clear away the dishes, it was announced that coffee would be served in the adjoining room. The guests rose and went through, and Danni was just wondering how she could overcome the problem of the missing panties, when Tonia floated gracefully to her and whispered that the car was waiting to take her back to Mr Wright.

Danni was surprised that she found that news just a little disappointing, and with a little reluctance, she slipped quietly away.

Chapter Twelve

Danni's strange life continued at Wright's mansion. The events of the decadent party seemed like a dream, but she knew it had all been real enough.

The days blurred into each other as she continued her role as Judith, dressing in outrageously brief clothes and never refusing her favours to any man who approached her. She saw little of Wright during that time, but the knowledge that the rooms in the house had hidden cameras was enough to assure her that he was taking a keen interest in her activities, a notion that she found oddly pleasing. Few days passed without her receiving messages from her host, telling her what to wear and where to be, though she was occasionally allowed to choose her own outfit, as long as it consisted of one of the sets in her wardrobe.

Tonia became a frequent visitor to the house. She seldom spoke to Danni, preferring to laze beside the pool or to amuse herself chatting to the other guests, but Danni knew that she took a close interest in her, and would often sense her eyes upon her as she moved about the house and grounds.

After a while Danni found herself actually settling into the life at the mansion. Strange though her role was, she was somehow becoming accustomed to Judith's sluttish ways and, just as Wright had predicted, the fact that the men who used her were all strangers made it easier for her to give herself in the ways she did. From time to time she wondered why and how Wright had a constant stream of guests, but decided it must be due to his business methods.

It was on a hot afternoon about ten days after her visit to Tonia's house that things suddenly changed for the young beauty.

Danni had received no instructions from Wright that

afternoon. On the occasions she found she had some time to herself, she generally took a stroll around the vast estate. She had discovered a route that led her far from the house through beautiful woodland, and she was in the habit of ambling along it when the weather allowed. So she put on a tiny miniskirt, a waistcoat, and a pair of sandals, and set off.

The outfit was, as always, far from modest. The skirt was very short indeed, sitting low down on her hips and leaving her midriff bare. The waistcoat was skimpy too, with no means of fastening it at the front so that it hung slightly open, revealing the pale swell of her breasts and barely hiding her nipples. But it was probably the most conservative outfit in the wardrobe.

She strolled along the gently winding paths, enjoying the plants and trees and the songs of the birds. Occasionally she would stop to smell the beautiful scent of a flower. She stretched her arms and savoured the brief respite from captivity. The grounds were peaceful and deserted, save for the occasional gardener, who would all take the opportunity for a rest from their labours and admire the luscious female as she wandered past. For Danni, the respite from Judith's antics was a welcome one, and she was glad of the relative solitude.

It was with some dismay, therefore, that she spotted a figure coming down the path towards her. It was a man. He was dressed in a black suit, a somewhat incongruous outfit, given the situation and the heat of the day. For a moment Danni considered turning off the path and trying to avoid the intrusion into her privacy, but decided against it. The man had almost certainly spotted her by now and, for all she knew, he might have been sent out by Wright to find her. So she kept walking towards him.

As he came closer, she realised that she'd seen him before somewhere, though she couldn't for the moment think where. Then the sunlight caught his glasses, and she remembered. It was the quiet man who had sat beside her at the dinner party, and who had appeared to be so disgusted by her behaviour. She wondered again if there was any way of avoiding him, but it was too late.

He stopped, blocking her path. Danni stopped too. He eyed her up and down with that same expression of disdain that she recognised from before, and she wished she was dressed more decently, instinctively pulling the waistcoat snugly around her breasts.

'Good afternoon,' she said, with more cheer than she really felt.

He nodded curtly.

She tried desperately to remember how Tonia had responded to her previous enquiry as to the name of the pious creep who'd sat next to her during that meal. 'It... it's Jeremiah isn't it?' she asked, trying to keep a pleasant note in her voice.

'That's right,' he responded, without any warmth.

'Jeremiah…?' she prompted.

'That's my surname.' He gazed off into the distance, as though remembering years gone by. His mood darkened visibly. 'I don't use my first name.'

'Oh…' The smile faltered on her lips as she offered him a handshake. 'I – I'm Judith. We met at Tonia's party… remember?'

He ignored her hand. 'Oh, how could I forget?'

His monotone voice made her shudder, and she hoped he hadn't noticed. His stare was intense, and she felt greatly unnerved as it conquered her and she felt compelled to look down at the mossy ground. She silently cursed herself for being so weak.

'Where are you going?' he asked suddenly, conversationally.

Danni brightened a little; perhaps he could be quite pleasant after all. 'I – I was just taking a little walk. I love it out here.'

'Perhaps I could walk with you?' he asked, and she thought

she detected the slightest flicker of a smile from his magnified eyes behind his glinting spectacles. The suggestion surprised her; her previous experience of the man had suggested that he would shun her company. If she was honest she would rather have been left alone, but perhaps she was being given the opportunity to repair some of the damage that had been done to her character – in his eyes, at least.

'That would be nice,' she said, trying to be bright and breezy.

They strolled along in silence. Despite an immense effort on her part, Danni still felt uncomfortable in his presence. He said nothing, but his eyes were constantly darting in her direction, surreptitiously eyeing her up, and she couldn't help but remember the state she had been in when he had last set eyes on her.

They walked on for some time, then came to a divide in the track. They were a long way from the house, she knew, and the left fork led back to it.

'I need to go left here,' she said. 'It's time I was getting back.'

'Why the hurry?' he asked.

'Charles will be looking for me. He always does at about this time of day.'

That was the truth. By late afternoon Wright was in the habit of giving her her instructions for that evening. While Danni knew he would probably just leave a written note in her room, it gave her the perfect excuse to get away from her taciturn walking companion.

'Can't we go a little further?'

'If I do I'll be late.'

He smiled thinly. 'My car is parked a short distance from here. If you come with me I'll drive you back.'

Danni eyed him warily. She hadn't been expecting that answer. In all honesty she would have preferred to walk, but she could scarcely justify refusing his offer. Besides, he might tell Wright that she was impolite.

'All right,' she said, though something told her she shouldn't have.

His smile widened, but it was clear that smiling didn't come naturally to him. 'Good. Come along then.'

They took the right fork. He was walking faster now, his steps more purposeful, and Danni wondered if he had planned the encounter. After all, it wouldn't have been difficult for him to discover the route that she took on her walks, and they were well beyond the range of Wright's ubiquitous cameras. Serious doubts festered as she followed him.

They came to the high fence that surrounded Wright's estate. There was a gate, and just beyond that was a car. The gates were normally kept bolted, but she saw that the padlock was missing. That surprised her, as Wright was very keen on security, and she had sometimes wondered if the locks were as much to keep her in as to keep intruders out. Such a precaution would have been pointless, though, since she had no intention of leaving the relative safety of the estate without Wright's say-so.

'Come on,' the man insisted, holding the gate open for her.

'I... I'm not sure,' she said, looking back over her shoulder in the direction of where the house lay out of sight beyond the wooded copse. 'I promised Charles I'd stay on the estate.'

'Don't be so silly,' he chided like a stern uncle. 'We're not going anywhere. I'll just give you a lift back... Come on,' he urged again.

Somewhat reluctantly she stepped through the gate. As she did so she stared about guiltily, suddenly reminded of how scantily dressed she was. On Wright's land she was able to wear the extraordinary outfits he gave her in the knowledge that the only people to see her would be Wright's guests, who relished her appearance, and his staff, who could offer no opinion anyway. Once she was off his property, though, none of that applied, and she found herself acutely aware of how the lower slopes of her buttocks nearly showed beneath the hem of the tiny skirt and the waistcoat did nothing to hide her cleavage.

Jeremiah closed the squeaky gate and led her across to his car. When they reached it he opened the door and she clambered in, then he walked round to the driver's side and got in beside her. It was a large car, with leather seats and a walnut dash, and Danni sat back, trying to enjoy the comfort.

He put the key in the ignition, but didn't start the engine. Instead, he turned to her.

'You're a very beautiful girl, Judith,' he said. 'May I call you Judith?'

'I...' Danni was taken aback by this sudden display of friendliness, but tried her best not to show it. 'Of course you can,' she replied.

There was an uncomfortable pause, and once more she was aware of his judgemental eyes upon her. It was warm in the car, and that combined with his simmering intensity made Danni shift awkwardly and blow her light fringe to cool herself.

'You like having men and women lust after you, don't you, Judith?' he said suddenly.

She twisted her hands in her lap. What was this bloke's problem? 'I don't mind,' she said.

'And men and women find you very attractive, don't they?'

Danni didn't know where his line of questioning was leading, and she began to wish she had never accepted his offer of a lift. 'I suppose so,' she said, to appease him. 'Do you think we could go no, please?'

'Oh, but they do,' he continued, ignoring her request. 'They find you *very* attractive.'

'If you say so.' He was making her feel increasingly uneasy.

'Would you mind if I photographed you?'

She stared at him in surprise. 'Photographed me? You want

to photograph me?'

'Yes, I do.' The thin smile was still fixed on his face. 'I would love to capture your image on film.'

'I... I don't know about that.'

'Why, what's the problem?'

'It – it's just that... well, the other night you didn't seem to approve of me at all.'

'That was because of all those other vultures. The way they drooled after you disgusted me. Now there's just the two of us.'

His monotone made her shudder again, despite the mounting warmth in the car. 'W-what sort of pictures do you want of me?'

'Shots of your body.' He spoke as though requesting nothing out of the ordinary.

'With no clothes on?'

'With no clothes on,' he confirmed confidently.

'And what would the photos be for?'

'Just a little keepsake for me.' His spectacles flashed again and hid his eyes from her.

'Would…' Danni tried to be careful what she said, sensing that it would be unwise to upset the volatile man, '…would you show them to anyone else?' She felt as though she was handling unstable explosives.

'Only to those who'd truly appreciate your beauty for the right reasons.'

'But I thought you disapproved of other people looking at my body?'

His face darkened, and for a moment she saw a flash of anger behind the spectacle lenses. 'Will you do it?' he asked bluntly, his mood shifting dangerously.

Danni eyed him cautiously. She knew she had little choice. She could make a dash from the car, but in her sandals and on the uneven ground it would be no distance before he brought her down like a hunted animal. And besides, perhaps she was being too sensitive and reading him all wrong;

154

perhaps he was okay. After all that had happened to her in the past few weeks she could hardly bulk about posing for a few photos. She made up her mind. 'We'll have to be quick, because I must be getting back… but where do you want me?'

'Get out of the car and take your clothes off.'

For a moment Danni did not move. Then she reached for the door handle and climbed out of the oppressively warm vehicle. An unexpected *frisson* of excitement churned her insides at the prospect of baring all, there in the open, and somehow the danger of being discovered by someone passing by only added to that excitement.

The man took a camera from the glove compartment and joined her. As he made adjustments to its settings she took one more look around, and then shrugged off her waistcoat and let it fall to the ground. She ran her fingers over her breasts, feeling the warmth of the sun on her perfect orbs. Then she loosened her skirt, held it in place for a moment, still a little reluctant to discard the final concession to modesty, and looked at the man. He was standing with his eyes fixed on her shapely young body, the camera held almost at the ready. Then she let the tiny garment flutter down her legs and stepped out of it. Taking a deep breath, she stood proudly before him and his impressive lens.

'What about the sandals?' she asked demurely.

'You can leave them on,' he said, a slight tremor in his voice. He raised the camera to his eye. Danni heard the click and whirr of the shutter.

'Stand by the car,' he directed. 'Lean back against it and face me.'

Danni did as she was told. The metal of the car's body felt pretty hot against her bare flesh and she squealed lightly.

'Open your legs a little further… that's better…' the camera clicked and whirred as he moved and ducked to get shots from different angles. 'That's good… *very* good,' he said over and over, his drab tone at last hinting towards a

155

little enthusiasm. Danni watched him repeatedly bobbing down onto one knee and then straightening up again, gradually moving in closer, and she suddenly felt like a timid animal being stalked by a voracious predator. She immediately tried to banish the feeling from her mind, but as the lens came within touching distance her eyes were drawn to the gradually increasing lump in the front of his trousers. She had thought he was some kind of prudish bigot, but he was no different to all the rest of them, and the evidence of that was growing brazenly before her eyes. He was a strange man and no mistake; he professed to disapprove of her behaviour at the very same time as he demanded and savoured it. She groaned inwardly, anticipating the next loathsome move in this extravagant seduction ritual.

The camera was eventually lowered, and hung from the strap around his neck. He stood close, his heavy breathing ruffling her wispy blonde fringe and the tip of his lens almost resting between her gently heaving breasts like a huge metal penis. Danni closed her eyes and awaited the first touch.

'Do you want me to fuck you?' he asked, his words so at odds with his Draconian image.

'I…' she opened her eyes and looked into his stern face. She shook her head.

'Slut!'

The venom in his voice took her aback. 'What—?'

'Cheap, shameless whore!' he hissed. 'Look at you, flaunting your body. And then you have the audacity to refuse me!'

'But I—'

'Cover yourself up, slattern!' His eyes were bulging from behind the glass. 'Stop your shameful and filthy behaviour.'

Danni was utterly shocked and confused by his unjust outburst. Tears threatened to burst and her chin quivered. She pushed past the brute and picked up her skirt.

The soft grass muted the sound of his strike. The first the

156

unsuspecting girl knew was when he grabbed her from behind and pressed the large cotton pad across her face. She struggled, but there was a harsh smell about the pad, and she felt her strength draining from her body. She was vaguely aware of a lump grinding against her hip as her struggles became more and more feeble. The trees span and seemed strangely out of focus. Then the darkness descended, and she collapsed limply in the arms that wrapped around her like a smothering boa constrictor.

Chapter Thirteen

Danni opened her eyes and blinked up into the bright, naked light hanging from the low ceiling. Her head ached and there was a strange taste at the back of her throat. Her vision was indistinct and she tried to rub her eyes, but for some reason she couldn't. She tried to sit up, but once again her limbs failed to obey. She let her head fall back, her mind a whirl of fuzzy thoughts as she tried to pull herself together, struggling to remember what had happened.

Slowly it came back to her. The woods, the weird man called Jeremiah, the photographs. She remembered being upset by him and then trying to dress herself... but then nothing. She tried to move her arms and legs again. Then she began to feel the pain in her wrists and ankles, and raised her pounding head once more.

What she saw made her heart plummet.

She was quite naked. Worse still, her wrists and ankles were manacled and chained to the four corners of the small cot upon which she lay. The chains were pulled tight, so that her limbs were stretched and useless.

She was in a tiny windowless cell with three plain white brick walls, and a forth of vertical metal bars set about four inches apart. Basically, she realised to her horror, she was in a cage!

Beyond the bars the room was a little larger, and there was a chair and table, a bizarre wooden frame festooned with metal chains, and something that resembled one of the trestles her dear parents would use to support a wall-papering table. It too had menacing chains and manacles hanging from it.

The thought of her parents threatened to bring the tears bursting forth, so she shoved it to the back of her mind and continued studying her surroundings.

The only way out of the room was a heavy wooden door, and that appeared to be firmly closed. There was nobody else around.

Danni was trussed on a thin mattress on a rough wooden cot. There were no other furnishings in the cell. She called for help, but the thick walls muffled her weak voice and the effort only made her head pound all the more.

Her eyes were drawn to a picture that was stuck on one wall with masking tape. It was clearly position where she could not fail to see it, and she stared for a moment before dreadful recognition dawned.

It was a photograph of her, posing lasciviously across that madman's car!

And beneath it was a sheet of paper with the single word *SLUT!!* scrawled across it in red.

Danni closed her eyes and struggled against the panic that threatened to overwhelm her. That weirdo had obviously abducted her!

Oh no – her life was a nightmare rapidly spiralling from bad to worse.

Her aching head was instantly a swirling mass of questions, the answers to which were just too awful to contemplate.

Where on earth was she? What horrible things did he have planned for her – and why? When would her torture begin? Would she ever see daylight again? It was all just too too dreadful to comprehend. She tugged at her bonds, but only succeeded in hurting her wrists and ankles. Tears burst forth and meandered down her cheeks. She was quite helpless.

A sudden scraping sound made her start and strain to see the door. Someone was unlocking it! Nausea churned her stomach as she watched the handle turn and the door swing slowly open.

It was Jeremiah. He was wearing a pair of black trousers and a black shirt buttoned right up to beneath his chin. He stood holding the cell bars, his body erect, staring down at her.

'So,' he said without emotion, 'you're awake.'

'Please…' Danni pleaded timidly, 'what am I doing here?'

Without responding to her question he produced a large key from his pocket and unlocked the door to the cage. He stepped in and sat on the edge of the cot. Danni cringed and tried to edge away from him. He smirked a little at her useless efforts.

He picked a jug and mug up from the floor, poured some water, lifted her head with one hand, and fed her the refreshing liquid. Danni realised just how parched she was, and drank gratefully. Some of the water dribbled onto her chin and throat. Jeremiah put the mug back down on the floor and tutted as though she was an incapable child. He then took a crisp white handkerchief from his other pocket and dabbed her lips, her chin, her throat… and then the upper slopes of her naked breasts. His eyes seemed even larger behind the spectacles, and a lizard-tongue flickered out over his lips. He seemed a little indecisive for a moment, and then he suddenly stood up and stuffed the hanky back into his pocket. Danni followed his hand, and groaned inwardly as she saw the beginnings of a lump within the black trousers. She felt more vulnerable than ever.

'Please,' she said, her voice stronger for the drink, 'could I have my clothes?'

'Clothes?' he snorted. 'You call those scraps clothes? No decent woman would dress the way you do. Those disgraceful garments were designed merely to tempt the weak and depraved.'

Danni could not believe what was happening to her. She was in the hands of a fanatic; some kind of religious freak. 'Look, I really think you should let me—'

'I have been sent me to save you,' he interrupted. 'Your salvation will be a painful one, but in the end you will see the error of your wicked ways.'

'Listen,' she said desperately, trying a different tack. 'You

160

have your photographs. Isn't that enough? Just let me go and I'll say nothing to—'

'Wicked temptress,' he said, his voice as cold as ice as his eyes crawled the length of her bound body. 'You want to lure me into the same trap as all the others.'

'No… I'm not trying to do anything of the kind,' she pleaded. 'I just want you to let me go.'

He shook his head. 'That's impossible. First you must be taught the error of your ways,' he said. 'And others must witness your conversion. The treatment will begin soon, when my students are here.'

'No… please…'

'I will not lock the cage,' he said smugly. 'I don't think you'll be going anywhere.'

'Please…' she begged again, but he turned and left, slamming and locking the heavy wooden door behind him.

Danni wasn't sure how long he left her there, her limbs aching and her mind in turmoil as she considered her situation. It seemed she had definitely fallen into the hands of a freak, and judging from his methods of ensuring she didn't escape, an extremely cunning madman. There was no way she could break free of the shackles that held her, and even if she did, there was still the heavy door to negotiate. For the time being she had to reconcile herself to being his prisoner, and to await an opportunity to escape, should one present itself.

After a long wait she heard voices, and the sound of the key turning in the lock. She watched as the door opened. It was Jeremiah again, and this time he was not alone. There were four young men with him, none of them more than eighteen or nineteen years old. They all looked like misfits in their untidy jeans and T-shirts. They shuffled around in front of the bars, and gawped at the lovely girl stretched and bound naked before them.

'Behold the strumpet,' announced Jeremiah theatrically. 'See how immodest she is. This is the one in the photographs

I showed you. Now you see that the camera did not lie. She is a sinful woman, and we must save her.'

Danni looked from youthful face to youthful face. The young men were clearly fascinated by what they saw, but appeared to be even less comfortable with the situation than she was.

'It is time to begin the punishment,' said Jeremiah. 'We must show her the error of her ways.'

Danni looked at him in consternation and wrenched hopelessly at the metal restraints. 'Punishment?' she gasped.

'First we must silence the temptress,' he said. He reached into his pocket and pulled out a ball gag fitted with a leather strap. He handed it to one of the spellbound young men. 'Here, put this on her,' he ordered.

The teenager looked at him hesitantly. 'Are you sure this is okay?'

'Of course it is. Do not question the work that we do here,' he threw a withering stare at each of them in turn, 'any of you.'

The four youths visibly shrank before him. There was a tense pause, and then the one with the gag shuffled into the cage and gazed down at her.

'You don't have to do it,' she whispered. 'He's mad.'

'Pay no attention,' Jeremiah said from behind the indecisive youth. 'It is the devil speaking. Silence the temptress.'

The young man hesitated for a moment longer, then knelt down beside the trapped beauty and, gripping her chin, he squeezed her mouth open and forced the ball inside. Danni tried to eject it, but in vain, and in no time the strap was buckled tightly around her head.

'Good,' said Jeremiah. 'Now let us begin her salvation. You two,' he clicked his fingers at two of his students, 'unshackle her and bring her to me.'

The pair stepped forward and set about the manacles at Danni's wrists. She noticed they were sweating slightly, and saw the way their crotches were already bulging. There was no doubt that the sight of her nude body was having an effect on them. Her whole predicament was rapidly shifting from the sublime to the ridiculous.

They lowered her stiff arms and re-cuffed them in front of her. Then they freed her legs and hauled her to her feet. Danni stood unsteadily as the feeling gradually returned to her limbs, before they took an arm each and dragged her from the cramped cage.

They presented her to Jeremiah, who eyed her up and down like an officer on parade. 'Strap her to the frame,' he ordered. 'And make a good job of it.'

The exhausted Danni was hauled over to the wooden configuration. It was rectangular, and anchored to the concrete floor. In the centre at the top was a metal ring from which hung a heavy chain, and there were more attached at the bottom corners. She tried to struggle and protest, but she still felt weak and the gag successfully suppressed any coherent outburst. Her ankles were dragged apart and shackled to the frame, and then her cuffed wrists were lifted above her head and fastened to the chain that hung from the ring. She tugged at the restraints, though she knew already that there was no escape. She strained to look over her shoulder, and groaned into the gag when she saw Jeremiah standing with his legs planted firmly apart, a long thin cane in his hand, and his four students standing in sombre fashion like witnesses at an execution. Even though the immediate outlook was bleak, she couldn't help but notice how ridiculous the five of them looked; one pair of black trousers and four pairs of jeans all tented at the groin.

Jeremiah stepped to her side and reached out with the weapon, running its vicious tip down her hot cheek, and then tracing the sweep of her throat down to the softness of her breasts. Danni tried to shy away as he used it to tease her nipples, and she groaned again with shame as the traitorous buds stiffened, despite her abhorrence of him and his stupid games.

He smiled triumphantly as he watched her body respond. 'See how the temptress behaves when she faces her nemesis,' he gloated. 'See how the harlot's lewd nipples welcome the kiss of the cane.' His gathered students shifted from foot to foot and mumbled uncomfortably. 'Well, let's see how the harlot's lewd nipples welcome the *sting* of the cane, shall we?'

Danni stared at him in disbelief. Surely he wasn't serious? She had resigned herself, reluctantly, to having her backside beaten by this maniac – but her breasts? He couldn't want to thrash those – could he?

He clearly saw the expression in her eyes, and he smiled a thin and humourless smile. 'At last she understands,' he said to his young followers. 'At last she understands that those salacious parts of her body that she gives so shamelessly to the corrupted must be chastised if she is to understand the many errors of her ways. First we must punish her breasts – breasts that thrust so provocatively to tempt the weak and the fallen. Then we must thrash her between those legs, to scourge that part that she gives so freely to one and all. Only then will she understand.'

'Um…' one of his students gingerly raised a hand and then lowered it again, 'shouldn't we allow her to repent first?' he ventured to ask.

The chains jangled as Danni strained further to look into his face, and those of his companions, and she saw the consternation there. Clearly even they hadn't been totally aware of what their leader was capable. She could see them fighting with their consciences.

Jeremiah turned on the young man. 'You fool,' he said, his voice still low and even. 'Don't you realise yet that we must beat the evil from this young lady in order to cleanse her soul? Do you still not understand that?'

The youth shrank back, clearly cowed by his leader's cold venom, and the others dropped their eyes and said nothing.

Jeremiah threw them each a disdainful look, then turned back to his victim.

'Now, young harlot, prepare to repent.'

Danni stared back at him, trying to maintain a defiant expression, though, incredibly, deep inside her extreme apprehension was slowly being eroded by a mounting arousal. Jeremiah's intention to beat her breasts, and then possibly worse, was clearly a serious threat, and yet the prospect of it was causing her stomach to knot with excitement.

'Raise your head,' the despicable persecutor warned her, 'unless you want your face whipped as well.'

Danni took a deep breath. Very slowly she arched her back and tilted her head, watching him as he lifted the cane, his eyes glued to her breasts as her new stance thrust them forward.

Thwack!

He swung the weapon down across the pale swellings of her vulnerable breasts. Danni gave a muffled scream of pain as it cut into the soft flesh, leaving a thin red stripe that darkened with every second.

Thwack!

He struck her again. For Danni the pain was like the sting of a thousand wasps, and the tears coursed down her cheeks as her naked body convulsed under the blows. A second angry stripe formed on her pale skin.

Thwack!

The third stroke caught her just above her nipples, the mark slicing an arc through the puckered moons of her areolae. To Danni's own surprise and chagrin the blow caused her teats to tauten in the same way that a lover's caress might have done. She heard muted gasps, and she knew his students had noticed her body's reaction.

Thwack!

The cane swept upwards, striking the underside of her pliable breasts and making them bounce and quiver before settling back into place.

Thwack!

Thwack!

Thwack!

He laid three more stripes across Danni's mouthwatering breasts, and then lowered his arm.

The sobs shook Danni's body as her breasts burned with pain. The once pale flesh was now criss-crossed with the thin red marks of the cane, though her nipples still stood stiffly to attention.

'Now you see the price you must pay for your lascivious pleasure,' Jeremiah said calmly, his chest heaving slightly from his exertion. 'Now you know what wrath is.' He turned to the four young men. 'Behold the wages of sin,' he announced piously, and through her cocktail of emotions Danni doubted that they knew what the hell he was on about. The four nodded dumbly, but despite her tear-misted eyes she could see that their expressions were doubtful. She wondered how they could have ever come to follow the hateful man in the first place. Whatever it was that had brought them there, they clearly hadn't expected what they had just witnessed.

'Bringing this harlot here was my destiny,' Jeremiah babbled on. 'I recently had a dream in which I was told to seek a woman called Judith, who is a sinner, and this is clearly she. I do my duty.'

As Danni listened to the words an idea struck her. She shook her head violently, mumbling into her gag as loudly as she was able.

'Be quiet,' he said calmly. 'It is time to punish that chasm of depravity between your legs. When I have finished you will never encourage another man to penetrate you again.'

He lifted the cane and ran it up and down Danni's tensed thighs. Once again she shook her head, trying her best to make herself understood through the debilitating gag. As Jeremiah drew back his arm, one of his students suddenly stepped forward.

'Wait… she's trying to say something,' he said defiantly.

Jeremiah threw him a withering glance. 'She's trying to beg for mercy,' he snapped. 'But it is not for me to grant that.'

'No, you don't know that,' insisted one of the others. 'Maybe she wishes to repent.'

Sensing the glimmer of an opportunity, Danni changed from shaking her head to nodding vigorously. Jeremiah eyed her with a doubtful expression.

'At least listen to what she has to say,' urged the first youth, his voice transmitting his growing confidence.

'Yeah,' said another, as though trying to absolve his own feelings of guilt by now helping the poor girl. 'At least give her a chance.'

Jeremiah lowered the cane once more. 'Very well,' he said, his suspicious stare fixed firmly on the trussed focal point of his obsessive fury. 'But don't think this will save you from the chastisement you so richly deserve.'

He reached behind her head and unbuckled the gag. The relief of being able to flex her jaw was immense, and for a moment all she could do was savour the sensation. Then she looked steadily into her persecutor's eyes.

'You're punishing the wrong girl,' she said, her voice wavering slightly.

'No,' he insisted. 'Didn't you hear me say that I'd been told I would meet you? I even knew what your name would be.'

'But my name's not Judith.'

He sneered at her. 'What nonsense are you trying to fool us with?'

'Honestly, my name's not Judith. It's Danni.'

'Foolish girl,' he laughed, 'Danny's a boy's name.'

'No. D-A-N-N-I. Danni. It's short for Danielle.'

'Then – then why do you call yourself Judith?' he asked, his demeanour suddenly lacking the immovable conviction

167

of before.

Danni sensed victory, and pressed home her advantage. 'It was that man Wright's idea. I'm pretending to be his cousin.'

Jeremiah eyed her doubtfully, clearly troubled that his faith just might have let him down. 'This is some sort of a trick,' he said.

'No, it isn't,' Danni urged.

'Then prove it,' he challenged, fighting back.

'I can't. I had my passport stolen when I was staying at some hotel.'

'A likely tale.'

'It's true.'

He snorted derisively. 'So what's the name of this hotel?'

'Oh…' Danni wracked her brains. 'The umm…'

'Well?' his confidence was returning.

'The… the… the Astra!' she announced gleefully. 'That's it – the Astra!'

'There is an Astra fairly near here,' confirmed one of the watching youths.

'Shut up!' snapped Jeremiah, turning his anger on him.

'So this Judith person who you were ordered to teach a lesson to isn't me!' exclaimed Danni.

'Well…' he paused. 'Well, I must punish you anyway. It is my duty.'

'No!' protested Danni.

'Hang on, sir,' said the fourth youth, who had remained silent until then.

'What is it now?' Jeremiah snapped.

'Well, if you really were told to punish Judith and that's not her name, maybe we really do have the wrong girl.'

Jeremiah shook his head impatiently. 'She called herself Judith. Isn't that enough?'

'Can't we at least check?' said one of the others.

'How?' The man was becoming increasingly exasperated. 'She claims to have lost her passport, remember?'

'If she was staying at the Astra she must have signed the register. You could check that.'

The other three chorused their agreement to the idea. There was a heated debate, and eventually Jeremiah had to relent and it was decided that it would be only right to check Danni's story.

As soon as he had stormed off in a foul temper, taking three of his students with him and leaving one to guard his captive, a new fear gripped poor Danni. She had no doubt that Hakis and Zuko would still be looking for her, and she feared that anyone making enquiries about her at the hotel would attract attention and lead them straight to her.

But it was too late to worry about that now – and at least she was saved from any further punishment from that nasty bigot. Her biggest concern now was finding a way to escape before he returned.

Chapter Fourteen

Now that his leader had gone, the remaining youth seemed embarrassed and uncomfortable by the presence of the naked girl trussed up before him, and at a loss as to what to do. Danni, meanwhile, considered her next move. She had successfully got Jeremiah out of the way for the time being, but she had to move fast if she was to escape.

She looked at the young man. 'Couldn't you release me from this for a while, please?' she asked. 'My arms and legs are awfully stiff.'

He looked at her uncomfortably, but didn't respond.

'Come on,' she persisted. 'It can't do any harm. I won't try to trick you, I promise.'

Still he didn't reply.

Silence fell over the horrible cellar and the time ticked by relentlessly while Danni fretfully considered her limited options. She decided to try a new tactic.

'What's your name,' she asked sweetly.

The youth looked up, and she could tell he almost answered her.

'Come over here,' she urged.

He hesitated, then slowly shuffled forward.

'Just feel how tight the muscles in my arms are,' she said. 'It's really very painful, being tied like this.'

Again he hesitated.

'Go on,' she coaxed. 'Feel them.'

He nervously stretched out a hand and ran it lightly down her tensed arm. He smiled weakly, clearly enjoying the feel of her soft flesh, but not sure quite what to do next.

'What's your name,' Danni whispered again, careful not to scare him away.

'J-Joseph,' he stammered clumsily.

She smiled at him again. 'Do you like me, Joseph?' she asked.

He nodded.

'Do you think I'm pretty?'

He blushed and nodded again.

She had to press on; time could be running short. 'Do you like my breasts?' She held her breath, hoping she hadn't pushed him too far too quickly.

'I – I guess so,' he admitted.

Danni was feeling more confident with him now. 'Even after they've been whipped? Feel the marks on them, Joseph. They hurt awfully.'

Joseph's hand had been resting on her arm. It lifted and hovered momentarily before her trussed body.

'Come on, Joseph,' she urged quietly. 'Touch my breasts.'

His hand shook slightly as his fingers traced one of the livid stripes that ran over the succulent flesh.

'Touch them properly,' she urged.

He opened his hand and placed it over her breast, squeezing it gently. Danni gave a sharp intake of breath as his touch brought back the pain of the beating, but the sensation of his strong hand sent a pulse of excitement through her body.

'Mmm… that feels so nice,' she encouraged.

'But…' he said, as though fighting with his emotions, 'Mr Jeremiah told us that lust is sinful.'

'Let me out of this, Joseph,' she said carefully, indicating the frame, 'and I'll show you there's nothing sinful about it. I promise you, I've done nothing to deserve this treatment.'

Torment raged in Joseph's eyes as he gazed at her for a long while, and although she was worried about the time, she knew it would be a mistake to rush him. Eventually he came to the decision she'd silently prayed he would, and set about undoing the chains.

Danni was quickly free. She flexed her limbs, luxuriating in the ability to do so at last. The young man stood close to her, watching as she loosened her muscles, then ran her hand

171

gingerly over her punished breasts, caressing them gently. At last she looked up at him.

'Look, Joseph,' she said, 'I really have to get out of here.'

The poor youth looked crestfallen. 'But you said...' he began.

'I know – I know.' Despite what she'd been through at the hands of Jeremiah, Danni suddenly felt sorry for Joseph. She considered doing something nice for him, but the thought of that creep returning at any minute stiffened her resolve. 'I'm sorry, but I have to get away before Jeremiah gets back. And I think you should do the same.' She held his hand and gave him a peck on the cheek.

'What the hell's going on here?'

Danni froze. It was Jeremiah. He was back already.

For a moment, nobody moved. Jeremiah stood in the doorway, staring at the two.

After a few moments he stepped into the dank cellar, and Joseph made his move with surprising agility. He pushed past Jeremiah and dashed out of the door and his hasty footsteps could be heard scurrying away. Jeremiah shouted after him, but there was no response.

Danni realised her chance of escape was vanishing before her eyes and tried to follow Joseph's example, but Jeremiah was too quick for her. He grabbed her by the arm and swung her round to face him.

'Filthy whore!' he shouted. 'What have you been doing with the lad?!'

'Let me go!' Danni squealed. His grip really hurt. 'Let me go, you're hurting me!'

'That's nothing to what I *will* do...' Veins in his neck were near bursting and his eyes bulged alarmingly. 'You've corrupted him with your wicked ways, you sinful creature!'

Danni tried to un-peel his crushing fingers from her poor bicep, but they were immovable. 'Rubbish!' she managed to protest through the pain. 'He was more than willing to free me!'

'Corrupt harlot!' he bellowed, his free hand raised threateningly. 'How dare you say such a thing?'

'It's you that's corrupt!' Danni shouted defiantly, closing her eyes and cringing as she awaited the blow across her face…

It never came.

Cautiously she opened her eyes again, and he was standing looking at her, his chest heaving, and the arm slowly lowering. His fury seemed to have abated, but she sensed he was no less dangerous.

'You'll pay for this,' he hissed quietly. 'I'll tie you down, and I'll—!'

His intent never did develop beyond a sick idea in his mind for, seizing her glimmer of an opportunity, Danni brought her knee up and crunched it as viciously as she could into his groin. He released her arm immediately, doubled up, and sank slowly to his knees like a felled tree. Clutching his assaulted balls with shock and agony paralysing his expression, he searched desperately for air like a landed fish on a riverbank and rolled onto his side. Whatever expletives he wanted to hurl in her direction struggled in vain to escape from his empty lungs.

Danni didn't waste another second. She dodged around the floundering hypocrite and darted out of the odious room.

She found herself at the foot of a narrow flight of concrete steps, which she bounded up, taking them two at a time. At the top was another door which, throwing caution to the wind, she burst through and into a kitchen. She glanced about for something – anything – to wear, but there was nothing in sight. To her right was another door. It was unlocked, and beyond it was a back yard. She stopped and turned her head in the direction of the cellar, trying to calm her breathing and the rapid heartbeat pounding in her chest, and listened for any pursuers. There was no sound of feet on the steps. It seemed the useless creep was still unable to respond to her audacious bid for freedom.

173

Feeling cautiously pleased with herself she turned to complete her escape, and bounced off a solid and immovable chest. She stumbled back, temporarily stunned, and then looked up at the substantial figure that blocked her way.

It was Zuko!

Danni stared, momentarily taken aback by the sight of him. He didn't look taken aback; he looked as though he was expecting to bump into her, though maybe not literally.

Danni took a step back, raising her hands defensively, but Zuko struck with the speed of a snake and pulled her close. She tried to struggle, but it was useless. Without any effort he twisted her arm up behind her back until she cried out from the pain.

'Hakis!' he shouted, his eyes not moving from hers. 'Come and see what I've found!'

Moments later his partner appeared. He smiled with grim satisfaction when he saw her.

'So,' he said. 'We find you at last. You've led us quite a merry dance, young lady.'

'Please let me go,' protested Danni. 'You have no right to—'

'Oh, we have every right,' cut in Zuko. 'You see, you took something that belongs to us, and now we want it back.'

'Let's get her into the house,' said Hakis.

Danni felt utterly defeated, but she kept her chin held high in a plucky display of defiance.

Just then Jeremiah staggered out of the house still clutching his crotch. At the unexpected sight of the two strangers he stopped in astonishment.

'What the...?'

'Hey, it's the guy who was making enquiries at the hotel,' said Hakis. 'We want to talk to you, boy.'

Clearly sensing the threat the two men represented, the hapless Jeremiah began backing into the kitchen, shaking his head and trying to smile apologetically. But he merely reversed into the doorframe, and when Hakis produced a pistol from inside his jacket he froze.

'Stay where you are, my friend,' growled the thug, pointing the gun threateningly. 'I've used this many times before, and I'll no doubt use it again.'

Zuko thrust Danni forward to stand beside the cowardly bigot.

'Put your hands on your heads,' he ordered, drawing his own gun.

Danni obeyed instantly. She felt extremely vulnerable, standing naked in the yard before the two dangerous men. She wanted to cover herself with her hands, but the sight of the gun muzzles pointed at her face persuaded her that it would not be a good idea.

'Right,' said Zuko. 'Get inside, the pair of you.'

The captives turned and the thugs followed.

'Where does that door lead?' asked Hakis.

'Th-the c-cellar...' whimpered Jeremiah.

'The cellar?' said Zuko. 'Excellent... get down there!'

As Danni retraced her steps down into the chilly gloom she cursed her continuing bad luck. Only a few minutes before she had been on her way to freedom, and now there she was, being forced back to the place of her recent captivity by two homicidal sadists pointing guns between her shoulder-blades.

As they entered the oppressive room, the dark-suited men whistled in surprise.

'Hey, this is quite a place,' said Zuko. 'What the hell's it all for?'

'It is a place of chastisement for sinners such as her,' said Jeremiah.

'Don't pay any attention to him, he's mad,' said Danni, sensing his returning confidence as he detected an inquisitive admiration from the two men for his methods. She feared an alliance against her. 'Look,' she said hastily, trying to draw their attention away from the barred cell and the whipping frame, 'can't you find me some clothes to put on?'

175

'Quiet!' barked Zuko. 'We've got some unfinished business with you, young lady.' He turned to Jeremiah, and the creep looked at him with an expectant leer. Danni's spirits sank even further than they already were. But then Zuko said, 'Meanwhile, you weirdo, get inside that cage.'

'But...' Jeremiah protested, '...but I can't. That place is for the confinement of sinners only. Don't you understand my work here? Can't you see—?'

'Just be quiet and do as we say,' said Hakis, like a parent just beginning to lose his patience with a stubborn child. 'Or we'll have to persuade you by other means.'

Jeremiah wisely fell silent. He backed into the cage, his hands still on his head, and Hakis closed the door and secured the padlock.

'Now, keep quiet,' he said.

Zuko, meanwhile, was pensively walking about the room, examining the equipment. He looked the whipping frame over, then moved to the trestle thing.

'Hey, this place really is pretty well equipped,' he said, tugging at one of the chains to test its strength. 'I reckon we can use some of this, my old friend.'

Hakis grinned at his partner.

'Good idea,' he said, then nodded at Danni. 'Looks like someone's already started on her, though. Who the hell put those stripes across your tits, baby?'

'It was that lunatic,' Danni sulked, indicating Jeremiah. 'He thinks he's some kind of messenger from the gods.'

'But that's exactly what I am,' protested the caged and not-so-brave man. 'This woman is a strumpet and a harlot. She must be chastised.'

'I thought I told you to keep quiet,' said Zuko. Although the weapons had been put away the two thugs were no less menacing, and they controlled their victims with little effort.

Jeremiah fell silent again, gazing sullenly at Danni.

'Right, baby,' said Zuko. 'You've got some explaining to do. Now where's our package?'

176

'I... I'm not sure.'

He smiled, but there was no humour there. 'And what do you mean by that?'

'I hid it. Some men were after me, so I hid it.'

'Men? What men?'

'They were from some kind of gang.'

'Killarneys?'

'Yes,' she said hopefully. 'At least, I think that's what they were called.'

'So they were onto you?' said Zuko, thoughtfully. 'How the hell did they find out?'

Danni told them how the pimp and his two prostitutes had picked her up. She shuddered when she thought of them and what they'd put her through. She described her escape from the apartment, and how she had hidden the shoulder-bag under the shed behind the bar.

'So what was the bar called?' asked Hakis.

'I don't know.'

'Well you must know where it is.'

'I don't. It's close to the pimp's apartment. But that's all I know.'

Zuko and Hakis looked at each other, communicating without words. Zuko picked up the cane Jeremiah had used earlier, and turned to the helpless girl.

'Then perhaps we can remind you.' He grinned sadistically. 'You know, jog your little memory.'

Danni shrank back. 'I tell you, I don't know where it is,' she protested. 'I'm not from here, so how should I know?'

'Get over there,' Zuko said casually.

Danni eyed him apprehensively, then looked at the trestle thing.

'Get a move on,' prompted Hakis.

Danni stepped hesitantly to where Zuko was waiting.

'Stand up against that,' he ordered, indicating the beam of wood that ran across the top of the trestle.

Danni did as she was told. The bar touched the top of her

177

thighs, and the wood felt uncompromising against her lower belly.

Zuko moved behind her and nudged her feet apart with the toe of a shoe. Then he crouched down and attached the shackles on the legs of the trestle to Danni's ankles. The youngster's heart sank as he did so. It was clear that something extremely unpleasant was in store for her, and she eyed the cane with some apprehension.

'Bend forward,' said Zuko.

'Look, I've told you all I know, honestly I – ahhh—!'

Her protests were cut short as he brought the flat of his hand down hard on her backside.

'Bend forward, I said!'

Reluctantly she did as she was told, until she was bent almost double. At once Zuko grabbed her hands and snapped manacles about her wrists. He tightened the chains relentlessly.

Danni was left in an extraordinary position, her body cruelly forced over the bar, her hips raised high so that the skin across her pert buttocks was stretched tight. She couldn't imagine a more vulnerable or uncomfortable position in which to be placed... but much worse was to come.

Zuko reached beneath her and cupped her gently heaving breasts. She winced slightly as she was reminded of the stripes that Jeremiah had put across them earlier. Zuko began to play with her nipples, rolling them between finger and thumb and gently teasing them to hardness. Danni could barely suppress a low moan of pleasure as he toyed with them, his fingers stroking and pinching the taut buds, causing them to swell and stiffen. Confusion swept over her; she couldn't understand the treatment. There was no doubt in her mind that he intended to thrash her. Why else would he have trussed her up like that? Yet he seemed to be intent on bringing her pleasure as his hands glided over her sensitive young breasts.

'Look what I've found,' she heard Hakis say, and then

some objects were handed to Zuko, who held them for her to see.

At first Danni's confusion continued; he held silver chains with what looked like little clamps on the ends. Then he pressed those clamps and she watched a pair of sprung jaws open – jaws barbed with tiny metal teeth! She stared, not wanting to accept his cruel intentions, and then he pressed them open again and moved them down towards her breasts.

'No!' Danni shook her head and whimpered, her eyes fearfully watching their slow approach. 'No!' she cried again. 'Please, not that!'

But already Zuko was positioning the clamp where he wanted it, and the youngster shivered as she felt the cold metal come into contact with her swollen and sensitive nipple.

'Ahhhh!' The jaws closed over her aching bud, the teeth biting and immediately spearing intense pain through her trussed body. She fought back the tears as the cruel object bit deeper, but already he was picking up a second one, and she braced herself as it closed over her other breast.

The pain was extraordinary, like nothing Danni had ever experienced before. Her nipples felt as if they were on fire.

Yet still Zuko was not finished. He began to tighten the chains to which the clamps were attached. Danni gave another yelp of pain as the teeth bit still deeper into her vulnerable skin, stretching the soft flesh of her breasts to an almost conical shape before he was finally satisfied.

He straightened up, eyeing his young captive.

'Ingenious,' he said. 'This wacko certainly has some interesting equipment down here. I've never seen a slut so well trussed.' He reached down, and cupped and lifted Danni's chin. 'Now baby…' he said, his tone without compassion, '…the truth.'

'But I *am* telling you the truth,' gasped Danni. 'It all happened just as I told you.'

Zuko shook his head and picked up the cane. 'You are a

very silly young lady. Perhaps this will remind you.'

Swish! Whack!

Swish! Whack!

Swish! Whack!

He laid three stripes across Danni's bare behind, the cane biting deep into her smooth flesh and bringing new cries of anguish from her. She tried to struggle, but only succeeded in sending new spasms of pain through her breasts as the clamps chewed still deeper.

'Where's our stuff?' barked Zuko.

'I tell you, I don't know,' she pleaded. 'You have to believe me. Please, I'm telling the truth.'

'Thrash her some more,' said Hakis.

'No, please...!'

Swish! Whack!

Swish! Whack!

Swish! Whack!

The cane cut down three more times, doubling Danni's agony as her punished flesh burned with pain. Tears were coursing down her cheeks and dripping from her chin onto the floor, her nude body racked with sobs.

'Tell us!'

'I don't know!' she wailed helplessly.

Swish! Whack!

Swish! Whack!

Swish! Whack!

Zuko raised his arm again and she braced herself for more... Then he lowered it.

'D'you think the silly little tart might be telling the truth?' he asked his partner.

Hakis shrugged. 'Maybe. But she sure as hell ain't going to tell us any more like this.'

'Well, if what she says is true, then we've got to find that pimp.'

'And to find him, we've got to find his whores.'

Zuko smacked Danni's scorched bottom with a heavy

palm.

'D'you reckon you could recognise those whores again?' he asked.

'I – I'm not s-sure,' she stammered through her sobs, sensing a reprieve. 'I – I think I m-might.'

'Let her up,' said Hakis.

Zuko undid the shackles at Danni's ankles, then at her wrists. Still the hapless girl couldn't move, held fast by the dreadful nipple clamps. Zuko released them one at a time, making the youngster gasp with relief as the pain in her breasts was finally alleviated. Zuko grabbed her shoulder and pulled her up straight.

Danni felt a complete and utter mess. Her hair was dishevelled. Her poor breasts were decorated with the thin red welts of the cane. Her nipples were throbbing and swollen from the bite of the vicious clamps. And she guessed her tenderised bottom was striped too. She turned her tearstained face to the two thugs, who eyed her with some amusement.

'We'd better take her back and get her cleaned up,' said Zuko.

Hakis nodded his agreement. 'Come on then,' he said. 'Better put some cuffs on her though. We don't want any stupid escape attempts, now do we?'

As Zuko dragged Danni's arms behind her and snapped on a pair of handcuffs, Jeremiah spoke.

'What about me?' he asked plaintively.

Zuko pulled out his gun and winked at his associate. 'What do you say,' he said, 'shall I blow the little shit's brains out?'

Hakis grinned. 'I'm not sure if he's got any.' He looked at Jeremiah, and the grin vanished. 'How about it, religious freak? You ready to meet your maker?'

'No…' whimpered the pitiful man, shrinking back against the cell wall. 'Please… no…'

'Looks like the faith ain't as strong as it should be,' sneered Zuko. 'What the hell, let's leave the bastard here.'

'B-but you can't leave me in this c-cell!' cried Jeremiah.

'I've – I've no food or water!'

'It's your set up,' said Zuko. 'You find a way out.'

'But—!'

One last threatening look from the two men and Jeremiah withered visibly and fell silent.

'Come on,' said Hakis, grabbing Danni by the arm. 'Get up those steps.'

With Jeremiah's sobbed prayers fading behind her, Danni was led out of the cellar and up to the outside world.

Chapter Fifteen

Danni gazed nervously from the window of the cab as it wove its way through the traffic. The sights she saw were familiar ones; dilapidated shops, colourless people and boarded-up windows. Her mind went back to the last time she had been in that area. Then she had been on foot, dressed as a prostitute, with a mysterious bag slung over her shoulder. Sitting there in the cab she felt not much more secure, and she wished she could be somewhere – anywhere – else.

On the side of the street she spotted two girls, dressed in short skirts and tight tops. The cabby obviously saw them too, as he slowed down.

'Those the hookers you're looking for, lady?' he asked over his shoulder, without taking his eyes off them.

Danni shook her head. 'No, not those two.'

'I don't know why you're bothered. After all, a whore's a whore.'

'Just keep driving, please.' Danni cringed, realising that the cabby thought she was looking for two girls for carnal reasons. What sort of a God-forsaken hell was she in?

She could sense the cabby's nervousness. Clearly even cab drivers were not immune from the dangers of the area. This was the third time they had driven down the street, and he had become more edgy with each pass. The mood was infectious, and she shifted anxiously on the seat.

She knew that Hakis and Zuko had gone to a great deal of trouble to set this up. They had obtained the cab from a company that was not controlled by either gang, and had ensured that its driver was from out of town. She was only too aware that to be on Killarney territory was extremely dangerous for a Dirango, and that recognition could lead to all kinds of trouble. Clearly the missing package was worth a great deal to them.

They passed another prostitute. The cabby glanced in his mirror at his lovely passenger and raised his eyebrows, but she shook her head. Perhaps the whole exercise was a waste of time. Perhaps the brunette and the blonde no longer worked that particular street. If that was so, she knew that her own position was a very unsafe one. The two prostitutes were her only connection back to that vile pimp, and therefore to the place where she had hidden the bag. That was why it was so important to find them.

Not for the first time the cabby surreptitiously used the rear-view mirror to admire the delectable curves of the girl sitting behind him, oblivious to the scrutiny she was undergoing. When he had picked his gorgeous passenger up, his eyes had positively bulged at the mouthwatering sight she presented. Now, as he lusted after her for the umpteenth time, he had to secretly shift to ease his aching erection.

She wore only a short dress made of white lace. The lace itself consisted of a sparse floral pattern on a completely transparent material, so that nothing was left to the imagination. It was tight about her breasts, the dark contours of her nipples as visible as if she wore nothing. Over the hips, too, it was a snug fit, outlining their shape perfectly, the pink of her flesh and the shadowy thatch of her pubic hair tantalisingly visible.

Danni shrank down in the seat a little, anxious to be seen by as few people as possible. Although the wig and the dark glasses meant that anyone seeing her was highly unlikely to recognise her, she still felt extremely vulnerable.

At last she thought she saw someone familiar loitering on a corner. She peered over the top of the sunglasses at the brunette hair and the tall, slender figure.

'There, on the right,' she said, her heart pounding from relief and trepidation. 'That's who I'm looking for.'

'You sure?' asked the cabby a little anxiously. 'Because I'd rather not stop here unless I really have to.'

'I'm positive. She's the one standing by the curb in that short dress. Please, pull over. I need to talk to her.'

'Whatever you say, lady. But I'm not hanging around here for long, I can tell you that.'

Danni composed herself. Then she wound down the window as the car stopped, and she was staring up into the brunette's face.

'Hi,' she said.

The prostitute glanced down at her. 'What do you want, honey?'

'Are you working?' Danni asked, hating what she was having to do, and certain that the woman would recognise her instantly.

The brunette chewed her gum languidly and eyed the girl in the cab suspiciously. 'What if I am?'

'I – I'm looking for some company.'

The brunette glanced at the cabby. 'You and your boyfriend here after a threesome?'

'He's not my boyfriend,' Danni said, what little confidence she had rapidly draining away. 'That's why he's in the front and I'm in the back.'

'Well,' the prostitute said impatiently, 'what are you after then?'

'I – I'm just looking for a little fun... that's all.' It all sounded so unbelievable. Surely the brunette would know something was up.

The woman narrowed her eyes and stared closely at Danni.

'What the fuck are you wearing?' she said.

Danni's face reddened. 'Not much,' she said.

'No kidding.'

'Listen… I'll pay you well.'

'Oh yeah?' the woman sneered sceptically. 'And how much is "well"?'

'F-five hundred.'

The prostitute looked to her left, and then to her right, clearly interested in the bait. 'Five hundred, you say?'

Danni opened her handbag and showed it to the woman. It contained a wad of twenty-dollar bills.

'Well?' she asked.

'Say, you're on the level, aren't you?'

Danni sat back. She took a deep breath, knowing there was nothing else for it. She placed a hand on her thigh and, in a slow smooth movement, ran it up her body until it reached her breast. She squeezed the soft flesh through the thin material.

'Well?' she asked huskily. 'What do you think?'

Without waiting for an answer she opened the door, then slid across the seat, patting it with her palm. 'Get in,' she said.

The prostitute stood where she was, an expression of doubt still on her face, and for a brief moment Danni thought she had failed to lure her into the trap. But then she shrugged and climbed in beside the young temptress.

'Where we going?' she asked, closing the door.

Danni couldn't believe what she was doing. 'J-just a little place I know,' she said.

The cabby slipped the car into gear and it purred away from the kerb. Danni turned to the prostitute. Now that she had successfully lured her target into the vehicle, she realised that the hardest part was yet to come. She had to convince the woman that she really did want to pay for her services. She ran her eyes over her body. There was no doubt that she was attractive. Her large breasts and slim waist and her long, slender legs would have been attractive to any man. But Danni was no man. On the other hand, with the threats of Zuko and Hakis echoing in her head, she had no other choice.

She moved a little closer to the wary prostitute.

'What's your name?' Danni asked.

'Lana,' she replied, without interrupting her chewing. 'What's yours?'

'Judith.'

'Well Judith, you seem a little young to be out on the streets paying for it.' Her eyes crawled over Danni's breasts and down to her thighs. 'As far as I can see, you'd have no problem picking up anyone you want. Especially in that outfit.'

She was suspicious! Danni's stomach knotted, and she was thankful for the dark glasses to hide the uncertainty she knew was in her eyes. 'You... you like it?' she said, trying to squirm sexily.

'Sure I like it. But like I say, it'd get you anyone you want.' Lana scrutinised her closely. 'You strictly a dyke, Judith, or do you swing both ways?'

Danni swallowed. 'I like men,' she said. 'B-but I like a woman more.'

'So why a whore like me?'

'Because you'll be discreet... And you won't ask questions.'

Lana laughed raucously, and Danni relaxed a little and laughed with her, sensing she had convinced her.

'Okay,' the woman said, between laughing and gum-chewing, 'point taken. So come here, you gorgeous little thing.'

She curled an arm around Danni's trim waist and pulled her close, kissing her lips experimentally. Her breath smelt pleasantly of spearmint as she whispered, 'I'm going to enjoy earning my five hundred, Judith,' and, clearly unconcerned about the drooling cabby spying in his mirror, she slipped a hand inside the entrapped girl's dress, and squeezed her firm breasts. Danni winced, and she knew the woman had felt the welts left by Jeremiah's cane.

'Hey,' she said huskily, 'someone been whipping your tits?'

Danni squirmed a little as the fingertips traced the tender stripes. 'Just a little bit of fun,' she said bravely, trying to ignore the discomfort.

Lana gave a low whistle of appreciation. 'Seems there's more to you than meets the eye, you horny little bitch,' she

187

said.

The rest of the journey passed in silence, with Danni moulded snugly against the older woman, who idly caressed her breasts and kissed her forehead. Danni was surprised at how arousing the woman's touch was, and allowed herself to relax and enjoy it.

They arrived at their destination. It was far outside the normal Dirango territory; an apartment block in one of the better areas of town. They climbed out of the cab and Lana gazed about.

'This is a long way from my usual stamping ground,' she said, showing just a little anxiety.

Danni paid the cabby, her face glowing as she bent and he leered blatantly at her cleavage.

'Let's go inside,' she said to Lana.

She led the way through the front door and into an entrance lobby. There was a bored-looking commissionaire, thumbing through a worn magazine. He eyed them up and down appreciatively, but said nothing as the pair stepped into the elevator. Danni pressed a button and the doors swished shut.

As soon as the lift began to move, Lana turned to her young companion. She pressed Danni back against the wall and slipped a hand up her dress, caressing her bare behind. The move took Danni completely by surprise, and she had to suppress her instinct to fight Lana off as she found herself being crushed into a corner, another hand squeezing between their bodies and stealing to her breasts.

'You've got the sexiest little body I've seen in a long, long time,' Lana whispered into her mouth. 'It's a rare treat to get paid for doing something I really enjoy. How did you know I prefer a bit of female ass to those useless male wankers?'

Danni was a little taken aback by the intensity of the woman. 'I—' she tried to answer, but her voice was smothered by an all-consuming kiss.

Lana ran her hand up Danni's spine, raising the hem of

her dress as she felt her soft flesh. Despite her apprehension, Danni felt her body respond still further to the skilful caresses. She had been dreading this part of the plan, but now she found an irresistible attraction towards the shapely woman that she hadn't suspected was possible.

She was surprised by the degree of disappointment she felt when the elevator came to a halt and the doors opened. For a moment Lana didn't move, trapping Danni in the corner. Their breasts heaved gently together and they looked deeply into each other's eyes, and Danni knew she secretly wanted the doors to close again and for Lana to continue where she had left off. But Lana suddenly stood back, and the flustered youngster smoothed her dress down and made her way unsteadily into the corridor, fumbling in her bag for the room key.

As she unlocked the door she peeped furtively from the corner of her eye, and saw the security camera along the corridor, the red light on top revealing that they were, even now, being watched by Hakis and Zuko. She knew that further cameras were concealed inside the apartment, because the two thugs had taken her into their temporary control room along the corridor and shown her the monitors. No corner was safe from the hidden cameras, and the microphones would pick up every word spoken. She had to play the whole thing straight, or risk getting even deeper into trouble.

She pushed open the door and stepped inside. The apartment was very well appointed, the carpets, wall coverings and furniture all of extremely good quality. She wondered who normally lived there. As she understood it, the owners were away on holiday, and the use of the place had been set up through the money-grabbing commissionaire.

Lana gave a low whistle of approval.

'Shit, this is quite a place, Judith,' she breathed. 'I gotta hand it to you, you've got taste.'

Danni smiled weakly. Now that she was alone with the woman, her stomach was churning, and suddenly she felt her bravery deserting her. Despite all of her recent experiences she felt suddenly unsure whether she could go through with the plan.

Lana must have sensed her uncertainty as she turned to her.

'You've never done this before, have you Judith?'

Danni knew she couldn't fool the experienced woman. She shook her head.

'No.'

'Why then?'

'An adventure I guess. I like being naughty.'

'Like having your tits whipped?'

'Yes... I suppose so.'

Lana studied her closely, and for a moment Danni feared she had blown it. But then the prostitute said, 'So why don't you take off that dress?'

Despite knowing that she had to see the plan through to a conclusion, Danni hesitated.

'Go on,' urged Lana, her own voice indicating the extent of her mounting arousal. 'I want to see your gorgeous body naked.'

Danni hesitated for a moment longer, but she knew the two hidden watchers would be getting furious, and so she reached up and brushed the straps off her shoulders. She peeled the tight-fitting garment down her body, then dropped it to the floor, so that she was left quite naked. Lana raised an appreciative eyebrow.

'Someone's been thrashing your arse too, I see.'

Danni's colour deepened, but she said nothing.

'You're an odd little thing, Judith,' said Lana. 'You act so shy and demure, yet you dress more outrageously than any of us working girls, and you clearly get up to some very interesting sex games.'

'I'm not paying you to psychoanalyse me,' said Danni

190

quietly.

The woman smiled. 'No, I guess you're not.'

She moved forward and, lifting Danni's sculptured chin, she kissed her. The English girl felt the woman's tongue pressing its way into her mouth and starting to lick at her own. Her body stiffened as Lana placed a hand over her breast and caressed it beautifully. The girl pulled her head back and gazed into her eyes.

'Hey, Judith, loosen up,' whispered the woman. 'Just go with it.'

She pushed Danni backwards, and the couch caught the back of her legs, making her sit down hard. At once Lana knelt down in front of her and pushed her knees apart.

'I love the way you shave your cunt,' she breathed. 'I hope it tastes as good as it looks.' She leaned forward, and Danni watched in fascination as the dark hair drew closer, and then gasped as she felt Lana lick the soft flesh of her thighs.

The prostitute took her time, running her tongue slowly over Danni's smooth skin, sending thrills through her as she moved toward the centre of the young beauty's desires. Once again Danni felt the stirrings of her own arousal as she gazed down at the woman who knelt before her as if worshipping her naked body, licking her thighs in long, even strokes.

'Ohhh…'

Danni was unable to suppress the cry as Lana's tongue burrowed between her wet labia and found her clitoris. A fire of passion swept through the youngster and she pressed her hips forward against the woman's face. Lana responded by licking harder at Danni's sex, her tongue flicking back and forth over her clitoris before delving inside her vagina. Danni had never experienced anything like it, the sense of a woman's soft hands on her body and the thrill of the tongue that lapped so insistently at her, bringing her to new heights of ecstasy.

Lana leaned back and rose to her feet. Danni whimpered in frustration, the saliva glistening on her pale flesh.

'All in good time, Judith,' smiled Lana. 'You're paying a lot for this, so I'm going to make it good for you.'

She reached behind and unzipped her dress. It fell to the floor. Beneath it she wore a small black bra that lifted and supported her breasts beautifully, accentuating their shape, and a pair of bikini briefs. Her black stockings were held up by a suspender belt, and the shapeliness of her long, slender legs were only accentuated by the black high heels she wore.

She unclipped the bra, and her breasts burst forth as she let the flimsy garment slide down her arms. Danni stared at her lovely soft breasts standing proudly from her chest, the nipples large and erect. The woman caught Danni's eye, and smiled at the reaction. Her hands went to the waistband of her panties and she sexily eased them down and stepped out of them. She stood with her legs slightly apart, her hands on her hips, gazing down at the young English girl.

'Well?' she said. 'Reckon you're getting your money's worth?'

Danni nodded silently, her eyes fixed on the older woman. Like Danni, she had shaved between her legs, leaving only a tiny neat triangle of soft curls. Her sex lips were thick and pink and inviting. Danni thought her extraordinarily beautiful, and the urge to reach out and touch her warm flesh was almost overwhelming.

'Come here, Judith,' Lana beckoned seductively.

As though in a trance, Danni rose slowly and stepped closer. Both were still wearing their shoes, but Lana stood a couple of inches taller than the English girl. She took Danni's hand, pulling her close until their breasts touched, Danni's pert nipples stroking silkily against the underside of Lana's beautiful mounds. They kissed again, and this time Danni reached for her companion, pulling her close and revelling in the warmth and feel of her soft flesh as it came into contact with her own. She ran her fingers down the curve of Lana's spine. Her flesh felt quite different from that of the men she had known; it was much softer and yielded delicately beneath her touch. She traced the contours of Lana's bottom, squeezing the fleshy globes.

Lana pulled her head back a little. Danni was still wearing the sunglasses, but now Lana took them off her. The wig remained in place, held there by numerous clips that were designed to ensure that, whatever she got up to, it remained intact. Even so, she suddenly feared being recognised. She consoled herself with the thought that her previous encounter with Lana had been a brief one, and had happened some time ago. She held her breath and waited, but thankfully the woman showed no signs of recognising her.

Lana put the glasses down on the coffee table beside them, then turned back to Danni. 'I want to taste you again, my little beauty,' she cooed. 'Lie down on the floor.'

She gently pressed down on the girl's shoulders, and Danni sank onto her back on the carpet. The luxurious pile was deep and soft, and seemed to caress her bare flesh as she relaxed into it. Lana knelt beside her and reached for her breasts, kneading and caressing them. Danni looked up at Lana. As the woman leaned forward her breasts swung down and swayed tantalisingly above the girl's flushed face, the large brown nipples still stiff and inviting. Hesitantly, Danni raised a hand and cupped one of the soft globes. She stroked it, loving the warmth of Lana's smooth, silky flesh.

Lana raised a leg and straddled Danni's body, her knees planted on each side of the supine girl's face, so that she was staring down at the girl's crotch. She ran her hands up Danni's thighs, nudging her legs gently apart to reveal the pale pink flower of her sex. Then she raised herself up onto all fours and slowly lowered her face between Danni's thighs.

'Mmmm...'

Danni couldn't suppress the sigh of sheer delight. The effect on her was electric as the woman's tongue once again sought out the little bud of her clitoris, taking it gently between her teeth and licking it with enthusiasm. Danni was instantly on fire with excitement, her dainty bottom rising

193

clear of the carpet as she urged the woman deeper. Her companion responded by licking harder, running her tongue up and down Danni's gaping sex then probing within, bringing a fresh flow of wetness from inside the gasping girl.

Danni opened her eyes and gazed up at Lana. Above her hovered the woman's succulent sex lips. She was immediately seized by an irresistible desire to taste them. The sight of her shaven slit so close to her was just too tempting. She reached up and ran her fingers over the woman's thighs. Then she raised her head.

In a moment she was engulfed by the scent and heat of female arousal, her senses filled by Lana's feminine attractions. She tentatively pushed out her tongue and licked at the woman's clitoris. It tasted divine, and she swooned. She licked again, loving the way the moist lips twitched at the touch. She moved higher, probing inside Lana's vagina and feeling the way her sex muscles contracted around her tongue. She tasted the juices that flowed from her partner, and was suddenly overcome with longing.

She began licking harder, devouring the soft, pliant flesh of the woman's vagina while her own body writhed with lustful pleasure under Lana's ministrations. She had never imagined that sex with another woman could be so good, but now the scent and softness of Lana's body was all she desired. Wrapping her arms tightly around her backside she pulled her closer.

The pair began to roll about on the carpet, first one on top, then the other, their naked bodies fused together as they licked hungrily at one another's crotches.

They came simultaneously, both emitting muffled shrieks of joy as they shuddered with mutual pleasure.

They remained locked together for long blissful minutes, each licking greedily at the other, until they could take no more and they flopped aside on their backs, their thighs glistening with spent juices, their breasts slowly rising and falling as they regained their composure.

As she lay there, Danni thought momentarily of the concealed cameras, and of Hakis and Zuko witnessing her passions, and she felt the heat in her cheeks rise. More importantly, though, the thought of the two thugs brought her back to her mission. It was time to move to the next stage of the plan. She rolled onto her stomach and gazed into Lana's eyes.

'That was great,' she breathed.

Lana smiled. 'You were pretty good, too.'

'Do you often get paid by women for sex?' Danni asked innocently.

'Hardly ever. It's nearly always men.'

'How do you find your customers?'

'Just pickups on the street. Like you were. And my pimp always finds me some.'

'Your pimp?'

Lana smiled patiently at the girl. 'You've got to have a pimp to be a whore in this town. It's a kind of insurance.'

'What's his name?' asked Danni, trying to appear innocently interested.

Lana smiled again. 'We don't know his name… nobody does. It's safer that way.'

'Oh…' Danni took a deep breath, ready to take the major plunge. 'I… I'd like to try it,' she said softly.

Lana chuckled dismissively. 'You'd like to try it?'

'Don't laugh at me,' Danni pouted, and then idly traced her fingertips around a still-erect nipple. 'I'd like to try being a prostitute. What's so funny about that?'

Lana lifted herself up on one elbow, and her breasts swung forward enticingly. She looked into Danni's eyes. 'You're serious, aren't you?'

Danni nodded.

'But…' Lana gazed around the apartment, '…but, with all this?'

'I'm bored,' Danni reasoned. 'I want a little excitement in

my life. I'm only young, but I'm already bored.'

'You're mad,' Lana said.

'I know.' Danni wanted to close the deal before the chance was lost. 'But I still want to try it... will you help me?'

'And how could I help?'

'You could introduce me to your pimp.'

Lana stared at her. 'You *are* serious.'

Danni nodded. 'Will you help?' She held her breath, desperate for the ploy to work.

'I suppose I could,' Lana eventually said.

'You'll introduce me to your pimp?'

Lana nodded.

'Oh yes!' Danni beamed triumphantly. 'And can we do it today?'

'I... I guess so,' Lana said hesitantly. 'But I've got to warn you, he's no Prince Charming.'

'Oh, I don't mind that...'

But now the plan had moved another step forward Danni knew, deep down, that she did mind, and fear once again gripped her insides. By trying to work her way out of her troubles, she seemed to be sinking deeper and deeper into them. She tried to imagine what perils now lay in store for her, and was barely aware of the fingers that moulded her breasts and the soft lips that nuzzled against her ear and throat.

Chapter Sixteen

Danni trembled with anticipation as the cab sped through the city streets. She knew she was entering the lion's den by returning to that vile pimp's apartment. She thought of the whipping she had received there on her previous visit, and a shiver ran through her. She only hoped that she could keep up the pretence of being Judith under his gimlet eye.

She glanced out of the rear window. Somewhere back there, the ever-watchful shadows of Hakis and Zuko were following. Her instructions had been to lead them to the pimp's apartment. That was the key to finding the shed under which the bag was hidden. She had given them the best directions, as she could remember them, from the apartment to that overgrown yard. Now she was the bait in the trap, leading them to it.

Danni was still wearing the lacy dress, at Lana's insistence. She had told Danni that it would go down well with her pimp. She then telephoned him before they left the apartment, telling him that she was bringing a new girl over.

Now, as they wove their way through the less salubrious part of town once again, Danni's heart was thumping against her ribs at the prospect of the impending encounter.

The cab slowed, and Danni's stomach tightened as she recognised the apartment block she had been taken to weeks before. She glanced across at Lana, who winked.

'Here we are,' she said.

Danni followed Lana into the building. A strange sense of being trapped overcame her as the door closed behind them, and it was all she could do to keep her nerve as she followed the woman up the stairs.

Lana knocked on the door of the apartment. There was silence for a moment, then it opened and Danni found herself staring into the face of the blonde who had helped take her there in the first place.

'Come on in,' she said, with little friendliness in her tone.

Danni entered, with Lana close behind her. The pimp was sitting in a chair by the window, and Lana led her across to him. He stared intensely, and she felt her legs weaken as his eyes bored into her.

'This is Judith,' said Lana. 'She wants to work with us.'

The blonde snorted derisively, and poured herself a large gin.

Danni said nothing. Now she had led Hakis and Zuko to the apartment her part in the whole sordid episode was complete. All she wanted to do now was to make a hasty retreat. But she had to be careful. She dared not make a mistake now.

The pimp's eyes crawled from her feet to her face, assessing every inch of her curvaceous body as they went. Danni shuddered under his vile inspection.

'Is this true?' he finally asked, his voice quietly hostile. 'You want to sell that cute little body of yours?'

Danni nodded, with a disturbing feeling that things were not working out as planned.

He considered her for a long time, and Danni's confidence evaporated in the unnerving silence. His distrustful eyes never left her. 'Let's have a proper look at you, then,' he said at last. 'Get the dress off.'

Danni hesitated.

'Come on, honey,' said the blonde, before taking a large mouthful of her gin. 'He's got to make sure the merchandise is all it appears to be.'

Trying to disguise her immense dislike for the weasel and her reluctance to do his bidding, Danni reached for the shoulder straps and eased them down her arms. She hesitated for a second, then she let the front of the dress fall away, baring her breasts to the trio.

'All the way off,' the pimp said. 'Come on, I'm a busy

man.'

Danni slid the dress down over her hips and let it fall and pool around her feet.

The pimp studied her for a while, Lana seemed keen to hear his opinion, and the indifferent blonde burped softly and returned her attention to the contents of her glass.

'Not bad,' he eventually said. Danni relaxed a little. 'Not bad at all. In fact… it's exactly as I remember you.'

Danni froze, her heart sinking. 'I – I – what do you mean?' she babbled.

'Don't fuck with me, baby,' he hissed viciously. 'You might fool these two dumb bitches with your wig, but I know exactly who you are.'

For a second Danni considered brazening it out with him, but she knew it was futile. There was nothing else for it. Spinning quickly she managed to make it to the door. She yanked it open and there, blocking her escape route, was a large man with a scar on his chin.

It was Malone!

He grabbed Danni's arm with a huge hand and propelled her back into the room. She stumbled and crashed into Lana, who pinned her arms behind her back. At the same time the blonde stepped forward and yanked the wig from her head, scattering clips in all directions.

'You didn't think that pathetic disguise had really fooled me, did you?' sneered Lana. 'As soon as I took the glasses off I knew it was you, you silly little bitch.'

Malone was staring coldly at the cringing girl. 'So what's your game, coming back here?' he said. 'You got a death wish or something?'

'I... I—'

'Don't bullshit us no more!' he snapped, making Danni flinch with his intensity. 'You running another errand for those fucking Dirangos?'

Danni opened her mouth to plead her innocence, but fear prevented anything from coming out.

'The word it that you were running an errand for those bastards when these three first brought you back here. Word is that you had a package that wasn't delivered.'

'I don't know what you're talking about—!' Danni shrieked as he brought the flat of a powerful hand sweeping down across her breasts.

'So what happened to that package?' he seethed, ignoring her denial.

'Please, I – I haven't got it,' Danni pleaded.

'You had it when you left here.'

'Wait... wait a minute,' the pimp suddenly said thoughtfully. 'She had it when she escaped from my apartment, and it's never been seen since. Now she comes back here. What the hell for?'

'I don't get it,' said Malone.

'Well, she was on the run when she left this place. What if she hid it somewhere near here?'

'But why come back to your apartment?'

'Because she'd forgotten where it was. She needed Lana to help her find the apartment again. Then she was going to grab the stuff. All that crap about wanting to work for me was just so we'd bring her back here. Then she was going to retrace her footsteps.'

Malone stared at him through narrowed eyes. Then he nodded.

'Shit,' he said quietly. 'That all makes sense.'

Danni looked from one to the other. It was clear that the pimp was cleverer than either Hakis or Zuko had given him credit for. He had very nearly guessed the plan in every detail. The only thing he had missed was that Hakis and Zuko were behind the plan, and that already they would be outside seeking the bag.

Malone moved close to the youngster, who was still being held immobile by Lana's arm-lock. He produced a knife from his pocket and flicked out the fearsome blade. It was long and glinted, and she shivered at the sight of it. He held

200

the blade close against her nipple, pressing slightly.

'Now listen,' he breathed. 'There's two ways we can do this. I can use my methods to persuade you to tell us where you hid that thing, or you can keep those pretty looks and tell us straight away.'

Danni looked up into his cruel eyes. There was no doubting he was serious. She was completely at his mercy, naked and trapped. There seemed little point in defying him.

'I'll take you,' she said quietly. 'But I can't be certain it'll still be there.'

'You'd better hope it is,' he said ominously. He lowered the knife and ran a cold hand over her soft breast. As he did so, Danni felt her nipple stiffen, and saw the amusement in his eyes as he felt it too. He slipped the knife into his pocket and fumbled crudely between her legs, his rough fingers seeking and agitating her clitoris. Danni bit her lip as she felt a tremor of arousal stirring her.

Malone turned to the pimp. 'I reckon she might make a good whore after all. When we've got the stuff I'm taking her back with me. A couple of weeks whoring for my boys will do her good. Then you can have her back and make some real money out of her.'

The pimp nodded. 'Sure,' he said. 'Whatever you say.'

Danni remained silent as she listened to Malone's plans. He was still groping her, and she found it difficult to suppress a moan. It was clear that the brutes considered her no more than a commodity to be used for their benefit. For the time being she had to go along with that.

Malone withdrew his hands, leaving the lascivious youngster panting slightly as he wiped the juices from his fingers across the bare skin of her belly.

'Get your dress on,' he said. 'You're going to show us where that package is.'

Chapter Seventeen

Danni stood beneath the window of the pimp's apartment, gazing up at it. She remembered the last time she had been in the same spot. Then, Malone had been staring down at her, a gun held in his hand. Now he was beside her, and the bulge in his pocket reminded her that he still had the weapon. Indeed he had made a point of showing it to her before they had left the building.

On that previous occasion, she recalled, she had been naked. Now, at least, she had the dress, though its transparent fabric made it virtually useless as a safeguard for her modesty.

'Okay,' said Malone. 'Which way now?' Danni thought carefully for a moment, not wanting to make any costly mistakes, and then pointed in the right direction.

They set off along the alley, Malone and the pimp walking on either side of her while the two women brought up the rear. As they progressed Danni felt her heart sinking. She had been hoping there might be some opportunity to slip away from them, but it was clear they had other ideas.

They walked on down the alley. Now that she saw it again, Danni realised how little she remembered of it. At the time she had been naked and scared, seeking any place to hide, and most of the alley had gone past as no more than a blur. Now the whole place seemed unfamiliar, and she glanced from side to side uncertainly, trying to recall some detail.

They rounded a corner, and relief flooded her as the memory of the boys playing ball came back to her.

'It's further down here,' she said, with a huge sigh.

'How far?' asked Malone, his eyes ever watchful.

'Not far,' she confirmed.

They walked on, and soon came within sight of the street

that crossed the alley. Danni pointed to the high wall and the tatty door to her left.

'It's there,' she said.

They moved cautiously to the door, just as two figures appeared at the end of the alley. The party stopped dead, and Danni recognised the figures as Zuko and Hakis.

'Shit!' spat Malone.

'What do we do now?' asked the pimp, without taking his alert black eyes from the ominous pair.

'Malone?' It was Hakis calling.

Malone made no response.

'Malone, leave the girl there and back off.'

'No way, Dirango,' he shouted back defiantly. 'This is my territory. You don't tell me what I can and can't do.'

'The merchandise is ours, Malone. You'd better leave it alone.'

'The hell with that. The bitch left it on our territory. You'd better get moving, Hakis, I've got more men on their way.'

'Don't bullshit us Malone.' That was Zuko.

Without warning Malone pulled his gun from his jacket and snatched a shot off in the general direction of the two figures. Hakis and Zuko melted away behind the corner, and then immediately returned his fire.

Danni and the other four ducked behind some overflowing garbage bins, and the shooting increased in intensity. Panic could be heard from the street near to where Hakis and Zuko were entrenched. Each side had the other pinned down. It was a stalemate. Danni doubted Malone's claim that he had reinforcements on the way. She certainly hadn't seen him order any. She wondered how on earth the showdown was to end.

Her answer came a few seconds later with a wail of police sirens in the distance.

'Shit!' cursed the blonde. 'We've got to get out of here, Malone.'

He in turn swore. 'If we go those bastards will get the

203

package,' he snapped.

'And if we stay the cops will get us. Come on. They'll be here in no time.'

Danni saw Malone hesitate for a second. Then the sirens wailed again, this time much louder.

'Bastards!' he spat. He jumped to his feet and sprinted back up the alley the way they'd come. The blonde and Lana did the same, struggling to keep up with him in their heels. Then Danni felt a hand squeeze around her wrist. It was the pimp.

'Come on,' he hissed. 'We haven't finished with you yet.'

Danni pulled back, but he was much too strong. He hauled her up and dragged her after the others. Danni felt her strength draining away as she tried to struggle against him. In an act of desperation she sank her teeth into his hand. He cursed with pain and released his vicious grip immediately. She scrambled to her feet and began backing away. He took a pace towards her, but the sirens drew ever nearer. He glanced over his shoulder, looked back at Danni and swore at her, then turned and ran.

Danni's heart leapt. There was no sign of Hakis or Zuko, but she couldn't risk running into them, so she ducked through the door and into the yard. Her only chance was to get amongst people, so despite the possible consequences, she scrambled for the bar and burst through the rear door. She slammed it shut and leaned back against it, her eyes closed, and her breasts heaving heavily as she fought to regain her breath.

Then she heard a familiar voice.

'Well, well. Our little English beauty decided to come back at last.'

She opened her eyes and glanced around, and her shoulders slumped as she recognised Larry, the man who had found her in the yard on the previous occasion. He stepped forward and loomed over her.

'So how's it going?' He licked his lips salaciously. 'I see

your dress sense has improved a little, but not much.'

The boozy audience sniggered.

Danni looked at him. For a second she contemplated escape, but there really was nowhere to go.

'Please… I need your help,' she panted.

'You do eh?' he gloated. 'Well, I'm not so sure you deserve it, after what happened last time.'

'I – I'm sorry…' she stammered desperately. 'Listen, you've got to hide me. I'm being chased by some thugs who really want to hurt me.'

'Mm,' he toyed with her, 'we thought we heard a bit of a commotion out there, didn't we boys?' There was a murmur of confirmation. 'But we just keep ourselves to ourselves in here – it's safer that way.' He licked his lips again, then placed a fingertip against her chin, and idly ran it down to her throat, lower to her cleavage, and then hooked it into her dress and pulled the lacy material out. He peered blatantly down at her firm, gently heaving breasts. He leaned closer and she felt a warm lump press against her hip, and could smell the alcohol on his breath. 'So what thanks will we get if we do decide to help you?' he asked.

Danni looked at him, then round at the other lecherous men in the bar. She recognised many of them as having been there on her previous visit. Now they were staring at her with expectant eyes. It was obvious what they wanted.

'Look,' she pleaded, knowing that Hakis and Zuko could burst in at any moment, 'I'll do whatever you ask. Please just hide me for a while.'

The customers mumbled in consultation. Larry smiled, then glanced across at the bar owner, who was standing in his customary place behind the bar. Danni cringed when she saw the grubby little rat and remembered the liberties he'd taken with her before.

'You got somewhere to hide the lady, Ed?' Larry asked.

'I guess she can come behind here,' the bar owner suggested.

Larry shook his head. 'Last time we did that she got away out the back.'

'I can lock the back door,' he said. 'She won't get away this time.'

'Hey,' said another man, slouching at a table by one of the grimy windows. 'There's two guys just coming through the yard. They the ones after you?'

Danni stared at him in alarm. 'That must be them,' she said. 'Please, you've got to hide me!'

Larry stared at her for a moment through suspicious eyes, then nodded. 'Okay,' he said. 'Get behind the bar.'

Danni darted to where the bar owner was holding open the flap. She darted behind and ducked down. Moments later she heard the door open.

There was silence in the room, broken only by the slow footfalls of the two thugs as they made their way across to the bar. Danni held her breath, pressing herself against the wooden shelves beneath the counter.

'You seen a girl around here?' The voice was Zuko's.

'We don't get many girls in this place,' replied the bar owner with a derisive chuckle. 'There was one in yesterday, though.'

'I'm talking about just now.' Zuko was not happy, and Danni willed the stupid bar owner not to provoke him.

'I ain't seen nobody,' he said. 'Anyone else seen a girl?'

'There was some chick came through the yard just now,' said a voice. 'Climbed over the side wall and disappeared. Sexy little thing.'

Zuko cursed. 'Where does that lead?'

'Out onto the street,' said the bar owner. 'She could be anywhere by now.'

Zuko cursed again, then Danni heard their footsteps retreating, and the door closed.

She waited for a few minutes, and then gingerly touched the bar owner's leg.

'Please, call Lucy,' she whispered up at him. 'Ask her to

tell Mr Wright where I am.'

The bar owner leered down at her. 'Sure,' he said, 'I can do that.'

Then another face appeared and grinned down at her.

'Well, baby,' said Larry. 'We kept our side of the bargain. Now it's your turn.'

Danni's legs were shaking slightly as she rose and emerged from behind the bar. The men had all moved closer, gathering round in a semicircle to watch the nervous young beauty in her skimpy frock. Larry was leaning on the bar, and he beckoned to her.

'Give the lady a drink,' he ordered. 'A large one.'

The bar owner placed a glass in front of Danni. It contained an amber liquid. She raised it nervously to her lips and sipped at it. It was whisky, and it warmed her throat as it slipped down. Knowing she needed some Dutch courage, she drained the glass with one mouthful.

'You ready?' asked Larry.

Danni saw two men close and bolt the front and back doors. She swallowed anxiously. 'I suppose so,' she whispered resignedly.

'Take off the dress.'

Danni looked around at the sea of faces. They were all watching her expectantly. There was no turning back now, she knew. She had given her word.

Slowly she reached up to her shoulders. She took the straps of her dress in her fingers and pulled them down, then let the garment drop to her waist. A low whistle sounded about the smoky room as the men drooled over her firm breasts. She paused for a moment, letting them take a good look. Then, closing her eyes, she hooked her thumbs inside the waistband and dragged the garment over her hips and off. She stood quietly, her cheeks burning as they feasted their eyes on her naked beauty.

For a moment there was no sound at all. Then Larry

207

reached out and, with surprising tenderness for such an oaf of a man, stroked Danni's breasts. Danni said nothing, though her heart was pounding under the surprisingly pleasurable explorations.

'You know what's going to happen?' he asked.

She nodded, not trusting herself to speak. Her mind was in turmoil. She knew she was about to be taken by the whole group of rough strangers – and probably in any and every way conceivable. Even now she could see two of them carrying a mattress out of what appeared to be a store cupboard. Tables and chairs scraped the floor as a space was hastily made, and the mattress was laid down. She knew too that she should protest, and should try to hide her body from their salacious gazes. But they had helped her, hadn't they? They had misled her dangerous pursuers and had saved her from their clutches. Surely they deserved her gratitude? And what else did she have to offer them but her body? Surely that was justification enough for her behaviour?

But deep inside she knew that something else was motivating her. Something much more fundamental than the debt she owed those men for helping her. The incongruity of her situation, the only woman amongst a gang of frustrated men, her breasts and sex bared to all, was having an effect that was becoming all too familiar to the wanton youngster. Even now she could feel the warm wetness seeping into her vagina as she contemplated what they were about to do to her. And the stiffening of her nipples betrayed her arousal to them, so that she lowered her head in shame of her own rampant desires.

Larry took her arm and led her forward, and the crowd parted before them. There, on the floor, lay the mattress, an old horsehair one stained with the records of previous adventures. She wondered how many other women had been a sexual sacrifice upon it, and if anyone had ever used it to take on as many men as she was expected to. She paused beside it, then looked around once more.

'Okay,' she said, 'do what you want with me.'

There was a moment of complete silence, then the drooling mob crowded in. Hands groped at her from all sides, grabbing at her soft breasts and rummaging up between her thighs. She felt her vagina penetrated by a finger, then another wormed its way between her buttocks and stabbed into her rear passage, twisting as it entered that tight hole. The dry entry made her squeal with pain, but a beery mouth closed over hers and stifled her whimpers. Fingers pinched her nipples, tweaking and pulling and rolling them back and forth, while others sought her clitoris, rubbing and making her wail into the humid mouth that engulfed her and threatened to deny her of oxygen. Her breasts swelled into the many gratefully grabbing hands as her lungs searched desperately to fill themselves. Then she was being dragged down onto the mattress, her legs pulled apart as they pinned her to the coarse material.

She looked up. Larry was standing between her legs, undoing his jeans. He let them fall to the floor, and she saw his penis. It was long and meaty and spearing up towards the nicotine-stained ceiling, a thick blue vein running up its underside. The end bulged, the foreskin folded back so that she could see the shiny surface of the helmet. He grinned down at her, working his hand back and forth along his shaft. Then he dropped to his knees and guided it between her immobilised thighs.

She bit her lip as she felt him press it against her, and her sex tightened as she anticipated what was to come. The bulbous tip nuzzled up against the pliant flesh of her nether lips, then began to push insistently.

He penetrated her with a grunt of satisfaction, his engorged crown suddenly gaining the access he needed. She gave a cry as he began to ease himself into her, his hefty organ forcing the walls of her sex apart. She looked up at the faces all around her. The slavering mob were watching with misty expressions of intense lust and, dropping her gaze, the young beauty saw that their crotches were bulging, evidence that they were all keenly anticipating their turn with her.

Larry began to move with short, aggressive jabs, driving his hips against hers and sending her to new peaks of arousal as she abandoned herself to the cacophony of undiluted lust that threatened to consume her. Fingers twisted into her hair and pulled her head to one side. For a second she was unsure what was happening, then a huge black penis bobbed just a few inches from her face. A muscular Negro was kneeling on the mattress beside her shoulder. As she watched he leaned over her, took his immense erection in his fist, and pressed it to her lips.

She opened her mouth and allowed the cock inside. He immediately began to move against her face, easing his hips back and forth as his erection squeezed in and out between the tight moist ring that was her stretched lips. She managed to wriggle her arm free from the mass of fumbling hands that held her down, and curled her fingers around that part of the throbbing shaft that the man was unable to cram into her full mouth. She masturbated him as she sucked valiantly.

Despite the intensity of the onslaught, Danni once again wondered at her own promiscuity. Never in her wildest dreams had she imagined herself in such a situation as she was in now, stretched naked on her back in a scruffy bar while one virtual stranger pounded his erect penis into her vagina and another into her mouth. And her overwhelming feeling was not one of shame or distress, but of desire. It was a desire that overwhelmed her, causing her to thrust her hips up against the man squatting between her thighs while simultaneously sucking at the other one with absolute relish.

Larry was fucking her still harder now, grunting with every stroke, his cock seeming to swell inside her as it continued to send exquisite sensations through her writhing body. It was all she could do to concentrate on pleasuring the hefty cock in her mouth as her own climax approached rapidly.

Larry came suddenly. The sensation was too much for the

wanton girl, and she shuddered with pleasure as her own orgasm swamped her, her lovely breasts quivering deliciously as she writhed about beneath the burly man. He came and came, sending exquisite sensations through her as he filled her with his seed.

As the last of his semen trickled from his wilting erection he began to withdraw. There was no respite for Danni, though. No sooner had he shuffled away than another man shoved into her.

As the new stranger began buffeting against her the kneeling man groaned and her mouth filled with his seed. She gulped down the viscous fluid with relish, swallowing enthusiastically as it continued to seep from his twitching organ. She worked his shaft back and forth in her fist, holding him between her lips until he was completely spent. Then he sank back into the throng and she was once again left to the mercy of the of sea bodies that swamped her.

She looked into the face of the man who was fucking her, seeing him properly for the first time. He was a burly young man, with a shaved head and a gold earring hanging from one ear. He was screwing her dispassionately, using her as he might an inflatable doll. Yet Danni didn't care. This was no place for romance. She was a brazen young slut stretched naked on the floor of a seedy bar and giving the patrons what they wanted, and taking her own pleasure without thought for those who were giving it to her.

The man's face was obscured again as another solid erection filled her vision and she reached for it, closing her lips about it and sucking keenly.

She satisfied two more men after that, one in her mouth and the other in her vagina. She lay back, waiting for the next, but instead she heard laughter, and found herself being pulled to her feet. They dragged her across to a table and pulled her forward over it, her breasts squashed down in a pool of spilt beer.

'Joe likes something a bit unorthodox,' said a voice in her

ear, followed by more laughter.

Then she felt her bottom cheeks being pulled apart, and a greasy ointment was rubbed into the tight star of her anus.

She knew then exactly what Joe wanted. In front of all those raucous men he was going to screw her bottom.

Danni felt his cock press between her buttocks. She strained to look over her shoulder at him. But strong hands held her down and she had no choice but to relax and accept him. The man pressed his glans against her anus, twisting it slightly to gain the access he required. He penetrated her suddenly, making her cry aloud with the shock and pain as his erection wormed its way into her rectum. She bit her lip, willing her sphincter to relax further as he pressed deeper and deeper, while his companions looked on, shouting their encouragement. At last he was buried to the hilt, and she felt his wiry hair against her stretched bottom. He paused there for a few moments, clearly relishing the tightness and heat of the English girl's back passage. Then he began to move, his hips grinding back and forth, shunting her exhausted body against the creaking table while the claustrophobic noise crescendoed around her.

But still there were more for her satisfy. As Joe grunted and rutted Danni found yet another penis pressed against her lips and, amid the whoops and hollers of those watching, was obliged to take it into her mouth.

This time both men came at once, and Danni's tormented body was once again a receptacle for their copious emissions. She clung to the edge of the table as they climaxed, rocked back and forth by the violence of their orgasms.

No sooner had they withdrawn than she was forced onto her back once again and invaded by more rampant revellers. Nobody wanted to miss out on their opportunity with the gorgeous English girl who was giving herself so gamely, and she could see yet more of them undoing their jeans as they awaited their turn to savour her.

Danni wasn't sure how many men took her that afternoon.

Her own orgasms came one after another, her small frame rocked by her insatiable desires as she responded to one turgid erection after another. At one point her poor bottom was thrashed by a thick leather belt, laying wide red stripes across her pale flesh while she whimpered with pain and delight.

When at last they were all satiated, they hauled her to her feet and helped her to the bar, where she gratefully drank another stiff whisky.

Then she was helped through to another room and laid on a musty-smelling couch. She stretched her aching limbs, and as she dozed she was aware of the dirty bar owner gently stroking her hair.

Chapter Eighteen

Danni dreamt that she was lying naked on a sun-kissed beach while an Adonis with long golden hair knelt beside her. He was stroking her head, his voice softly calling her name.

'Danni... Danni.'

'Mmmm?' she murmured.

'Danni, it's me. Wake up.'

The beach, the sun and the blue sky seemed to fade away as the strong young man's face seemed to distort, then turned into one that was much more familiar. She blinked, trying to focus on him.

'Oh...' she murmured, disappointedly. 'It's you.'

Charles Wright brushed the hair back from her eyes. 'That's right,' he said. 'It's me.'

'Where am I?'

'You're still in the bar,' he said. 'It looks like you've been through quite a lot.'

Danni stared at him uncomprehendingly for a moment. Then she glanced down at herself, and gave a little cry of dismay.

She was still quite naked. Her pale skin was stained by dirty marks where she had lain on the grimy mattress or been held down over the tables while the drunken mob had their wicked way with her. Her backside still ached from the thrashing she had received with the belt, and her breasts felt swollen from the incessant groping and mauling.

She turned away from Wright's gaze as the enormity of what she had done sank home. And yet she saw no signs of disgust in his expression – simply concern.

'Where have you been?' he asked quietly.

'I... I'm sorry,' she stammered. 'I didn't mean to leave you. That creep Jeremiah, he was the one. He...'

Wright placed a fingertip to her lips. 'All in good time,' he said. 'The important thing is that you're safe.'

'Those men who were after me,' she said, suddenly panicking as she remembered them, 'where are they?'

'Pretty well scattered by now, I should think,' he said calmly. 'The police have been combing the area. They found some kind of a package that they seemed very pleased about. You wouldn't know anything about that would you?'

'The package?'

'Whatever was in it, it must have been worth quite a bit. They've been rounding up suspects all evening.'

'But… but I put it there,' Danni admitted hesitantly, not sure whether it was wise to or not.

Wright smiled and nodded. 'I thought you might have been involved. That's why we need to get you out of here. Do you feel strong enough to get up?'

'I… I need to clean myself up.'

'There's a washroom over there.' He indicated a door on the far side of the room. 'Go ahead. I'll wait for you here.'

Danni lifted herself and swung her legs over the side of the couch. Her limbs were stiff, but otherwise she was okay. She rose to her feet and crossed a little unsteadily to the washroom, closing the door behind her.

The hot water from the shower felt wonderful on her body, and she let it cascade over her, her face turned up into the spray as it splashed down onto her breasts. She took the bar of soap from the rack and began to wash away the grime and memories of the afternoon. When she was scrubbed and refreshed she found a bottle of shampoo and washed her hair. Then she turned off the shower and dried herself with a slightly threadbare towel that hung from the rail on the wall.

The brush she found on a shelf beneath the chipped wall-mirror was a little grubby, as she expected, but she used it anyway. Then she wrapped the towel around her revitalised body, knotted it in her cleavage, and walked back into the bedroom.

215

Wright was sitting on the couch. Beside him sat another figure, and Danni's eyes widened as she recognised Tonia. She blushed at her nudity, but said nothing as Wright beckoned her forward.

'Is that better?' he asked.

'Much,' she nodded. 'Thank you.'

'How are you feeling now?' He seemed genuinely interested, but after recent weeks, Danni was still a little wary.

'I'm still a little tired,' she admitted.

'Well, we'd better get you away from here,' he said. 'Those people you don't want to meet will be back looking for you, probably sooner rather than later.'

Danni shivered. 'Yes,' she agreed, 'I think you're right.'

Wright got to his feet and moved closer to her.

'Listen,' he said, 'I think your days of playing Judith at my house are over. It's just too dangerous for you to stay anywhere near here.'

'It's a pity, though,' said Tonia. 'I was getting rather fond of Judith and her liberated ways.'

Danni said nothing, feeling suddenly very insecure before the well-dressed and confident couple.

'So,' went on Wright. 'The question is, what happens next?'

'What will you do if you go home?' asked Tonia.

'I don't know really,' she said, feeling very alone. 'I haven't any family. I guess I'll just have to go back to the temping agencies.'

'Well there can't be very much potential in that,' Tonia derided.

'No…' Danni conceded, 'but enough to rent a bed-sit somewhere, and for me to rethink my future.'

Wright reached out and stroked her cheek. It was the first real sign of affection she had received for a very long time, and tears threatened to burst forth at the touch.

'Listen, Danni,' he said. 'I'd like to make you a

216

proposition.'

'W-what sort of a proposition?' she asked, tensing a little and fearing the worst.

He smiled kindly. 'Nothing for you to worry about. This is something I rather think you'll like.'

She looked hopefully into his eyes.

'I own an island in the Caribbean,' he said.

'You—'

He held up a hand and she obediently fell silent. 'Now it's not a very big island, but it has a large house on it and I'm often entertaining important guests out there. I'd like you to live there... as Judith.'

'I...' Danni couldn't quite believe her ears. 'I... you... want me... as Judith?'

'Yes. The same rules would apply, but this would be a more permanent position.'

'What do you mean, more permanent?'

'I'd still expect you to be considerate to my friends and associates, as you have been in the past. You'd still be Judith, my wanton young cousin, but this time there'd be a contract, and a more than generous salary.'

Danni was excited but confused. 'Why – why are you offering this to me?'

'Quite simply,' he said breezily, 'because you are the single most delicious young lady I have met for a very long time, and my friends and associates will adore you.' The gentle fingers left her cheek, tugged at the knot nestling between her breasts, let the towel drop to the floor, and then delicately teased her nipple until it stiffened and she sighed instinctively. 'You're a natural, Danni,' he whispered, his expensive cologne and his experienced fingers making her swoon.

Through swirling clouds of pleasure she made her mind up, but she felt she should show at least some resistance. 'I...' she blurted, her mouth suddenly dry, 'I don't know.'

'Yes you do,' urged Tonia. 'You know very well you do.

217

Some men and women are born to be successful in many different ways. And you, my darling Danni, were born to be successful in giving pleasure. You've an exquisite body and an appetite for sex like I've never seen before.'

'Listen to Tonia,' the urbane man said as he continued to tease her swollen nipple. 'She's absolutely right.'

'And if I wanted to leave…' Danni asked, finding it more and more difficult to concentrate, 'say, after a year?'

'You'd be free to do so. While you're there, though, you'll do as I ask – much as it has been up to now.'

Danni stared at the pair of them. What they'd said was true, she knew that. Even now she was aroused by her nakedness and by his touch. Even now she wanted him to seduce her there and then, in front of Tonia if necessary, despite her orgiastic afternoon of total abandon. And he was offering her exactly what she wanted.

'All right…' she said at last. 'I'll be Judith on your island. I'll look after your guests, however they want me.'

Wright smiled. 'That's my girl,' he said. 'I'll arrange to have you flown out as soon as possible.'

'And I'll come and visit you,' said Tonia, gliding close and running her fingers through Danni's hair in a way that made the young beauty shiver with desire.

'We'd better get going then,' said Wright. 'We've lots of arrangements to make.'

'Just one thing before we go,' said Danni.

'And that is?' asked Wright.

She sank to her knees between the couple, and one hand moulded itself over the growing bulge in his trousers, and the other slipped beneath the hem of Tonia's elegant skirt and slid lightly up between the woman's stockinged thighs.

'I'd like to show my appreciation for all your help,' Danni said huskily and smiled up at them. 'In the best way I know how.'

More exciting titles available from Chimera

1-901388-09-3*	Net Asset	*Pope*
1-901388-18-2*	Hall of Infamy	*Virosa*
1-901388-21-2*	Dr Casswell's Student	*Fisher*
1-901388-28-X*	Assignment for Alison	*Pope*
1-901388-39-5*	Susie Learns the Hard Way	*Quine*
1-901388-44-1*	Vesta – Painworld	*Pope*
1-901388-45-X*	The Slaves of New York	*Hughes*
1-901388-46-8*	Rough Justice	*Hastings*
1-901388-47-6*	Perfect Slave Abroad	*Bell*
1-901388-48-4*	Whip Hands	*Hazel*
1-901388-50-6*	Slave of Darkness	*Lewis*
1-901388-51-4*	Savage Bonds	*Beaufort*
1-901388-52-2*	Darkest Fantasies	*Raines*
1-901388-53-0*	Wages of Sin	*Benedict*
1-901388-55-7*	Slave to Cabal	*McLachlan*
1-901388-56-5*	Susie Follows Orders	*Quine*
1-901388-57-3*	Forbidden Fantasies	*Gerrard*
1-901388-58-1*	Chain Reaction	*Pope*
1-901388-61-1*	Moonspawn	*McLachlan*
1-901388-59-X*	The Bridle Path	*Eden*
1-901388-65-4*	The Collector	*Steel*
1-901388-66-2*	Prisoners of Passion	*Dere*
1-901388-67-0*	Sweet Submission	*Anderssen*
1-901388-69-7*	Rachael's Training	*Ward*
1-901388-71-9*	Learning to Crawl	*Argus*
1-901388-36-0*	Out of Her Depth	*Challis*
1-901388-68-9*	Moonslave	*McLachlan*
1-901388-72-7*	Nordic Bound	*Morgan*
1-901388-80-8*	Cauldron of Fear	*Pope*
1-901388-77-8*	The Piano Teacher	*Elliot*
1-901388-25-5*	Afghan Bound	*Morgan*
1-901388-76-X*	Sinful Seduction	*Benedict*
1-901388-70-0*	Babala's Correction	*Amber*
1-901388-06-9*	Schooling Sylvia	*Beaufort*
1-901388-78-6*	Thorns	*Scott*
1-901388-79-4*	Indecent Intent	*Amber*
1-903931-00-2*	Thorsday Night	*Pita*
1-903931-01-0*	Teena Thyme	*Pope*
1-903931-02-9*	Servants of the Cane	*Ashton*
1-903931-03-7*	Forever Chained	*Beaufort*
1-903931-05-3*	In Service	*Challis*
1-903931-06-1*	Bridled Lust	*Pope*
1-903931-08-8*	Dr Casswell's Plaything	*Fisher*

****

All **Chimera** titles are available from your local bookshop or newsagent, or direct from our mail order department. Please send your order with your credit card details, a cheque or postal order (made payable to *Chimera Publishing Ltd*) to: **Chimera Publishing Ltd., Readers' Services, PO Box 152, Waterlooville, Hants, PO8 9FS.** Or call our **24 hour telephone/fax credit card hotline: +44 (0)23 92 646062** (Visa, Mastercard, Switch, JCB and Solo only).

UK & BFPO - Aimed delivery within three working days.
- · A delivery charge of £3.00.
- · An item charge of £0.20 per item, up to a maximum of five items.

For example, a customer ordering two items for delivery within the UK will be charged £3.00 delivery + £0.40 items charge, totalling a delivery charge of £3.40. The maximum delivery cost for a UK customer is £4.00. Therefore if you order more than five items for delivery within the UK you will not be charged more than a total of £4.00 for delivery.

Western Europe - Aimed delivery within five to ten working days.
- · A delivery charge of £3.00.
- · An item charge of £1.25 per item.

For example, a customer ordering two items for delivery to W. Europe, will be charged £3.00 delivery + £2.50 items charge, totalling a delivery charge of £5.50.

USA - Aimed delivery within twelve to fifteen working days.
- · A delivery charge of £3.00.
- · An item charge of £2.00 per item.

For example, a customer ordering two items for delivery to the USA, will be charged £3.00 delivery + £4.00 item charge, totalling a delivery charge of £7.00.

Rest of the World - Aimed delivery within fifteen to twenty-two working days.
- · A delivery charge of £3.00.
- · An item charge of £2.75 per item.

For example, a customer ordering two items for delivery to the ROW, will be charged £3.00 delivery + £5.50 item charge, totalling a delivery charge of £8.50.

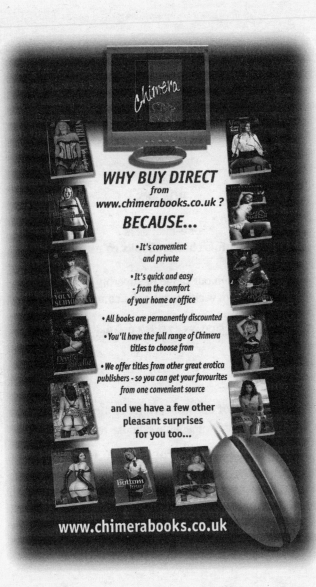